DEATH CALL

His phone rang. As soon as Wexford heard the voice he knew an attempt was being made to disguise it.

"I'm not prepared to give my name," the voice said. "I've written to you twice."

"Your letters were received."

"You played around with me this morning. That's not going to happen tomorrow."

"Tomorrow?" Wexford said evenly.

"I shall be on the grounds of Saltram House tomorrow by the fountains. At six p.m. with John. And I want the mother to come for him. *Alone.*"

"You haven't got John," Wexford said. "That hair you sent me wasn't John's." Scorn and rage made him forget caution. "You are an ignorant man. Hair can be as precisely identified as blood these days."

There was heavy breathing, then the voice said, "D'you think I don't know that? I cut that hair from Stella Rivers."

NO MORE DYING THEN

Ruth Rendell

BANTAM BOOKS
TORONTO • NEW YORK • LONDON • SYDNEY • AUCKLAND

NO MORE DYING THEN

A Bantam Book / published by arrangement with
Doubleday & Company, Inc.

PRINTING HISTORY

Doubleday edition published April 1972
Bantam edition / September 1974
2nd printing ... January 1980
3rd printing ... February 1980
4th printing ...... June 1980
5th printing ...... June 1986

ISBN 0-553-25968-7

Bantam Books are published by Bantam Books, Inc. Its trademark, consisting of the words "Bantam Books" and the por-
trayal of a rooster, is Registered in U.S. Patent and Trademark
Office and in other countries. Marca Registrada. Bantam
Books, Inc., 666 Fifth Avenue, New York, New York 10103.

PRINTED IN THE UNITED STATES OF AMERICA

H   14 13 12 11 10 9 8 7 6

For Gerald Austin

So shalt thou feed on death that feeds on men,
And death, once dead, there's no more dying then.

—Shakespeare, Sonnet 146

No More Dying Then

1

The spell of fine weather which so often occurs in the middle of October is known as St. Luke's Little Summer. The "little summer" part needs no explanation; the St. Luke bit derives from its coincidence with the eighteenth, which is that saint's day. Basking in the warm autumn sunlight, Station Sergeant Camb delivered this piece of interesting but useless information to Harry Wild and smiled sententiously.

"Is that so? Maybe I'll do a diary note on it." Wild sucked at his smelly old pipe and rested leather-patched elbows on the counter top. He yawned. "Haven't you got anything more exciting for me?"

Camb caught the yawn and yawned himself. He remarked for the third time on the closeness of the weather and then he opened his book.

"Two vehicles in collision at the junction of Kingsmarkham High Street and Queen Street," he read. "Nobody hurt. That was Sunday. Nothing in that for the *Courier*, is there? Girl of seventeen missing, but we know where she is all right. Oh, and there's a baboon got lost from the pet shop . . ." Wild looked up, lazily enquiring. ". . . Only they found it up on their balcony, tucking in to the waste bin."

"What a dump," said Wild. He put away his notebook. "Still, I opted for the quiet life. I could be up in Fleet Street tomorrow if I fancied it. Only got to say the word and I'd be up there where it's all happening."

"Sure you would." Camb knew very well that Wild remained as chief reporter of the *Kingsmarkham Courier* because idleness and general ineptitude, as well now as his advancing years, made him unfit

1

for any more illustrious newspaper. Wild had been coming into the police station for more years than Camb cared to remember and every time he came he talked about Fleet Street as if he had rejected it and not it him. But they sustained the fiction for the sake of peace and pleasantness. "Much the same for me," he said. "Many a time in the old days Mr. Wexford begged me to consider the C.I.D. but I wouldn't. I'm not ambitious. I don't say I wouldn't have had the ability, mind."

"Of course you would've." Playing fair, Wild returned praise for praise. "Where does it get you, though, ambition? Look at Inspector Burden, just to take an example. Worn out, and not forty yet, I daresay."

"Well, he's had a lot of trouble, hasn't he? Losing his wife like that and two kids to bring up."

Wild gave a heavy lugubrious sigh. "That," he said, "was a tragic business. Cancer, wasn't it?"

"That's right. Fit as a fiddle this time last year and dead by Christmas. Only thirty-five. It makes you think."

"In the midst of life. Looks to me as if he's taken it hard. I suppose they were a devoted couple?"

"More like sweethearts than man and wife." Camb cleared his throat and stood up straighter as the lift opened and Chief Inspector Wexford marched out.

"Gossiping again, Sergeant? Good afternoon, Harry." Wexford just glanced at the two empty teacups on the counter. "This place," he said, "gets more like a Mothers' Union bun fight every week."

"I was just telling Mr. Wild," said Camb with dignity, "about our escaped baboon."

"My God, that's hot news. There's a story in that, Harry. Terrorising the populace, mothers afraid to let their kids out of their sight. Is any woman safe while this wild beast roams our meadows?"

"It's been found, sir. In a dustbin."

"Sergeant, if I didn't know you to be incapable of it, I should say you were mocking me." Wexford quivered with silent laughter. "When Inspector Burden comes in, tell him I've gone, will you? I want a few hours to enjoy our Indian Summer."

"St. Luke's Little Summer, sir."

"Indeed? I stand corrected. I wish I had the time to devote to digging up these fascinating pieces of meteorological lore. I'll give you a lift, Harry, if you've finished your monkey business."

Camb sniggered. "Thanks very much," said Wild.

It was gone five but still very warm. The sergeant stretched and wished Constable Peach would appear so that he could send him to the canteen for another cup of tea. Half an hour and he would knock off.

Presently the phone rang.

A woman's voice, low and rich. Actressy, Camb thought. "I'm sorry to trouble you, but my little boy . . . He's—well, he was out playing and he's—he's disappeared. I don't . . . Am I making a fuss over nothing?"

"Not at all, madam," said Camb soothingly. "That's what we're here for, to be troubled. What name is it?"

"Lawrence. I live at 61 Fontaine Road, Stowerton."

Camb hesitated for a second. Then he remembered Wexford had told him all cases of missing children must be reported to C.I.D. They didn't want another Stella Rivers . . .

"Don't worry, Mrs. Lawrence. I'm going to put you through to someone who will help you." He got the switchboard and heard Sergeant Martin's voice, put down the receiver.

Sergeant Camb sighed. It was a pity Harry had gone like that, just when the only piece of news had come in for weeks. He could give poor old Harry a ring . . . Tomorrow would do. The kid would be found, come to that, like that monkey had been. Missing people and things usually were found in Kingsmarkham and in more or less good order. Camb turned his head in the sunlight like someone turning a piece of toast in the red light of a fire. It was twenty past five. By six he'd be sitting down to his dinner in Severn Court, Station Road; then a little jaunt out with the wife to the Dragon, then telly . . .

"Having a nice little kip, Sergeant?" said a cold voice with an edge to it like a freshly unwrapped razor blade. Camb nearly jumped out of his skin.

"Sorry, Mr. Burden. It's the heat, makes you sleepy. St. Luke's Little Summer, they call it, on account of . . ."

"Are you off your bloody head?" Burden had never sworn in the old days. It had been quite a joke in the police station the way he never took the name of the Lord in vain or said bloody or any of the things everyone else said. Camb liked the old days better. He felt his face reddening and it wasn't the sun. "Any messages for me?" Burden snapped.

Camb looked at him sadly. He was terribly sorry for Inspector Burden, his heart ached for his bereaved colleague, and that was why he forgave Burden for humiliating him and showing him up in front of Martin and Gates and even Peach. Camb couldn't imagine what it must be like to lose one's wife, the mother of one's children, and be alone and desolate. Burden was so thin. The sharp high cheekbones jutted out of his taut skin and his eyes glittered nastily when you glanced at them but they were unbearable when you looked deeper. Once he had been rather a handsome man, English-looking, blond and ruddy, but now all the colour and life had gone out of him and he was a sort of grey. He still wore a black tie, pulled so tight you thought it would choke him.

Once, when it had first happened, the sergeant had expressed his sympathy along with everyone else, and that was all right, that was expected. And then, later, he had tried to say something more sincere and more personal, and Burden had swung on him like a man drawing a sword. He had said terrible things. It was more terrible to hear them coming from those mild cool lips than from the mouths of the Kingsmarkham roughs who used them habitually. It was like opening a nice book written by someone whose books you liked and asked the library to keep for you, opening it and reading a word that used to be printed with an f and a dash.

So, although Camb wanted at this moment to say something kind—wasn't he old enough to be this man's father?—he only sighed and replied in a blank official voice, "Mr. Wexford went home, sir. He said he . . ."

"That's all?"

"No, sir. There's a child missing and . . ."

"Why the hell didn't you say so before?"

"It's all taken care of," Camb stammered. "Martin knows and he's bound to have phoned Mr. Wexford. Look, sir, it's not for me to interfere, but—well, why don't you just go home, sir?"

"When I require your instructions, Sergeant, I'll ask for them. The last child that went missing here was never found. *I am not going home.*" I have nothing to go home for. He didn't say it, but the words were there and the sergeant heard them. "Get me an outside line, will you?"

Camb did so and Burden said, "My home." When Grace Woodville answered, Camb gave the phone to her brother-in-law. "Grace? Mike. Don't wait dinner for me. There's a child missing, I should be in by ten."

Burden crashed down the receiver and made for the lift. Camb watched the doors blankly for ten minutes and then Sergeant Mathers came down to take over the desk.

The bungalow in Tabard Road looked exactly as it had done in Jean Burden's lifetime. the floors gleamed, the windows shone and there were flowers —chrysanthemums at this season—in the Poole pottery vases. Plain English food was served at regular times and the children had the cared-for look of children who have a loving mother. The beds were made by eight-thirty, the washing was on the line by nine and a pleasant cheerful voice sounded a greeting to those who came home.

Grace Woodville had seen to all this. It had seemed to her the only way, to keep the house as her sister had done, to act with the children as her sister had done. She already looked as much like her sister as is possible for two women who are not twins. And it had worked. Sometimes she thought John and Pat almost forgot. They came to her when they were hurt or in trouble or had something interesting to tell just as they had gone to Jean. They seemed happy, recovered from the wound of Christmas. It had worked for them and the house and the practical business of running things, but it hadn't worked for Mike. Of course it hadn't. Had she really thought it would?

She put down the phone and looked into the glass where she saw Jean's face looking back at her. Her own face had never seemed like Jean's while Jean was alive, but quite different, squarer and stronger and more fulfilled and—well, why not say it?—more intelligent. It was like Jean's now. The liveliness had gone out of it, the sharp wit, and that wasn't surprising when she thought how she spent her days, cooking and cleaning and comforting and waiting at home for a man who took it all for granted.

She called out, "John? That was your father. He won't be home till ten. I think we'll eat, shall we?" His sister was in the garden, gathering caterpillars for the collection she kept in the garage. Grace was more afraid of caterpillars than most women are of mice or spiders, but she had to pretend to like them, even to gloat over them, because she was all Pat had for a mother. "Pat! Food, darling. Don't be long."

The little girl was eleven. She came in and opened the matchbox she was holding. Grace's heart squeezed and chilled at the sight of the fat green thing inside. "Lovely," she said faintly. "A lime hawk?" she had done her homework, and Pat, like all children, valued adults who bothered.

"Look at his sweet face."

"Yes, I am. I hope he'll grow into a chrysalis before the leaves die off. Daddy won't be home for dinner."

Pat gave an indifferent shrug. She didn't love her father much at present. He had loved her mother more than her, she knew that now, and she also knew that he ought to love her to make up for what she had lost. One of the teachers at school had told her that he would, that all fathers did that. She had waited and he hadn't. He had always stayed out late working but now he stayed out nearly all the time. She transferred her simple animal-like love to her Aunt Grace. Privately she thought it would be nice if John and her father went away and left her with her aunt and then the two of them would have a lovely time collecting better and rarer caterpillars and reading books on natural history and science and the Bolshoi Ballet.

She sat down at the table next to her aunt and then began to eat the chicken-and-ham pie which was just like the ones Jean used to make.

Her brother said, "We had a debate at school today on the equality of the sexes."

"That was interesting," said Grace. "What did you have to say?"

"I left most of the talking to the others. One thing I did say, women's brains don't weigh as much as men's."

"They do," said Pat.

"No, they don't. They don't, do they, Auntie Grace?"

"I'm afraid they don't," said Grace, who had been a nurse. "But that doesn't mean they aren't as good."

"I bet," said Pat with a vindictive look at her brother, "I bet mine weighs more than yours. My head's bigger. Anyway, it's all boring, discussions and stuff. A lot of talk."

"Come along, darling, eat your pie."

"When I am grown up," said Pat, beginning on a perennial theme, "I'm not going to talk and argue and do boring things. I'm going to get my degree—no, maybe I'll wait till I've got my doctorate—and then I'm going to go to Scotland and make a big investigation of the lochs, all the very deep lochs, and discover the monsters that live in them, and then I'm ..."

"There aren't any monsters. They looked and they never found one."

Pat ignored her brother. "I'll have divers and a special boat and a whole staff and Auntie Grace will be at the station looking after us and cooking for us."

They began to argue fiercely. It could happen, Grace thought. That was the horrible thing, it could just happen. Sometimes she could see herself staying here until they were grown up and she was old and then tagging along after Pat, being her housekeeper. What else would she be fit for then? And what did it matter whether her brain weighed less than a man's or more or the same when it was stuck in a little house in the depths of Sussex, atrophying away?

She had been a sister in a big London teaching hospital when Jean died and she had taken the six weeks' leave that was owing to her to come here and care for Mike and Mike's children. Just six weeks she was going to stay. You didn't spend years of your life studying, taking cuts in salary, to study for more qualifications, going to the States for two years to learn the latest obstetric methods at a Boston clinic, and then just give it all up. The hospital board had told her not to and she had laughed at the very idea. But the six weeks had lengthened into six months, into nine, ten, and now her post at the hospital had been filled by someone else.

She looked thoughtfully at the children. How could she leave them now? How could she even think of leaving them for five years? And then Pat would be only sixteen.

It was all Mike's fault. A hard thing to think, but true. Other men lost their wives. Other men adjusted. On Mike's salary and with his allowances he could afford a housekeeper. And it wasn't only that. A man as intelligent as Mike ought to realise what he was doing to her and the children. She had come at his invitation, his passionate plea, thinking that she would have his support in her task, certain that he would make an effort to be home in the evenings, take the children out at weekends, compensate them in some measure for the loss of their mother. He had done none of this. How long was it now since he'd spent one evening at home? Three weeks? Four? And he wasn't always working. One night when she could no longer stand the sight of John's bitter rebellious face she had phoned Wexford and the chief inspector had told her Mike went off duty at five. A neighbour had told her later where Mike went. She had seen him sitting in his car on one of the paths in Cheriton Forest, just sitting still and staring at the straight, parallel, endless trees.

"Shall we have some television?" she said, trying to keep the weariness out of her voice. "There's quite a good film on, I believe."

"Too much homework," John said, "and I can't do the maths till my father comes. Did you say he'd be back at ten?"

"He said about ten."

"I think I'll go into my room, then."

Grace and Pat sat on the sofa and watched the film. It was all about the domestic lives of policemen and bore little relation to reality.

Burden drove to Stowerton, through the new part and into the old High Street. Fontaine Road was parallel with Wincanton Road, and there, years and years ago when they were first married, he and Jean had for six months rented a flat. Wherever he went in Kingsmarkham and its environs he kept coming on places that he and Jean had been to or visited on some special occasion. He couldn't avoid them, but the sight of them brought fresh hurt every time and the pain did not diminish. Since her death he had avoided Wincanton Road, for there they had been especially happy, young lovers learning what love was. Today had been a bad day, bad in that for some reason he was ultra-sensitive and prickly, and he felt that the sight of the house where their flat had been would be the last straw. Control might go utterly and he would stand at the gate and weep.

He didn't even look at the street name as he passed it but kept his eyes fixed straight ahead. He turned left into Fontaine Road and stopped outside number 61.

It was a very ugly house, built about eighty years ago, and surrounded by a wild untended garden full of old fruit trees whose leaves lay in drifts on the grass. The house itself was built of khaki-coloured bricks with a shallow, almost flat, slate roof. Its windows were the sash kind and very small, but the front door was enormous, quite out of proportion, a great heavy thing with inset panels of red and blue stained glass. It was slightly ajar.

Burden didn't go into the house at once. Wexford's car, among other police cars, was parked against the fence which divided the end of the street from the field Stowerton Council had turned into a children's playground. Beyond this came more fields, woods, the rolling countryside.

Wexford was sitting in his car, studying an ordnance survey map. He looked up as Burden approached and said:

"Good of you to get here so fast. I've only just arrived myself. Will you talk to the mother or shall I?"

"I will," said Burden.

There was a heavy knocker on the front door of number 61, shaped like a lion's head with a ring in its mouth. Burden touched it lightly and then he pushed open the door.

2

A young woman was standing in the hall, holding her hands clasped in front of her. The first thing Burden noticed about her was her hair which was the same colour as the dead apple leaves that had blown in on to the tiled passage floor. It was fiery copper hair, neither straight nor curly but massy and glittering like fine wire or thread spun on a distaff, and it stood out from her small white face and fell to the middle of her back.

"Mrs. Lawrence?"

She nodded.

"My name is Burden, Inspector Burden, C.I.D. Before we talk about this I'd like a photograph of your son and some article of clothing he's recently worn."

She looked at him, wide-eyed, as if he were a clairvoyant who could sense the missing boy's whereabouts from handling his garments.

"For the dogs," he said gently.

She went upstairs and he heard her banging about feverishly, opening drawers. Yes, he thought, it would be an untidy house with nothing in its place, nothing to hand. She came back, running, with a dark green school blazer and an enlarged snapshot. Burden looked at the photograph as he hurried up the road. It was of a big sturdy child, neither very clean nor very tidy, but undeniably beautiful, with thick light hair and large dark eyes.

The men who had come to search for him stood about in groups, some in the swings field, some clustered around the police cars. There were sixty or seventy of them, neighbours, friends and relatives of

11

neighbours, and others who had arrived on bicycles from further afield. The speed with which news of this kind travels always amazed Burden. It was scarcely six o'clock. The police themselves had only been alerted half an hour before.

He approached Sergeant Martin, who seemed to be involved in some kind of altercation with one of the men, and handed him the photograph.

"What was all that about?" said Wexford.

"Chap told me to mind my own business because I advised him he'd need thicker shoes. That's the trouble with getting the public in, sir. They always think they know best."

"We can't do without them, Sergeant," Wexford snapped. "We need every available man at a time like this, police and public."

The two most efficient and experienced searchers belonged, properly speaking, in neither category. They sat a little apart from the men and viewed them with wary scorn. The labrador bitch's coat gleamed like satin in the last of the sun, but the alsatian's thick pelt was dull and rough and wolflike. With a quick word to the man Sergeant Martin had admonished not to go near the dogs—he appeared to be about to caress the alsatian—Wexford passed the blazer over to the labrador's handler.

While the dogs explored the blazer with expert noses, Martin formed the men into parties, a dozen or so in each and each with its leader. There were too few torches to go round and Wexford cursed the season with its deceptive daytime heat and its cold nights that rushed in early. Already dark fingers of cloud were creeping across the redness of the sky and a sharp bite of frost threatened. It would be dark before the search parties reached the wood that crouched like a black and furry bear over the edges of the fields.

Burden watched the small armies enter the wide swings field and begin the long hunt that would take them to Forby and beyond. A frosty oval moon, just beginning to wane from the full, showed above the woods. If only it would shine bright, unobscured by that blue-black floating cloud, it would be a greater asset than all their torches.

The women of Fontaine Road who had hung over their gates to see the men go now strayed lingeringly back into their houses. Each one of them would have to be questioned. Had she seen anything? Anyone? Had anything at all out of the way happened that day? On Wexford's orders, Loring and Gates were beginning a house-to-house investigation. Burden went back to Mrs. Lawrence and followed her into the front room, a big room full of ugly Victorian furniture to match the house. Toys and books and magazines were scattered everywhere and there were clothes about, shawls and scarves draped over the furniture. A long patchwork dress on a hanger hung from a picture rail.

The place looked even dirtier and frowstier when she switched on the standard lamp, and she looked stranger. She wore jeans, a satin shirt and strings of tarnished chains around her neck. He didn't need to admire her, but he would have liked to be able to feel sympathy. This woman with her wild hair and her strange clothes made him immediately feel that she was no fit person to be in charge of a child and even that her appearance and all he associated with it had perhaps contributed to that child's disappearance. He told himself not to jump to conclusions, not yet.

"Now, what is the boy's name and how old is he?"

"John. He's five."

"Not at school today?"

"It's half-term for the primary schools," she said. "I'll tell you about this afternoon, shall I?"

"Please."

"Well, we had our lunch, John and I, and after lunch at about two his friend from next door came to call for him. He's called Gary Dean and he's five too." She was very composed, but now she swallowed and

cleared her throat. "They were going to play in the
street on their tricycles. It's quite safe. They know
they have to stay on the pavement.

"When John goes out to play I look out of the
window every half-hour or so to see he's all right and
I did that today. You can see all the street and the
field where the swings are from my landing window.
Well, for a bit they played on the pavement with the
other boys, all boys from around here, but when I
looked out at half past three they'd gone into the
swings field."

"You could make out your son from this distance?"

"He's wearing a dark blue sweater and he's got fair
hair."

"Go on, Mrs. Lawrence."

She took a deep breath and clasped the fingers of
one hand tightly in the other.

"They'd left their tricycles in a sort of huddle on
the pavement. The next time I looked they were all
on the swings and I could pick out John by his hair
and his sweater. Or—or I thought I could. There were
six boys there, you see. Anyway, when I looked out
again they'd all gone and I went down to open the
front door for John. I thought he must be coming in
for his tea."

"But he wasn't?"

"No, his tricycle was on the pavement by itself."
She bit her lip, her face very white now. "There
weren't any children in the street. I thought John must
have gone into someone else's house—he does that
sometimes although he's not supposed to without telling me so I waited—oh, five minutes, not more—and
then I went into the Deans to see if he was there.
It gave me a shock," she said, half-whispering. "That
was when I first started getting frightened. Gary was
there, having his tea, and there was a boy with him
in a blue sweater and with fair hair, but it wasn't
John. It was his cousin who'd come over for the afternoon. You see, I realised then that the boy I'd been
thinking was John ever since half past three was this
cousin."

"What did you do next?"

"I asked Gary where John was and he said he didn't know. He'd gone some hours ago, he said—that was how he put it, hours ago—and they thought he was with me. Well, I went to another boy's house then, a boy called Julian Crantock at 59, and Mrs. Crantock and I, we got it out of Julian. He said Gary and the cousin had started on John, just silly children's teasing, but you know what they're like, how they hurt each other and get hurt. They picked on John about his sweater, said it was a girl's because of the way the buttons do up at the neck, and John—well, Julian said he sat on the roundabout by himself for a bit and then he just walked off towards the road."

"This road? Fontaine Road?"

"No. The lane that runs between the swings field and the farm fields. It goes from Stowerton to Forby."

"I know it," Burden said, "Mill Lane. There's a drop into it from those fields, down a bank, and there are trees all along the top of the bank."

She nodded. "But why would he go there? Why? He's been told again and again he's never to leave the street or the swings field."

"Little boys don't always do as they are told, Mrs. Lawrence. Was it after this that you phoned us?"

"Not at once," she said. She lifted her eyes and met Burden's. They were greenish-grey eyes and they held a terrified bewilderment, but she kept her voice low and even. "I went to the houses of all the boys. Mrs. Crantock came with me and when they all said the same, about the quarrel and John going off, Mrs. Crantock got out her car and we drove along Mill Lane all the way to Forby and back, looking for John. We met a man with cows and we asked him, and a postman and someone delivering vegetables, but nobody had seen him. And then I phoned you."

"So John has been missing since about three-thirty?"

She nodded. "But why would he go there? Why? He's afraid of the dark."

Her composure remained and yet Burden felt that the wrong word or gesture from him, perhaps even a sudden sound, would puncture it and release a scream of terror. He didn't quite know what to make of her. She looked peculiar, the kind of woman who belonged to a world he knew of only through newspapers. He had seen pictures of her, or of women who closely resembled her, leaving London courts after being found guilty of possessing cannabis. Such as she were found dead in furnished rooms after an overdose of barbiturates and drink. Such as she? The face was the same, pinched and pale, and the wild hair and the repellent clothes. It was her control which puzzled him and the sweet soft voice which didn't fit the image he had made of her of eccentric conduct and an unsound life.

"Mrs. Lawrence," he began, "we get dozens of cases of missing children in the course of our work and more than ninety per cent of them are found safe and sound." He wasn't going to mention the girl who hadn't been found at all. Someone else probably would, some interfering neighbour, but perhaps by then the boy would be back with his mother. "Do you know what happens to most of them? They wander away out of pique or bravado and get lost and exhausted, so they lie down in some warm hole and—sleep."

Her eyes dismayed him. They were so large and staring and she hardly seemed to blink at all. Now he saw in them a faint gleam of hope. "You are very kind to me," she said gravely. "I trust you."

Burden said awkwardly, "That's good. You trust us and let us do the worrying, eh? Now what time does your husband get home?"

"I'm divorced. I live alone."

"Yes, well, my chief will want to know about that, see your—er, ex-husband and so on." She would be divorced, he thought. She couldn't be more than twenty-eight and by the time she was thirty-eight she would probably have been married and divorced

twice more. God knew what combination of circumstances had brought her to the depths of Sussex from
London where she rightly belonged, to live in squa-
lour and cause untold trouble to the police by her
negligence.

Her quiet voice, grown rather shaky, broke into his
harsh and perhaps unjust reverie. "John's all I've got.
I've no one in the world but John."

And whose fault was that? "We'll find him," said
Burden firmly. "I'll find a woman to be with you. Perhaps this Mrs. Crantock?"

"Would you? She's very nice. Most of the people
around here are nice, although they're not . . ." She
paused and considered. "They're not quite like any
people I've known before."

I'll bet they're not, thought Burden. He glanced at
the patchwork dress. For what respectable social occasion would any woman choose to wear a thing like
that?

She didn't come to the door with him. He left her
staring into space, playing with the long chain of
beads that hung round her neck. But when he was
outside he looked back and saw her white face at the
window, a smeared dirty window that those thin
hands had never polished. Their eyes met for a moment and convention forced him to grin uneasily. She
gave no answering smile but only stared, her face
as pale and wan as the moon between clouds of
heavy hair.

Mrs. Crantock was a neat and cheerful woman who
wore her greying black hair in crisp curls and a string
of cultured pearls against her pink twinset. At Burden's request she left immediately to keep Mrs. Lawrence company. Her husband had already gone off
with the search parties and only Julian and his four-
teen-year-old sister remained in the house.

"Julian, when you saw John walk off towards Mill
Lane, did you see anything else? Did anyone speak to
him?"

The boy shook his head. "He just went off."

"And then what did he do? Did he stand under the trees or go down the lane?"

"Don't know." Julian fidgeted and looked down. "I was on the swings."

"Did you look over towards the lane? Didn't you look to see where he was?"

"He'd gone," said Julian. "Gary said he'd gone and a jolly good thing because we didn't want babies."

"I see."

"Honestly, he doesn't know," said the sister. "We've been on and on at him but he really doesn't know."

Burden gave up and went to the Deans at 63.

"I'm not having Gary hounded," said Mrs. Dean, a hard-looking young woman with an aggressive manner. "Children quarrel all the time. Gary's not to be blamed because John Lawrence is so sensitive that a bit of teasing makes him run off. The child's disturbed. That's what's at the root of the trouble. He comes from a broken home, so what can you expect?"

These were Burden's own sentiments. "I'm not blaming Gary," he said. "I just want to ask him some questions."

"I'm not having him bullied."

These days the least bit of opposition was liable to set him off.

"You're at liberty," he said sharply, "to report me to the Chief Constable, madam, if I bully him."

The boy was in bed but not asleep. He came down in his dressing-gown, his eyes sulky and his lip stuck out.

"Now, Gary, I'm not angry with you. No one's angry. We just want to find John. You understand that, don't you?"

The boy didn't answer.

"He's tired," said his mother. "He's told you he didn't see anyone and that ought to be enough."

Burden ignored her. He leant towards the boy. "Look at me, Gary." The eyes which met his were full of tears. "Don't cry. You could help us, Gary. Wouldn't you like everyone to think of you as the boy who helped the police to find John? All I want you to tell me is if you saw anyone at all, any grown-up, by the lane when John went away."

"I didn't see them today," said Gary. He screamed and threw himself on his mother. "I didn't see them, I didn't!"

"I hope you're satisfied," said Mrs. Dean. "I'm warning you, I shall take this further."

"I didn't see that person," Gary sobbed.

"Well, Mike?" said Wexford.

"It looks as if a man's been hanging about that playing field. I thought I might have a go at the people in the end houses overlooking the swings field."

"All right, and I'll try the two end ones in Wincanton."

Did Wexford remember that he and Jean had once lived there? Burden wondered if he was attributing an excess of sensitivity to the chief inspector. Probably. A policeman has no private life when on a case. He made his way to the bottom of Fontaine Road. The fields were dark now but occasionally in the far distance, he could make out the gleam from a torch.

The last two houses faced each other. One was a detached bungalow, vintage 1035, the other a tall narrow Victorian place. Both had side windows facing the field. Burden knocked at the bungalow and a girl came to the door.

"I'm out at work all day," she said. "I've only just got in and my husband isn't home yet. What's happened? Has something awful happened?"

Burden told her.

"You can see the field from my window," she said, "but I'm never here."

"I won't waste your time, then."

"I hope you find him," the girl said.

The door of the Victorian house was opened before he reached it. As soon as he saw the face of the woman who was waiting for him he knew she had something to tell him. She was elderly, sharp-eyed and spry.

"It wasn't that man, was it? I'll never forgive myself if it was him and I . . ."

"Perhaps I could come in a minute? And may I have your name?"

"Mrs. Mitchell." She took him into a neat, newly decorated room. "I ought to have gone to the police before but you know how it is. He never did anything, he never even spoke to any of the children. I did mention it to young Mrs. Rushworth because her Andrew plays there, but she's always so busy, out at work all day, and I expect she forgot to tell the other mothers. And then when he didn't come back and the children went back to school . . ."

"Let's begin at the beginning, shall we, Mrs. Mitchell? You saw a man hanging about the swings field. When did you first see him?"

Mrs. Mitchell sat down and took a deep breath. "It was in August, during the school holidays. I always clean my upstairs windows on a Wednesday afternoon and one Wednesday I was doing the landing window and I saw this man."

"Where did you see him?"

"Over by the Forby road, Mill Lane, under the trees. He was standing there, looking at the children. Let me see, there was Julian Crantock and Gary Dean and poor little John Lawrence and Andrew Rushworth and the McDowell twins, and they were all playing on the swings and this man was looking at them. Oh, I should have gone to the police!"

"You spoke to one of the mothers, Mrs. Mitchell. You mustn't reproach yourself. I take it you saw this man again?"

"Oh, yes, the next Wednesday, and I made a point of looking the next day, the Thursday, and he was there again, and it was then I spoke to Mrs. Rushworth."

"So, in fact, you saw him often throughout the August holiday?"

"We had a spell of bad weather after that and the children couldn't go into the field, and then it was

time to go back to school. I forgot all about the man
after that. Until yesterday."

"You saw him *yesterday?*"

Mrs. Mitchell nodded. "It was Wednesday and I was
doing the landing window. I saw the children come
into the field and then this man appeared. It gave me
a shock, seeing him again after two months. I thought
to myself, I'm going to stand at this window and
watch you and see what you do. But he didn't do
anything. He walked around the field and he picked
some leaves, branches of autumn leaves, you know,
and then he stood still for a bit, looking at the boys.
He was there for about half an hour and when I was
just thinking, I'll have to get a chair because my legs
won't hold me up, he went down over the bank."

"Had he a car?" Burden asked quickly. "In the
lane?"

"I couldn't see. I *think* I heard a car start up, but it
mightn't have been his, might it?"

"Did you see him today, Mrs. Mitchell?"

"I should have looked, I know that. But I *had* told
Mrs. Rushworth and it was her responsibility. Besides,
I'd never seen this man do anything." She sighed. "I
went out at two today," she said. "I went to see my
married daughter in Kingsmarkham."

"Describe this man to me, Mrs. Mitchell."

"I can do that," she said, pleased. "He was young,
hardly more than a boy himself. Very slim, you
know, and sort of slight. Not as tall as you, not nearly.
About five feet six. He always wore the same clothes,
one of those—what d'you call them?—duffel coats,
black or very dark grey, and those jeans they all wear.
Dark hair, not long for these days, but a lot longer
than yours. I couldn't see his face, not from this distance, but he had very little hands. And he limps."

"*Limps?*"

"When he was walking round the field," said Mrs.
Mitchell earnestly, "I noticed that he dragged one of
his feet. Just slightly. Just a slight little limp."

3

The next parallel street was called Chiltern Avenue and access to it was by a footpath which ran along the side of Mrs. Mitchell's house between her garden and the field. Burden went down Chiltern Avenue, calling at every house. The McDowell family lived at number 38 and the twins, Stewart and Ian, were still up.

Stewart had never seen the man, for during most of August he had been confined indoors with tonsillitis and today he had been with his mother to the dentist. But Ian had seen him and had even discussed him with Gary Dean, his special friend.

"He kept right under the trees all the time," said Ian. "Gary said he was a spy. Gary went to talk to him one day but he ran into Mill Lane."

Burden asked the boy to describe him, but Ian lacked Mrs. Mitchell's powers of observation.

"Just a man," he said. "About as big as my brother." The brother in question was fifteen. Burden asked about the limp.

"What's limp?"

Burden explained. "Dunno," said Ian.

Further down, in a house of the same vintage as Mrs. Lawrence's, he encountered the Rushworth family. Rushworth, it appeared, was an estate agent in Kingsmarkham, and he had gone off with the search parties, but his wife was at home with her four unruly children, all of whom were still up. Why hadn't she come to the police when Mrs. Mitchell had first warned her back in August?

A little blonde woman whose stilt heels and long fingernails combined with a bouncing crest of hair gave her the look of a delicate game bird, Mrs. Rush-worth burst into tears.

"I meant to." She choked. "I had every intention. I work so hard. I work in my husband's office, you know. There's never a moment to do *anything!*"

It was almost eight and John Lawrence had been missing for four and a half hours. Burden shivered a little less from the frosty chill of the night than from the sense of impending tragedy, of coming events casting a long cold shadow before them. He went over to the car and got in beside Wexford.

The chief inspector's driver had left him alone and he sat in the back of the black official car, not making notes, no longer studying his map, but pondering deeply. There was very little light—he hadn't switched on the interior light—and in the shadows he might have been a figure of stone. From head to foot he was grey —grey sparse hair, old grey raincoat, shoes that were always a little dusty. His face was deeply lined and in the half-dark it too looked grey. He turned slightly as Burden came in and fixed on him a pair of grey eyes which were the only brilliant sharp thing about him. Burden said nothing and for a few moments the two men were silent. Then Wexford said:

"A penny for them, Mike."

"I was thinking of Stella Rivers."

"Of course you were. Aren't we all?"

"It was her half-term holiday too," Burden said. "She was an only child of divorced parents. She also disappeared in Mill Lane. There are a good many similarities."

"And a good many dissimilarities too. For one thing, she was a girl and older. You don't know much about the Stella Rivers case. You were off sick when it happened."

They had thought he was going to have a break-down. Back in February it had been when the first shock of Jean's death had abated, leaving grief and panic and the horror of his situation to pour in. He had lain in bed, sleeping when Dr. Crocker drugged him, shouting out when he was conscious that it was only the flu he had, that he must get up and go back to work. But he had been off work for three weeks and when at last he was better he had lost nearly two stone. Still, he had been alive, while Stella Rivers was dead or vanished from the face of her small earth.

"She also lived with her mother," said Wexford, "and her stepfather. On Thursday, February 25th, she had a riding lesson at Equita, the riding school in Mill Lane near Forby. She had her regular lessons on Saturdays, but this was an extra one, arranged to take advantage of her half-term holiday. The stepfather, Ivor Swan, drove her to Equita from their home at Hall Farm in Kingsmarkham, but there was some doubt as to how she was to get home again."

"What d'you mean, doubt?"

"After she disappeared both Ivor and Rosalind Swan said Stella had told them she would get a lift home in a friend's car, as she sometimes did as far as Kingsmarkham, but it appeared that Stella had had no such idea and expected Swan to pick her up. When it got to six o'clock—the lesson ended at four-fifteen—Rosalind Swan, having checked with the friend, phoned us.

"We went first to Equita, saw Miss Williams who runs the school and her assistant, a Mrs. Fenn, and were told that Stella had left alone at four-thirty. By now it was raining hard and the rain had begun at about four-forty. Eventually we made contact with a man who had passed Stella at four-forty and offered her a lift to Stowerton. At this time she was walking along Mill Lane towards Stowerton. She refused his offer which made us think she was a sensible girl who wouldn't take lifts from strangers."

"She was twelve, wasn't she?" Burden put in.

"Twelve, slight and fair-haired. The man who offered her the lift is called Walter Hill and he's the manager of that little branch of the Midland Bank in Forby. If misguided, he's perfectly respectable and had nothing to do with her disappearance. We checked and double-checked him. No one else ever came forward to say he had seen Stella. She walked out of Equita, apparently believing she would meet her stepfather, and vanished into thin air.

"I can't go into all the details now, but of course we investigated Ivor Swan with the utmost care. Apart from the fact that he had no real alibi for that afternoon, we had no real reason to believe he wished harm to Stella. She liked Swan, she even seemed to have had a sort of crush on him. Not one relative or friend of the Swans could tell of any trouble whatsoever in their household. And yet . . ."

"And yet what?"

Wexford hesitated. "You know those feelings I get, Mike, those almost supernatural sensations that something isn't, well—well, quite right?"

Burden nodded. He did.

"I felt it there. But it was only a feeling. People boast of their intuition because they only care to remember the times they've been proved right. I never let myself forget the numberless times my premonitions have been wrong. We never found the least thing to pin on Swan. We shall have to resurrect the case tomorrow. Where are you going?"

"Back to Mrs. Lawrence," said Burden.

An anxious-looking Mrs. Crantock admitted him to the house.

"I don't think I've been much help," she whispered to him in the hall. "We aren't very close, you see, just neighbours whose children play with each other. I didn't know what to say to her. I mean, normally we'd discuss our little boys, but now—well, I didn't feel . . ." She gave a helpless shrug. "And you can't talk to her about ordinary things, you know. You never can. Not about the house or what goes on in the neighborhood." Her forehead wrinkled as she made a mammoth effort to explain the inexplicable. "Perhaps if I could talk about books or—or something. She just isn't like anyone else I know."

"I'm sure you've done very well," said Burden. He thought he knew very well what Mrs. Lawrence would like to talk about. Her idea of conversation would be an endless analysis of the emotions.

"Well, I tried," Mrs. Crantock raised her voice. "I'm going now, Gemma, but I'll come back later if you want me."

Gemma. A curious name. He didn't think he had ever come across it before. She *would* have an outlandish name, either because her equally eccentric parents had labelled her with it or—more likely—she had adopted it herself on the grounds of its originality. Suddenly impatient with himself, he wondered why he kept speculating about her in this irritating way, why every new piece of knowledge of her he acquired gave immediate rise to enquiry. Because she is, or soon will be, involved in a murder case, he told himself. He pushed open the living-room door, his mind full of the flamboyant, wild and outrageous image he had made, and stopped, taken aback at what he saw. Yet it was only what he had left behind, a white-faced frightened girl, crouched in a chair, waiting, waiting . . .

She had switched on an electric fire, but it had done little to warm the room and she had wrapped herself in one of the shawls he had seen, a heavy black-and-gold thing with a long fringe. He found he couldn't picture her with a child or imagine her reading bedtime stories or pouring out cornflakes. Sitting in some club, yes, singing and playing a guitar.

"Would you like some tea?" she said, turning to him. "Some sandwiches? I can easily make sandwiches."

"Don't bother for me."

"Will your wife have something for you when you get home?"

"My sister-in-law," he said. "My wife's dead."

He didn't like having to say it. People immediately became embarrassed, blushing or even recoiling slightly as if he had some infectious disease. Then came the rush of awkward insincere sympathy, meaningless words to be gabbled through and then as soon forgotten. No one ever looked as if they really cared, or no one had until now.

Gemma Lawrence said quietly and slowly, "I'm so sorry. She must have been quite young. That was a great tragedy for you. Now I can see what has taught you to be kind to other people who are in trouble."

He felt ashamed of himself and shame made him stammer. "I—well . . . I think I would like those sandwiches if it isn't any trouble."

"How could it be?" she asked wonderingly, as if the polite conventional phrase was new to her. "Naturally I want to do something in return for all you're doing for me."

She brought the sandwiches in a very short time. It was evident they hadn't taken long to make. Ham had been roughly placed between two doorsteps of bread and the tea was in mugs without saucers.

Women had been spoiling Burden all his life, serving him food on dainty china from trays covered with lace cloths, and he took a sandwich without much enthusiasm, but when he bit into it he found that the ham was tasty and not too salty and the bread fresh.

She sat on the floor and rested her back against the armchair opposite to him. He had told Wexford there were many more questions he wanted to ask her and he hazarded a few of them, routine enquiries as to John's adult acquaintances, the parents of his school friends, her own friends. She responded calmly and intelligently and the policeman's part of his mind registered her answers automatically. But something strange had happened to him. He was absorbing with a curious unease a fact which the average man would have observed as soon as he laid eyes on her. She was beautiful. Thinking the word made him look away, yet carry with him, as if imprinted on his retina, a brilliant impression of that white face with its good bones and, more disturbingly, her long legs and full firm breasts.

Her hair was vermilion in the red firelight, her eyes the clear water-washed green of jewels that are found under the sea. The shawl gave her an exotic look as if she were set within the frame of a Pre-Raphaelite portrait, posed, unreal, unfitted for any ordinary daily task. And yet there was about her something entirely natural and impulsive. Too natural, he thought, suddenly alarmed, too real. She is more real and more aware and more natural than any woman has a right to be.

Quickly he said, "Mrs. Lawrence, I'm sure you told John never to speak to strange men."

The face whitened. "Oh, yes."

"But did he ever tell you that a man had spoken to him?"

"No, never. I take him to school and fetch him home. He's only alone when he goes out to play and then the other boys are with him." She lifted her face and now there was no guard on it. "What do you mean?"

Why did she have to ask so directly? "No one has told me they saw any stranger speak to John," he said truthfully, "but I have to check."

She said in the same uncompromising level voice, "Mrs. Dean told me a child was lost in Kingsmarkham last February and never found. She came in to tell me while Mrs. Crantock was here."

Burden forgot that he had ever allied himself with Mrs. Dean. In savage, unpoliceman-like tones he burst out before he could stop himself, "Why the hell don't these busybodies keep their mouths shut?" He bit his lip, wondering why what she had said brought out so much violence in him and the desire to go next door and strike the Dean woman. "That child was a girl," he said, "and much older. The kind of—er—pervert who needs to attack girls isn't likely to be interested in a small boy." But was that true? Who could yet understand the mysteries of a sane mind, let alone a diseased one?

She drew the shawl more closely about her and said, "How shall I get through the night?"

"I shall get you a doctor." Burden finished his tea

and got up. "Didn't I see a doctor's plate in Chiltern Avenue?"

"Yes. Dr. Lomax."

"Well, we'll get some sleeping pills out of this Lomax, and a woman to stay the night with you. I'll see you're not left alone."

"I don't know how to thank you." She bowed her head and he saw that at last she began to cry. "You'll say it's only your job and your duty, but it's more than that. I—I do thank you. When I look at you I think, Nothing can happen to John while he's there."

She was looking at him as a child should look at its father but as he could never remember his own children looking at him. Such trust was a terrible responsibility and he knew he shouldn't foster it. There was more than a fifty-fifty chance now that the child was dead and he wasn't God to bring the dead to life. He ought to say that she mustn't worry, mustn't think about it—how cruel and stupid and insensitive!—but all he could say in the face of those eyes was, "I'll go for the doctor now and he'll see you get a good night." There was no need to add anything but he added, "Don't sleep too long. I'll be back with you by nine."

Then he said good night. He didn't mean to look back. Something impelled him. She was standing in the doorway, framed in yellow light, a curious outlandish figure in that gypsy gilded shawl, her hair so bright that it seemed on fire. She waved to him tentatively, rather shyly, her other hand smoothing away the tears from under her eyes. He had seen pictures of women like her but never known them, never spoken to them. Briefly he wondered if he wanted the child found, wanted it so passionately, because that would mean he need never see her again. He turned sharply towards the street and went to summon Dr. Lomax.

A great moon drifted above the fields, pale and misty as if it drifted in a pool of water. Burden waited until the searchers got back at midnight. They had found nothing.

Grace had left a note for him: "John waited up till eleven for you to help him with his maths. Could you just glance at it? He was in quite a state. G."

It took Burden a couple of seconds to adjust to the fact that his own son was also called John. He glanced at the homework and, as far as he could see, the algebra was correct. A lot of fuss about nothing. These little nagging notes of Grace's were getting a bit much. He opened the door of his son's room and saw that he was fast asleep. Grace and Pat slept in the room that had been his and Jean's—impossible as his bedroom after her death—and he couldn't very well open that door. In his own room, once Pat's, a little room with ballet dancers cavorting on the walls as appropriate for an eleven-year-old, he sat on the bed and felt the tiredness ebb away, leaving him as alert as at eight in the morning. He could be weary to the point of collapse, but let him come in here, be alone with himself, and immediately he would be filled with this frightful, degrading urgency.

He put his head in his hands. They all thought he missed Jean as a companion, as someone to talk to and share trouble with. And so he did, terribly. But what assailed him most every day and every night, without respite, was sexual desire, which, because it had had no release in ten months, had become sealed-up, tormented sexual madness.

He knew very well how they all thought of him. To them he was a cold fish, stern when confronted by licence, mourning Jean only because he had become used to marriage and was what Wexford called uxorious. Probably, if they had ever thought of it, they imagined him and Jean making love once a fortnight with the light out. It was the way people did think about you if you were the sort of man who shied away from dirty jokes and found this permissive society foul.

They never seemed to dream that you could hate promiscuity and adultery because you knew what marriage could be and had experienced it to such a degree of excellence that anything else was a

mockery, a poor imitation. You were lucky but . . .
Ah, God, you were unlucky too!—cast adrift and sick
when it was over. Jean had been a virgin when he
married her and so had he. People said—stupid people and the stupid things they said—that it made it
hard when you married, but it hadn't for him and
Jean. They had been patient and giving and full of
love and they had been so fulsomely rewarded that,
looking back as from a desert, Burden could hardly
believe it had been so good almost from the start, with
no failures, no disappointments. But he could believe
it because he knew and remembered and suffered.

And if they knew? He was aware what their advice
would be. Get yourself a girl friend, Mike. Nothing
serious. Just a nice easy girl to have a bit of fun with.
Perhaps you could do that if you'd been used to kick-
ing over the traces. He had never been any woman's
lover but Jean's. Sex for him had been Jean. They
didn't realise that telling him to get another woman
would be like telling Gemma Lawrence to get another child.

He took off his clothes and lay face downwards, his
fists carefully clenched and pushed under the pillow.

4

If Mike made the slightest effort at an apology, Grace decided, she wouldn't say a word. Of course, he had to work and many times he couldn't get away without putting his job in jeopardy. She knew what that meant. Before she came to be his housekeeper she had had men friends, some who were just friends and some, a few, who were lovers, and often she had had to break a date because there was an emergency on at the hospital. But the next day she had always phoned or written a note to explain why.

Mike wasn't her lover but only her brother-in-law. Did that mean he owed her nothing, not even common politeness? And had you the right to stand up your children without a word, even when your son was trembling with nerves at nearly midnight because he couldn't believe he'd got his algebra right and old Parminter, the maths man, would put him in detention if he hadn't?

She cooked eggs and bacon for the lot of them and laid the dining table with a clean cloth. Not for the first time she wished her sister hadn't been such an excellent housekeeper, so correct and near-perfect in everything she did, but at least slackened to the extent of serving breakfast in the kitchen. Living up to Jean made life a bit of a burden.

She hadn't meant to make a pun and she didn't laugh. Her face hardened when Mike came down, grunted to the children and took his place at the table without a word. He wasn't going to mention last night. Well, she would.

"That algebra was perfectly O.K., John."

32

The boy's face lit as it always did when Burden spoke to him.

"I reckoned it was. I don't really care about it, only old Mint Face will keep me in if it's not. I don't suppose you'd give me a lift to school."

"Too busy," said Burden. "The walk does you good." He smiled, but not too kindly, at his daughter. "And you too, miss," he said. "Right, get going. It's nearly half past."

Grace didn't usually see them to the door but she did today to make up for their father's hardness. When she came back Burden was on his second cup of tea and before she could stop herself she had burst into a long tirade all about John's nerves and Pat's bewilderment and the way he left them all alone.

He heard her out and then he said, "Why is it that women"—he corrected himself, making the inevitable exception—"most women—can't realise men have to work? If I didn't work God knows what would happen to the lot of you."

"Were you working when Mrs. Finch saw you sitting in the car in Cheriton Forest?"

"Mrs. Finch," he flared, "can mind her own bloody business!"

Grace turned her back. She found she was slowly counting to ten. Then she said, "Mike, I do understand. I can imagine how you feel."

"I doubt that."

"Well, I think I can. But John and Pat can't. John needs you and he needs you cheerful and matter-of-fact and—and like you used to be. Mike, couldn't you get home early tonight? There's a film they'd both like to see. It doesn't start till seven-thirty, so you wouldn't have to be home till seven. We could all go. It would mean so much to them."

"All right," he said. "I'll do my best. Don't look like that, Grace. I'll be home by seven."

Her face lit up. She did something she hadn't done since his wedding. She bent over and kissed his cheek. Then she began quickly to clear the table.

Her back was to him so that she didn't see the shiver
he gave and the way he put his hand up to his face
like a man who has been stung.

Gemma Lawrence had put on clean jeans and a clean
thick sweater. Her hair was tied back in a bunch
with a piece of ribbon and she smelt of soap like a
good clean child.

"I slept all night."

He smiled at her. "Cheers for Dr. Lomax," he
said.

"Are they still searching?"

"Of course. Didn't I promise you? We've borrowed
a whole army of coppers from all the surrounding districts."

"Dr. Lomax was very kind. D'you know, he said
that when he was living in Scotland before he came
here his own little boy was missing and they found
him in a shepherd's hut lying asleep, cuddling the
sheep-dog. He'd wandered for miles and this dog had
found him and looked after him like a lost lamb. It
reminded me of Romulus and Remus and the wolf."

Burden didn't know who Romulus and Remus
were, but he laughed and said, "Well, what did I tell
you?" He wasn't going to spoil her hopes now by
pointing out that this wasn't Scotland, a place of
lonely mountains and friendly dogs. "What are you
going to do today? I don't want you to be alone."

"Mrs. Crantock's asked me to lunch and the neighbours keep coming in. People are very kind. I wish I
had some closer friends here. All my friends are in
London."

"The best thing for worry," he said, "is work. Take
your mind off things."

"I don't have any work to do, unfortunately."

He had meant housework, cleaning, tidying, sew-
ing, tasks which he thought of as naturally a
woman's work, and there was plenty of that to be
done. But he could hardly tell her that.

"I expect I'll just sit and play records," she said,

shifting a dirty cup from the record player to the floor. "Or read or something."

"As soon as we have any news, I'll come to you. I won't phone, I'll come."

Her eyes shone. "If I were the Prime Minister," she said, "I'd make you a superintendent."

He drove to Cheriton Forest where the search was now centred and found Wexford sitting on a log. It was misty this morning and the chief inspector was wrapped in an old raincoat, a battered felt hat pulled down over his eyes.

"We've got a lead on the car, Mike."

"What car?"

"Last night when they were out in the fields one of the search party told Martin he'd seen a car parked on Mill Lane. Apparently, he had a week off in August and he took his dog walking regularly up Mill Lane and three times he noticed a car parked near the spot where Mrs. Mitchell saw the man. He noticed it because it was obstructing the lane, only leaving room for single-line traffic. A red Jaguar. Needless to say, he didn't get the number."

"Did he see the man?"

"He didn't see anyone. What we want now is to find someone who regularly uses that road. A baker, for instance."

"I'll see to that," said Burden.

In the course of the morning he found a baker's roundsman who used the road every day and the driver of a van delivering soft drinks who used it only on Wednesdays and Fridays. The baker had seen the car because, coming round a corner one afternoon, he had almost hit it. A red Jaguar, he confirmed, but he hadn't taken the number either. And although he had been on the road the day before, he had passed the swings-field hedge at two and the car wasn't there then. At half-past four two women in a car had asked him if he had seen a little boy, but he was almost into Forby by then. The red Jaguar might have passed him, might have contained a child, but he couldn't remember.

The soft-drinks man was less observant. He had
never noticed anything out of the way on that road,
either recently or in August.

Burden went back to the station and had a quick
lunch in Wexford's office. They spent the afternoon interviewing a sad little stream of men, all shifty and
most undersized, who at some time or other had
made overtures to children. There was the retarded
nineteen-year-old whose speciality was waiting outside school gates; the middle-aged primary-school
teacher, sacked by the authority years ago; the
draper's assistant who got into train compartments
that contained a solitary child; the schizophrenic who
had raped his own little daughter and since been dis-
charged from mental hospital.

"Lovely job, ours," said Burden. "I feel slimy all
over."

"There but for the grace of God . . ." said Wexford.
"You might have been one of them if your parents
had rejected you. I might if I'd responded to the
advances made to me in the school cloakroom. They
sit in darkness, they're born, as Blake or some clever
sod said, to endless night. Pity doesn't cost anything,
Mike, and it's a damn sight more edifying than shouting about flogging and hanging and castrating and
what you will."

"I'm not shouting, sir. I just happen to believe in
the cultivation of self-control. And my pity is for the
mother and that poor kid."

"Yes, but the quality of mercy is not strained. The
trouble with you is you're a blocked-up colander and
your mercy strains through a couple of miserable little
holes. Still, none of these wretched drop-outs was near
Mill Lane yesterday and I don't see any of them living it up in a red Jaguar."

If you haven't been out in the evening once in ten
months the prospect of a trip to the cinema in the
company of your brother-in-law and two children can
seem like high living. Grace Woodville went to the

hairdresser's at three and when she came out she felt more elated than she had the first day Pat came to kiss her of her own accord. There was a nice golden-brown sweater in Moran's window, and Grace, who hadn't bought a garment in months, decided on an impulse to have it.

Mike should have a special dinner tonight, curried chicken. Jean had never cooked that because she didn't like it, but Mike and the children did. She bought a chicken and by the time John and Pat came home the bungalow was filled with the rich scents of curry sauce and sweet-sour pineapple.

She had laid the table by six and changed into the new sweater. By five to seven they were all sitting in the living room, all dressed-up and rather self-conscious, more like people waiting to be taken to a party than a family off to the local cinema.

The telephone calls had begun. They came in to Kingsmarkham police station not only from people in the district, not only in Sussex, but from Birmingham and Newcastle and the north of Scotland. All the callers claimed to have seen John Lawrence alone or with a man or with two men or two women. A woman in Carlisle had seen him, she averred, with Stella Rivers; a shopkeeper in Cardiff had sold him an ice-cream. A lorry-driver had given him and his companion, a middle-aged man, a lift to Grantham. All these stories had to be checked, though all seemed to be without foundation.

People poured into the station with tales of suspicious persons and cars seen in Mill Lane. By now not only red Jaguars were suspect but black ones and green ones, black vans, three-wheelers. And meanwhile the arduous search went on. Working without a break, Wexford's force continued a systematic house-to-house investigation, questioning most particularly every male person over sixteen.

Five to seven found Burden outside the Olive and Dove Hotel in Kingsmarkham High Street, facing the cinema, and he remembered his date with Grace and the children, remembered, too, that he must see Gemma Lawrence before he went off duty.

The phone box outside the hotel was occupied and a small queue of people waited. By the time they had all finished, Burden judged, a good ten minutes would have passed. He glanced again at the cinema and saw that whereas the last programme began at seven-thirty, the big picture didn't start until an hour later. No need to phone Grace when he could easily drive to Stowerton, find out how things were with Mrs. Lawrence and be home by a quarter to eight. Grace wouldn't expect him on time. She knew better than that. And surely even his two wouldn't want to sit through a film about touring in East Anglia, the news and all the trailers.

For once the front door wasn't open. The street was empty, almost every house well-lit. It seemed for all the world as if nothing had happened yesterday to disturb the peace of this quiet country street. Time passed, men and women laughed and talked and worked and watched television and said, What can you do? That's life.

There were no lights on in her house. He knocked on the door and no one came. She must have gone out. When her only child was missing, perhaps murdered? He remembered the way she dressed, the state of her house. A good-time girl, he thought, not much of a mother. Very likely one of those London friends had come and she'd gone out with him.

He knocked again and then he heard something, a kind of shuffling. Footsteps dragged to the door, hesitated.

He called, "Mrs. Lawrence, are you all right?"

A little answering sound came to him, half a sob and half a moan. The door quivered, then swung inwards.

Her face was ravaged and swollen and sodden with crying. She was crying now, sobbing, the tears streaming down her face. He shut the door behind him and switched on a light.

"What's happened?"

She twisted away from him, threw herself against the wall and beat on it with her fists. "Oh God, what shall I do?"

"I know it's hard," he said helplessly, "but we're doing everything that's humanly possible. We're . . ."

"Your people," she sobbed, "they've been in and out all day, searching and—and asking me things. They searched this house! And people kept phoning, awful people. There was a woman—a *woman* . . . Oh my God! She said John was dead and she—she described how he died and she said it was my fault! I can't bear it, I can't bear it, I shall gas myself, I shall cut my wrists . . ."

"You must stop this," he shouted. She turned to him and screamed into his face. He raised his hand and slapped her stingingly on the cheek. She gagged, gulped and crumpled, collapsing against him. To stop her falling, he put his arms round her and for a moment she clung to him, as in a lover's embrace, her wet face buried in his neck. Then she stepped back, the red hair flying as she shook herself.

"Forgive me," she said. Her voice was hoarse with crying. "I'm mad. I think I'm going mad."

"Come in here and tell me. You were optimistic earlier."

"That was this morning." She spoke quietly now in a thin broken voice. Gradually and not very coherently she told him about the policeman who had searched her cupboards and tramped through the attics, how they had torn away the undergrowth that swamped the roots of old trees in that wild garden. She told him, gasping, of the obscene phone calls and of the letters, inspired by last night's evening-paper story, the second post had brought.

"You are not to open any letters unless you recognise the handwriting," he said. "Everything else we'll look at first. As to the phone calls . . ."

"Your sergeant said you'd have an arrangement to get my phone monitored." She sighed deeply, calmer now, but the tears were still falling.

"Have you got any brandy in this—er—place?"

"In the dining room." She managed a damp, weak smile. "It belonged to my great-aunt. This—er—place, as you call it, was hers. Brandy keeps for years and years, doesn't it?"

"Years and years make it all the better," said Burden.

The dining room was cavernous, cold and smelling of dust. He wondered what combination of circumstances had brought her to this house and why she stayed. The brandy was in a sideboard that looked more like a wooden mansion than a piece of furniture, it was so ornamented with carved pillars and arches and niches and balconies.

"You have some too," she said.

He hesitated. "All right. Thank you." He made his way back to the armchair he had occupied before going to the dining room, but she sat down on the floor, curling her legs under her and staring up at him with a curious blind trust. Only one lamp was alight, making a little golden glow behind her head.

She drank her brandy and for a long time they sat without talking. Then, warmed and calmed, she began to speak about the lost boy, the things he liked doing, the things he said, his little precocious cleverness. She spoke of London and of the strangeness of Stowerton to herself and her son. At last she fell silent, her eyes fixed on his face, but he had lost the embarrassment which this trusting childlike stare had at first occasioned in him and it didn't return even when, leaning forward with quick impulsiveness, she reached for his hand and held it tightly.

He wasn't embarrassed, but the touch of her hand electrified him. It brought him such a shock and such sudden turbulence that instead of the normal reactions of a normal man enclosing the hand of a pretty woman in his own he had the illusion that his whole body was holding her body. The effect of this was to make him tremble. He loosened his fingers and said abruptly, breaking the now heavy and languorous silence, "You're a Londoner. You like London. Why do you live here?"

"It is rather ghastly, isn't it?" All the harshness and terror had gone from her voice and once more it was soft and rich. Although he had known she was bound to speak in answer to his question, the sound of her beautiful voice, quite normal now, disturbed him almost as much as the touch of her hand. "A dreadful old white elephant of a house," she said.

"It's no business of mine," he muttered.

"But it's no secret either. I didn't even know I had this great-aunt. She died three years ago and left this house to my father, but he was dying himself of cancer." With a peculiarly graceful but unstudied movement she raised her hand and pushed away the mass of hair from her face. The full embroidered sleeve of the strange tunic she wore fell away from her arm and the skin glowed whitely, faint golden down gleaming in the lamplight. "I tried to sell it for my father, but no one wanted it, and then he died and Matthew —my husband—left me. Where else could I go but here? I couldn't afford the rent of our flat and Matthew's money had run out." It seemed like hours since those eyes had first begun staring at him, but now at last she turned them away. "The police," she said very softly, "thought Matthew might have taken John."

"I know. It's something we always have to check on when the child of—er—estranged or divorced parents is missing."

"They went to see him, or they tried to. He's in hospital, having his appendix out. I believe they talked to his wife. He married again, you see."

Burden nodded. With more than a policeman's natural curiosity he passionately wanted to know whether this Matthew had divorced her or she him, what he did for a living, how it had all come about. He couldn't ask her. His voice felt strangled.

She edged a little closer towards him, not reaching out for his hand this time. Her hair curtained her face. "I want you to know," she said, "how you've helped me. What a comfort you've been. I should have broken down completely tonight if you hadn't come. I should have done something dreadful."

"You mustn't be alone."

"I've got my sleeping tablets," she said, "and Mrs. Crantock is coming in at ten." Slowly she got to her feet, reached out and switched on the standard lamp. "She'll be here in a minute. It's five to now."

Her words and the sudden brightness brought Burden sharply back to reality. He blinked and shook himself.

"Five to ten? I've just remembered, I'm supposed to be taking my family to the pictures."

"And I've stopped you? Would you like to phone? Please do. Use my phone."

"Too late, I'm afraid."

"I'm dreadfully sorry."

"I think my being here was more important, don't you?"

"It was important to me. But you must go now. Will you come again tomorrow? I mean you yourself."

He was standing in the doorway as she spoke. She put her hand lightly on his arm and they were close together, their faces only a foot apart. "I—yes . . . Yes, of course." He was stammering badly. "Of course I'll come."

"Inspector Burden . . . No, I can't keep calling you that. What's your first name?"

"I think it will be best if you . . ." he began, and then, almost desperately, "It's Michael. People call me Mike."

"Mike," she said, and at that moment, as she dwelt on the name, repeating it softly, Mrs. Crantock rang the bell.

Grace was curled up on the sofa and he could see that she had been crying. The enormity of what he had done for a moment overcame that other enormity, the urgency of his body.

"I'm terribly sorry," he said, going over to her. "The phone box was full and later . . ."

She lifted her head and faced him. "We sat here and we waited for you. When you hadn't come by eight we had our meal, though it was ruined. I said, 'Let's go just the same,' and John said, 'We can't go without Dad. We can't let him come home and find us gone.'"

"I said I'm sorry," said Burden.

"You could have phoned!" Grace said passionately. "I wouldn't say a word if you'd phoned. Don't you realise, if you go on like this, you'll—you'll destroy those children!"

She went out and the door closed behind her, leaving Burden to thoughts that were neither of her nor his children.

5

Burden looked at the sheet of paper Wexford had handed him. Written on it in a bold, large but child-like hand were the names of every man, woman and child Gemma Lawrence had known during the past ten years.

"When did she write all that out?"

Wexford eyed him briefly and narrowly. "This morning with Loring's help. You aren't her exclusive private eye, you know."

Burden flushed. What hundreds of people she knew and what extraordinary names they had! Artists and models and theatre folk, he supposed, suddenly bad-tempered. "Have we got to interview all this lot?"

"The Met are going to help us there. I asked Mrs. Lawrence to write down every name because I want to show the list to the Swans."

"You are connecting the two cases, then?"

Wexford didn't answer directly. He took the list from Burden, gave him another piece of paper and said, "This came. It's been gone over for fingerprints, so you needn't worry about touching it. Of course there weren't any prints."

"John Lawrence is safe and well with me," Burden read. "He is happy playing with my rabbits on the farm. To show you this is not a hoax, I am enclosing a lock of his hair." The note, written in block capitals on a sheet of lined paper, was correctly spelt and punctuated. "His mother can have him back on Monday. I will bring him to the southern end of Myfleet Ride in Cheriton Forest at 9 a.m. If anyone tries to collect him before nine-thirty, I will know and I will

44

shoot John dead. This is a serious warning. I will not break my promise if you co-operate."

Burden dropped it in disgust. Used as he was to such things, he could still not read them without a shudder. "Was there a lock of hair?" he asked.

"Here."

It had been twisted into a smooth neat circle like a woman's pin curl. Burden lifted it in tweezers, noting the delicacy of each red-gold strand, the absence of those kinks and ridges which occur in adult hair.

"It's human," said Wexford. "I got Crocker on to it at once. He says it's the child's hair, but, of course, we shall have to have more expert tests."

"Has Mrs. Lawrence been told?"

"Thank God he's safe," she said when she had read the first lines. She held the letter momentarily to her breast but she didn't cry. "He's safe and well on a farm somewhere. Oh my God, and what agonies I've been through! Imagine, all that for nothing and he'll be back with me on Monday."

Burden was appalled. He had already told her not to bank on the letter at all, that in ninety-nine cases out of a hundred such letters are cruel hoaxes. For all the notice she took, he might not have spoken.

"Let me see the hair," she said.

Reluctantly he took the envelope which contained it from his briefcase. She gasped when she saw the small golden curl. So far it had been handled carefully with tweezers, but she took it, stroked it and pressed it to her mouth. "Come upstairs."

He followed her into John's bedroom, noticing that the child's bed hadn't been made since his disappearance. It was a nice bedroom, though, full of toys and with a beautiful expensive wallpaper of Dürer animals reproduced in line and wash. However much she might neglect the rest of the house, she had cared for this room and probably done the papering herself. Burden's opinion of her as a mother rose.

She went over to a small blue-painted chest of

drawers and picked up John's hairbrush. A few fine blond hairs were caught in its bristles and, with an earnest concentrated expression, she compared them with the lock in her hand. Then she turned and smiled radiantly.

Burden had never seen her really smile before. Until then her smiles had been brief and watery, reminding him, he thought suddenly, of a faint sun coming out after rain. Such metaphors were very unusual with him, fanciful and not in his line. But he thought it now as he received the full force of her brilliant happy smile and saw again how beautiful she was.

"It is the same, isn't it?" she said, the smile fading as she almost pleaded, "Isn't it?"

"I don't know." There was certainly a strong similarity, but Burden didn't know whether he wanted the hairs to be the same or not. If this man really had John and if he had really cut that lock from John's head, was it likely that he would let the boy go otherwise unharmed? Would he risk the boy's identifying him? On the other hand, he had demanded no money . . . "You're his mother," he murmured. "I wouldn't like to say."

"I know he's safe," she said. "I feel it. I've only got to get through two more days."

He hadn't the heart to say any more then. Only a brute, he thought, would destroy such shining happiness. So that she shouldn't read the last lines he wanted to take the letter from her, but she read it to the end.

"I've heard about cases like this," she said, a little fear returning to her voice as she gazed at him, "and what the police do. You wouldn't—you wouldn't do—do what he says you're not to do? You wouldn't try to trap him? Because then John . . ."

"I promise you," he said, "that we shall do nothing which might in any way endanger John's life." She had said nothing vindictive about the writer of the letter, he noticed. Other women in her position would have raged and screamed for revenge. She had merely been filled with joy. "We shall go there on Monday morning, at nine-thirty, and if he is there we shall bring him back to you."

"He'll be there," she said. "I trust this man. I've got a feeling he's genuine. Really, I have, Mike." Her use of his Christian name brought colour into his face. He felt his cheeks burn. "He's probably dreadfully lonely," she said gently. "I know what it is to be lonely. If John has given him a few days' respite from his loneliness I don't grudge John to him."

It was incredible and Burden couldn't understand. If it had been his child, his John, he would have wanted to kill the man, to see him die a lingering death. As it was, his feelings towards the letter-writer were so violent that they frightened him. Let me get at him, he thought, give me five minutes alone in the cell with him and, by God, if I lose my job for it . . . He pulled himself up with a jerk and saw that her eyes were on him, kind, sweet and compassionate.

In his haste to see Gemma, Burden had forgotten the Swans, but now he remembered Wexford saying the note helped to establish a connection between the two cases. The chief inspector was still in his office.

"Swan lives on a farm," he said. "I phoned but he's out till three."

"Does he keep rabbits?"

"Don't mention rabbits to me. I've only just got over an hour with the secretary of the local rabbit club. Rabbits! The place is crawling with them, Old English, Blue Beverens, you name 'em, we got 'em. I tell you, Mike, it's like the Apocrypha says, 'The coneys are a feeble folk, but they make their houses in the rocks!' "

"And every fancier being checked?" said Burden, unsmiling.

Wexford nodded. "And I know the bloody thing's a hoax," he said. "I shall spend the best part of my weekend—and so will dozens of other policemen—chasing rabbits and farmers and checking shot-gun licences and being polite to human hair experts, but I know very well it's a hoax and what I'm doing is an utter waste of time."

"But it has to be done."

"Of course it has to be done. Let's go to lunch."

At the Carousel Café only ham and salad was left on the menu. Wexford picked without enthusiasm at the salad in which lettuce leaves were economically eked out with shreds of cabbage and carrot. "Can't get away from rabbits," he muttered. "Want me to tell you about Swan and his wife?"

"I suppose I ought to have a bit of background."

"Usually," Wexford began, "you feel too much sympathy with the parents of a lost child. You find your emotions getting involved." He shifted his gaze from his plate to Burden's face and pursed his lips. "Which doesn't help," he said. "I didn't feel particularly sorry for them. You'll see why not in a minute." Clearing his throat, he went on, "After Stella disappeared, we did more research into the life and background of Ivor Swan than I can ever remember doing with anyone. I could write his biography.

"He was born in India, the son of one General Sir Rodney Swan, and he was sent home to school and then to Oxford. Being in possession of what he calls small private means, he never took up any particular career but dabbled at various things. At one time he managed an estate for someone, but he soon got the sack. He wrote a novel which sold three hundred copies, so he never repeated that experiment. Instead he had a spell in P.R. and in three months lost his firm an account worth twenty thousand a year. Utter ingrained laziness is what characterises Ivor Swan. He is indolence incarnate. Oh, and he's good-looking, staggeringly so, in fact. Wait till you see."

Burden poured himself a glass of water but said nothing. He was watching Wexford's expression warm and liven as he pursued his theme. Once he too had been able to involve himself as raptly in the characters of suspects.

"Swan rarely had any settled home," Wexford said.

"Sometimes he lived with his widowed mother at her house in Bedfordshire, sometimes with an uncle who had been some sort of big brass in the Air Force. And now I come to an interesting point about him. Wherever he goes he seems to leave disaster behind him. Not because of what he does but because of what he *doesn't* do. There was a bad fire at his mother's house while he was staying there. Swan had fallen asleep with a cigarette burning in his fingers. Then there was the loss of the P.R. account because of what he didn't do; the sacking from the estate management job—he left a pretty mess behind him there—on account of his laziness.

"About two years ago he found himself in Karachi. At that time he was calling himself a free-lance journalist and the purpose of his visit was to enquire into the alleged smuggling of gold by airline staff. Any story he concocted would probably have been libellous, but, as it happened, it was never written or, at any rate, no newspaper printed it.

"Peter Rivers worked for an airline in Karachi, not as a pilot but among the ground staff, meeting aircraft, weighing baggage, that sort of thing, and he lived with his wife and daughter in a company house. In the course of his snooping Swan made friends with Rivers. It would be more to the point to say he made friends with Rivers' wife."

"You mean he took her away from him?" Burden hazarded.

"If you can imagine Swan doing anything as active as taking anyone or anything away from anyone else. I should rather say that the fair Rosalind—'From the East to Western Ind, no jewel is like Rosalind'—fastened herself to Swan and held on tight. The upshot was that Swan returned to England plus Rosalind and Stella and about a year later Rivers got his decree.

"The three of them all lived in a poky flat Swan took in Maida Vale, but after they were married Swan, or more likely Rosalind, decided the place wasn't big enough and they came out here to Hall Farm."

"Where did he get the money to buy a farm?"

"Well, in the first place it isn't a farm any more but a chichi tarted-up farm*house* with all the land let off. Secondly, he didn't buy it. It was part of the property held under a family trust. Swan put out feelers to his uncle and he let him have Hall Farm at a nominal rent."

"Life's very easy for some people, isn't it?" said Burden, thinking of mortgages and hire purchase and grudgingly granted bank loans. "No money worries, no housing problems."

"They came here last October, a year ago. Stella was sent to the convent at Sewingbury—uncle paid the fees—and Swan let her have these riding lessons. He rides himself and hunts a bit. Nothing in a big way, but then he doesn't do anything in a big way.

"As to Rivers, he'd been having it off on the quiet with some air hostess and he also has married again. Swan, Rosalind and Stella plus an *au pair* girl settled down quite comfortably at Hall Farm, and then, bang in the middle of all this bliss, Stella disappears. Beyond a doubt, Stella is dead, murdered."

"It seems clear," said Burden, "that Swan can have had nothing to do with it."

Wexford said obstinately, "He had no alibi. And there was something else, something less tangible, something in the personality of the man himself."

"He sounds too lazy ever to commit an aggressive act."

"I know, I know." Wexford almost groaned the words. "And he had led, in the eyes of the law, a blameless life. No history of violence, mental disturbance or even bad temper. He hadn't even the reputation of a philanderer. Casual girl friends, yes, but until he met Rosalind he had never been married or engaged to be married or even lived with a woman. But he had a history of a sort, a history of disaster. There's a line in rather a sinister sonnet—'They that have power to hurt and yet do none.' I don't think that means they don't do any hurt but that they do *nothing*. That's Swan. If he didn't do this killing it happened because of him or through him or because he is what he is. D'you think that's all airyfairy moon-shine?"

"Yes," said Burden firmly.

St. Luke's Little Summer maintained its glory, at least by day. The hedges were a delicate green-gold and frost had not yet bitten into blackness the chrysan-themums and michaelmas daisies in cottage gardens. The year was growing old gracefully.

The farm was approached by a narrow lane scat-tered with fallen leaves and overhung by hedges of Old Man's Beard, the vapourish, thistledown seed heads of the wild clematis, and here and there, be-hind the fluffy masses, rose Scotch pines, their trunks a rich coral pink where the sun caught them. A long low building of stone and slate stood at the end of this lane, but most of its stonework was obscured by the flame and scarlet virginia creeper which covered it.

"Du coté de chez Swan," said Wexford softly.

Proustian references were lost on Burden. He was looking at the man who had come round from the back of the house, leading a big chestnut gelding.

Wexford left the car and went up to him. "We're a little early, Mr. Swan. I hope we're not putting you out?"

"No," said Swan. "We got back sooner than we ex-pected. I was going to exercise Sherry but that can wait."

"This is Inspector Burden."

"How do you do?" said Swan, extending a hand. "Very pleasant, all this sunshine, isn't it? D'you mind coming round the back way?"

He was certainly an extremely handsome man. Bur-den decided this without being able to say in what his handsomeness lay, for Ivor Swan was neither tall nor short, dark nor fair, and his eyes were of that indeter-minate colour men call grey for want of more ac-curate term. His features had no special regularity, his figure, though lean, no sign of athletic muscular devel-opment. But he moved with an entirely masculine grace, exuded a vague lazy charm and had about him an air of attractiveness, of making himself immediately noticed.

His voice was soft and beautiful, the words he used slowly enunciated. He seemed to have all the time in the world, a procrastinator who would always put off till tomorrow what he couldn't bring himself to do today. About thirty-three or thirty-four, Burden thought, but he could easily pass for twenty-five to a less discerning observer.

The two policemen followed him into a kind of lobby or back kitchen where a couple of guns and an assortment of fishing tackle hung above neat rows of riding boots and wellingtons.

"Don't keep rabbits, do you, Mr. Swan?" Wexford asked.

Swan shook his head. "I shoot them, or try to, if they come on my land."

In the kitchen proper two women were engaged on feminine tasks. The younger, an ungainly dark girl, was preparing—if the heaps of vegetables, tins of dried herbs, eggs and mincemeat spread on the counter in front of her were anything to go by—what Burden chauvinistically thought of as a continental mess. Well away from the chopping and splashing, a minute doll-like blonde was ironing shirts. Five or six had already been ironed. There were at least that number remaining. Burden noticed that she was taking extreme care not to cause a horizontal crease to appear under the yoke of the shirt she was at present attending to, an error into which hasty or careless women often fall and which makes the removal of a jacket by its wearer an embarrassment.

"Good afternoon, Mrs. Swan. I wonder if I may trouble you for a few minutes?"

Rosalind Swan had a girlish air, a featherlight "bovver" haircut and nothing in her face or manner to show that eight months before she had been deprived of her only child. She wore white tights and pink buckled shoes, but Burden thought she was as old as he.

"I like to see personally to all my husband's laundry," she declared in a manner Burden could only describe as merry, "and Gudrun can't be expected to give his shirts that little extra wifely touch, can she?"

From long experience Burden had learnt that if a man is having an affair with another woman and, in that woman's presence, his wife makes a more than usually coquettish and absurd remark, he will instinctively exchange a glance of disgust with his mistress. He had no reason to suppose Gudrun was anything more than an employee to Swan—she was no beauty, that was certain—but, as Mrs. Swan spoke, he watched the other two. Gudrun didn't look up and Swan's eyes were on his wife. It was an appreciative, affectionate glance he gave her and he seemed to find nothing ridiculous in what she had said.

"You can leave my shirts till later, Rozzy."

Burden felt that Swan often made remarks of this nature. Everything could be put off till another day, another time. Idleness or chat took precedence over activity always with him. He nearly jumped out of his skin when Mrs. Swan said gaily:

"Shall we go into the lounge, my lover?"

Wexford just looked at him, his face impassive.

The "lounge" was furnished with chintzy chairs, doubtful antiques, and, hanging here and there, brass utensils of no apparent use to a modern or, come to that, ancient household. It reflected no particular taste, had no individuality, and Burden remembered that Hall Farm, doubtless with all its contents, had been supplied to Swan by an uncle because he had nowhere else to live.

Linking her arm into her husband's, Mrs. Swan led him to a sofa where she perched beside him, disengaged arms and took his hand. Swan allowed himself to be thus manipulated in a passive fashion and seemed to admire his wife.

"None of these names mean anything to me, Chief Inspector," he said when he had looked at the list. "What about you, Roz?"

"I don't think so, my lover."

Her lover said, "I saw in the paper about the missing boy. You think the cases have some connection?"

"Very possibly, Mr. Swan. You say you don't know any of the people on this list. Do you know Mrs. Gemma Lawrence?"

"We hardly know anyone around here," said Rosalind Swan. "You might say we'll still on our honeymoon, really."

Burden thought this a tasteless remark. The woman was all of thirty-eight and married a year. He waited for her to say something about the child who had never been found, to show some feeling for her, but Mrs. Swan was looking with voracious pride at her husband. He thought it time to put his own spoke in and he said flatly:

"Can you account for your movements on Thursday afternoon, sir?"

The man wasn't very tall, had small hands, and anyone could fake a limp. Besides, Wexford had said he hadn't had an alibi for that other Thursday afternoon . . .

"You've quite cast me for the role of kidnapper, haven't you?" Swan said to Wexford.

"It was Mr. Burden who asked you," Wexford said imperturbably.

"I shall never forget the way you hounded me when we lost poor little Stella."

"Poor little Stella," Mrs. Swan echoed comfortably.

"Don't get upset, Rozzy. You know I don't like it when you're upset. All right, what was I doing on Thursday afternoon? Every time you add anyone to your missing persons list I suppose I must expect this sort of inquisition. I was here last Thursday. My wife was in London and Gudrun had the afternoon off. I was here all alone. I read for a bit and had a nap." A flicker of temper crossed his face. "Oh, and at about four I rode over to Stowerton and murdered a couple of tots that were making the streets look untidy."

"Oh, Ivor, darling!"

"That sort of thing isn't amusing, Mr. Swan."

"No, and it's not amusing for me to be suspected of making away with two children, one of them my own wife's."

No more could be got out of him. "I've been meaning to ask," said Burden as they drove back, "did she go on calling herself Rivers after her mother remarried?"

"Sometimes she was one, sometimes the other, as far as I could gather. When she became a missing person she was Stella Rivers to us because that was her real name. Swan said he intended to have the name changed by deed poll, but he hadn't taken any steps towards it. Typical of him."

"Tell me about this non-existent alibi," said Burden.

6

Martin, Loring and their helpers were still interviewing rabbitkeepers, Bryant, Gates and half a dozen others continuing a house-to-house search of Stowerton. During the chief inspector's absence Constable Peach had brought in a child's plimsoll which he had found in a field near Flagford, but it was the wrong size, and, anyway, John Lawrence hadn't been wearing plimsolls.

Wexford read the messages which had been left on his desk, but most were negative and some needed immediate attention. He scanned the anonymous note again, then put it back in its envelope with a sigh.

"We had enough letters in the Stella Rivers case to paper the walls of this office," he said, "and we followed them all up. We had five hundred and twenty-three phone calls. The fantasies that go on in people's minds, Mike, the power of their imaginations! They were nearly all well intentioned. Ninety per cent of them really thought they had seen Stella and ..."

Burden interrupted him. "I want to hear about Swan's alibi."

"Swan drove Stella to Equita at two-thirty. Silly sort of name, isn't it? Whether it's supposed to mean all the pupils are equal or the only thing they teach is horse-riding, I wouldn't know."

Burden was always impatient with these digressions. "What kind of a car does he drive?"

"Not a red Jag. An oldish Ford shooting brake. He left Stella at the gates, believing, he said, that friends would bring her home, and went back home himself. At three-thirty he also got on a horse, that Sherry thing, and rode to Myfleet to see, believe it or not, a man about a dog."

"You're joking."

"Would I, about a thing like this? There's a fellow in Myfleet called Blain who breeds pointers. Swan went to look at some puppies with an eye to buying one for Stella. Of course, he didn't buy one, any more than he ever got her the pony he promised or got her name changed. Swan's always 'just going to do something.' One of the Four Just Men, he is."

"But he did call on this man?"

"Blain told us Swan was with him from ten to four until four-fifteen, but he didn't get back to Hall Farm until five-thirty."

"Where did he say he had been in that hour and a quarter?"

"Just riding round. The horse, he said, needed exercise. Maybe it also needed a wash, for both rider and mount must have been wet through when Swan got home. But odd though this sounds, it is the kind of thing Swan would do. He *would* moon about on horseback in the rain. His ride, he said, took him through Cheriton Forest, but he couldn't produce a single person to corroborate this. On the other hand, he could have got to Mill Lane in the time and killed Stella. But if he did, why did he? And what did he do with her body? His wife hasn't an alibi either. She says she was at Hall Farm and she can't drive. At any rate, she hasn't a driving licence."

Burden digested all this carefully. Then, he decided, he wanted to know more about Stella's departure from Equita. He wanted the details Wexford hadn't had time to give him when they had sat together in the car in Fontaine Road.

"The children," said Wexford, "had an hour's riding lesson and a further hour they spent messing about with the horses. Miss Williams, the owner of Equita, who lives in that house adjoining the stables, saw Stella that afternoon but says she didn't speak to her and we have no reason to doubt her word. It was Mrs. Margaret Fenn who took the children out for their ride. She's a widow of about forty and she lives in what used to be the lodge to Saltram House. Know it?"

Burden knew it. Ruined Saltram House and its grounds, now turned to wilderness, had been a favorite resort of his and Jean's. For them it had been a place of romance, a lost domain, where they had gone for evening walks in the early days of their marriage and where they had later returned many times to bring their children on picnics.

All that day he had hardly thought about Jean and his happy past with her. His misery had been suspended by the present tumultuous events. But now again he saw her face before him and heard her call his name as they explored the gardens that time had laid waste and, hand in hand, entered the dark cold shell of the house. He shivered.

"You all right, Mike?" Wexford gave him a brief anxious glance and then he went on. "Stella said goodbye to Mrs. Fenn and said that as her step-father—incidentally, she always referred to him as her father—hadn't yet arrived, she would walk along Mill Lane to meet him. Mrs. Fenn didn't much like letting the girl go alone, but it was still light and she couldn't go with her as she still had another hour and a half at Equita in which to clear up. She watched Stella go through the gates of Equita, thus becoming the last person but one to see her before she disappeared."

"The last but one?"

"Don't forget the man who offered her a lift. Now for the houses in Mill Lane. There are only three between Equita and Stowerton, all widely separated, Saltram Lodge and two cottages. Before Hill offered her the lift she had passed one of these cottages, the one that is occupied only at week-ends, and, this being a Thursday, it was empty. We know no more of what happened to her after she was seen by Hill, but if she walked on unmolested she would next have come to the second cottage which has a tenant, not an owner occupier. This tenant, a single man, was out at work and didn't return until six. Again this was carefully checked because both this cottage and Saltram Lodge have telephones and one of the possibilities which occurred to me was that Stella might have called at a house and asked to phone Hall Farm. The third and last house, Saltram Lodge, was also empty until Mrs. Fenn got home at six. She had had some relatives staying with her, but they had left for London by the three-forty-five train from Stowerton. A taxi-driver confirmed that he had picked them up at the lodge at twenty past three."

"And was that all?" Burden said. "No more leads?"

Wexford shook his head. "Not what you'd call leads. The usual flock of people came forward with unhelpful evidence. A woman had picked up a child's glove outside one of the cottages but it wasn't Stella's. There was another of those free-lift merchants who said he had picked up an elderly man near Saltram Lodge at five-thirty and driven him into Stowerton, but this driver was a shifty sort of fellow and he impressed me as a sensation-monger rather than someone whose word you could rely on.

"A van-driver claimed to have seen a boy come out of the back door of the rented cottage and perhaps he did. They all leave their back doors unlocked in this part of the world. They think there's no crime in the country. But the van-driver also said he heard screams coming from behind the hedge just outside Equita, and we *know* Stella was alive and unharmed until she had refused Hill's offer. I doubt if we shall ever find out any more."

Wexford looked tired, his jowly face heavier, and more drooping than usual. "I shall take a couple of hours off tomorrow morning, Mike, and I advise you to do the same. We're both dead-beat. Have a lie-in."

Burden nodded abstractedly. He didn't say that there is no point in lying-in when there is no one to lie in with, but he thought it. Wearily he found himself recalling as he went out to his car those rare but delightful Sunday mornings when Jean, usually an early riser, consented to remain in bed with him until nine. Lying in each other's arms, they had listened to

the sound of Pat making tea for them in the kitchen,
and had sat bolt upright, jerking away from each other
when she came in with the tray. Those had been the
days, but he hadn't known it at the time, hadn't ap-
preciated and treasured each moment as he should
have done. And now he would have given ten years of
his life for one of those mornings back again.

His memories brought him a dull misery, his only
consolation that soon he would be in the company of
someone as wretched as himself, but when he walked
up to the always open door he heard her call out to
him gaily and as intimately as if they were old friends,
"I'm on the phone, Mike. Go in and sit down. Make
yourself at home."

The telephone must be in the dining room, he
thought. He sat down in the other room, feeling uncomfortable because untidiness always made him ill-
at-ease. He wondered how anyone as beautiful and as
charming as she could bear to live in such disorder
and wondered more when she came in, for she was a
changed woman, brilliantly smiling, almost elegant.

"You needn't have run off on my account," he said,
trying not to stare too hard at the short kingfisher-blue
dress she wore, the long silver chains, the silver comb
in her high-piled hair.

"That was Matthew," she said. "They brought him a
phone and he phoned me from his bed. He's terribly
worried about John, but I told him it was all right. I
told him everything would be all right on Monday. He
has so many worries, poor boy. He's ill and his wife's
expecting a baby and he's out of work and now this."

"Out of work? What sort of work does he do?"

She sat down opposite him and crossed the best pair
of legs Burden thought he had ever seen. He stared
at a patch of floor some inches from her feet.

"He's a television actor, or he is when he can get
work. He so terribly wants to be a household word.
The trouble is his face is wrong. Oh, I don't mean he
isn't good-looking. He was born too late. He looks just
like Valentino and that won't do these days. John's
going to be just like him. He's very like him now."

Matthew Lawrence . . . it rang some sort of bell. "I think I may have seen his picture in the papers," said Burden.

She nodded earnestly. "Squiring Leonie West about, I expect. She used to be photographed wherever she went."

"I know her. She's a ballet dancer. My daughter's crazy about ballet. As a matter of fact, I think that's where I've seen your ex-husband, in pictures with Leonie West."

"Matthew and Leonie were lovers for years. Then he met me. I was a drama student and I had a small part in a television series he was in. When we got married he said he wouldn't see Leonie any more, but he really only married me because he wanted a child. Leonie couldn't have children, otherwise he'd have married her."

She had been speaking in a very cool practical voice, but now she sighed and fell silent. Burden waited, no longer tired, even more interested than usual in other people's life stories, although this one perturbed him strangely.

After a while she went on. "I tried to keep our marriage going and when John was born I thought we had a chance. Then I found out Matthew was still seeing Leonie. At last he asked me to divorce him and I did. The judge expedited the decree because there was a child on the way."

"But you said Leonie West couldn't . . ."

"Oh, not Leonie. He didn't marry her. She was years older than he was. She must be well into her forties by now. He married a girl of nineteen he met at a party."

"Good God," said Burden.

"She had the baby, but it only lived two days. That's why I'm keeping my fingers crossed for them now. This one just must be all right."

Burden couldn't keep his feelings to himself any longer. "Don't you bear any malice?" he said. "I should have thought you'd hate him and his wife and that West woman."

She shrugged. "Poor Leonie. She's too pathetic now to hate. Besides, I always rather liked her. I don't hate Matthew or his wife. They couldn't help themselves. They did what they had to do. You couldn't expect them all to spoil their lives for me."

"I'm afraid I'm rather old-fashioned in these things," said Burden. "I believe in self-discipline. They spoiled your life, didn't they?"

"Oh, *no!* I've got John and he makes me very very happy."

"Mrs. Lawrence ..."

"Gemma!"

"Gemma," he said awkwardly. "I must warn you not to bank too much on Monday. I don't think you should bank on it at all. My chief—Chief Inspector Wexford —has absolutely no faith in the veracity of this letter. He's sure it's a hoax."

She paled a little and clasped her hands. "No one would write a letter like that," she said innocently, "if it wasn't true. Nobody could be so cruel."

"But people are cruel. Surely you must know that?"

"I won't believe it. I know John is going to be there on Monday. Please—please don't spoil it for me. I'm holding on to it, it's made me so happy."

He shook his head helplessly. Her eyes were beseeching, imploring him to give her one word of encouragement. And then, to his horror, she fell on her knees in front of him, seizing both his hands in hers.

"Please, Mike, tell me you think it'll be all right. Just say there's a chance. There could be, couldn't there? Please, Mike!"

Her nails dug into his wrists. "There's always a chance ..."

"More than that, more than that! Smile at me, show me there's a chance." He smiled, almost desperately. She sprang up. "Stay there. I'm going to make coffee."

The evening was dying away. Soon it would be quite dark. He knew that he should go away now, follow her outside and say briskly, "Well, if you're all right, I must be on my way." Staying here was wrong, entirely overstepping the bounds of his duty. If she needed company it ought to be Mrs. Crantock or one of those strange friends of hers.

He couldn't go. It was impossible. What a hypocrite he was with his talk of self-discipline. Jean? he said, savouring her name experimentally. If Jean had been at home there would have been no staying, no need for control.

She came back with the coffee and they drank it in the dusk. Soon he could hardly see her and yet somehow he felt her presence more forcefully. In one way he wanted her to turn on the light, but at the same time he prayed that she wouldn't and thus destroy the atmosphere, warm, dark and scented with her scent, a tension and yet a peace.

She poured him more coffee and their hands touched. "Tell me about your wife," she said.

He had never told anyone. He wasn't the kind of man to open his heart and relieve his soul. Grace had tried to draw him out. That idiot Camb had tried and, in a more subtle and tactful way, Wexford himself. And yet he would have liked to tell someone, if only the right listener could be found. This beautiful kind woman wasn't the right listener. What would she with her strange past, her peculiar permissiveness, understand of his notions of monogamy, his one-woman life? How could he talk to her of his simple gentle Jean, her quiet existence and her abominable death?

"It's all over now," he said shortly. "Best forgotten." Too late he realised the impression his words had made.

"Even if you haven't been too happy," she said, "you don't just miss the person, you miss love."

He saw the truth of it. Even for him it was true. But love wasn't quite the word. There was no love in those dreams of his and Jean never entered them. As if to deny his own thoughts, he said harshly, "They say you can find a substitute, but you can't. I can't."

"Not a substitute. That's the wrong word. But someone else for another way of love perhaps."

"I don't know. I have to go now. Don't put on the light." Light would show her too much, his face after suppressed pain had worked on it, and worse than that, the hunger for her he could no longer hide. "Don't put on the light!"

"I wasn't going to," she said softly. "Come here."

It was a little light kiss on the cheek she gave him, such as a woman may give a man she has known for years, the husband of a friend perhaps, and, returning it, touching her cheek, he still meant to kiss her in the same way with a comradely reassurance. But he felt his heart beating and hers beside it as if he had two hearts of his own. Their mouths met and his long control broke.

He kissed her with everything he had, crushing her in his arms and forcing her back against the wall, his tongue thrusting down into her mouth.

When he let her go and moved away shivering, she stood still with her head bowed, saying nothing. He opened the front door and ran from her, not looking back.

7

Sunday, the morning of his lie-in. He had passed a horrible night, filled with dreams so disgusting that if he had read them in some work on psychology—the kind that Grace was always on about—he would have had no difficulty in believing they were the product of a diseased and perverted mind. Even thinking of them made him shudder with shame.

If you lie wakeful in bed when it is already light you have to think. But of what? Jean who was gone for ever? Dreams that made you wonder if inside you were as bad as all those local deviates? Gemma Lawrence? What a fool he had been to kiss her, to stay sitting there with her in the dark, to get involved!

He got up quickly. It was only seven-thirty when he came into the kitchen and no one else was about. He made a pot of tea and took a cup in to each of the others. It was another beautiful clear day.

Grace sat up in bed and took the teacup. She wore a nightgown just like Jean's. Her morning face was a little puffy with sleep, dreamy and vague just as Jean's had always been. He hated her.

"I have to go out," he said. "Work."

"I didn't hear the phone," said Grace.

"You were asleep."

His children didn't stir when he put their teacups beside them. They were heavy sleepers and it was only natural. Burden knew all that, but it seemed to him that they no longer cared for him. Their mother was dead but they had a mother substitute, a mother facsimile. It was all one to them, he thought, whether their father was there or not.

He got out his car and drove off, but with no clear

picture of where he was going. Perhaps to Cheriton
Forest to sit and think and torture himself. But instead of taking the Pomfret road he found himself
heading towards Stowerton. All the control he had left
was needed to stop him going towards Fontaine Road,
but he kept his control and turned instead into Mill
Lane.

It was here that the red Jaguar had been seen. Behind those trees the young duffel-coated man with the
small hands had strolled picking leaves. Were they
connected, the car and the youth? And was it possible
in this wicked and cynical world that the leaf-picker
kept rabbits—perhaps he had been picking leaves for
his rabbits—and needed a child only for the pleasure
of that child's company and the sight of its happy face
when a small eager hand stroked thick smooth fur?

On such a morning even this improbable and Peter
Pan-like notion seemed feasible. In the distance, ahead
of him, he could hear the bells of St. Jude, Forby, ringing for early Communion. He knew now where he was
going. He rounded a bend in the road and Saltram
House came suddenly and gloriously into view.

Who would have supposed, looking at it from this
distance as it proudly crowned the hill, that those
windows were not glazed, those rooms not inhabited,
but that the great stone edifice was merely a shell,
the skeleton, so to speak, of a palace? It was golden-
grey in the morning sun, a palladian house, late eighteenth century, and in its splendid proportions it
seemed both to smile and to frown on the valley below.

Fifty years old now, the tale of its destruction was
known to everyone in Kingsmarkham. During the
First World War it had been. Whoever had owned the
house, and this was now forgotten, had given a house
party and his guests had gone out on to a flat area of
the roof to watch a Zeppelin pass over. One of them
had dropped a cigar butt over the parapet and the
butt had set fire to the shrubs below. There was nothing now behind those blank exquisite windows, nothing but trees and bushes which had grown up out

of the burnt foundations to thrust their branches where once women in Paris gowns had walked, looking at pictures and trailing their fans.

He started the car again and drove slowly up to the iron gates where the drive to Saltram House began. On the left of the gates stood a small one-storey white house with a thatched roof. A woman was in the garden, picking mushrooms from the lawn. Mrs. Fenn, he supposed. She hadn't lived there in the days when he and Jean used to come picnicking in the grounds. The lodge had stood empty for years.

Of course, these grounds would have been thoroughly searched back in February and then again by the search parties on Thursday night and Friday. But did the searchers know the place as he knew it? Would they know the secret places as he knew them?

Burden opened the gates and they creaked dully on their hinges.

Wexford and his friend Dr. Crocker, the police doctor, sometimes played golf together on Sunday mornings. They had been friends since boyhood, these two, although Wexford was the senior by seven years and the doctor was a spry lean fellow who looked quite young when seen from a distance, whereas Wexford was a huge man, gone to seed and stout, with dangerously high blood pressure.

It was on account of his hypertension that Crocker had suggested the Sunday golf sessions and prescribed a rigorous diet. Wexford lapsed from his diet twice a week on average, but he didn't greatly object to the golf, although his handicap was disgracefully around thirty-six. It got him out of going to church with his wife.

"You wouldn't fancy a little drop of something?" he asked wistfully in the club bar.

"At this hour?" said Crocker, the disciplinarian.

"It's the effect that counts, not the hour."

"If my sphyg wasn't about the best you can buy," said the doctor, "it would have busted last time I took your blood pressure. I kid you not, it would have

snapped in sheer despair. You wouldn't put a thermom-
eter under the hot tap now, would you? What you need
isn't alcohol but a few brisk swings under the pro's
eagle eye."

"Not that," Wexford pleaded. "Anything but that."

They went on to the first tee. His expression inscru-
table, Crocker watched his friend fumbling in his golf
bag and then he handed him a five iron without a
word.

Wexford drove. The ball disappeared, but nowhere
in the direction of the first hole. "It's so bloody unfair,"
he said. "You've been at this ridiculous pastime all
your life and I'm a mere novice. It's giving me a hell
of an inferiority complex. Now if we were to fetch
someone else in on this, Mike Burden, for instance . . ."

"Do Mike good, I daresay."

"I worry about him," said Wexford, glad of a respite
before having to witness one of the doctor's perfect
drives. "I wonder sometimes if he isn't heading for a
nervous breakdown."

"Men lose their wives. They get over it. D'you know
what? Mike will marry his sister-in-law. It's right on
the cards. She looks like Jean, she acts like Jean. Mike
can marry her and almost stay monogamous. Enough
of this nonsense. We're here to play golf, remember."

"I mustn't go too far from the club-house. They may
want to reach me at any time if anything comes up
about that missing boy."

It was a genuine anxiety on Wexford's part and not
an excuse, but he had cried wolf on the golf course too
often. The doctor grinned nastily "Then they can come
and fetch you. Some members of this club can actually
run, you know. Now watch me carefully." He took his
own well-seasoned five and drove with beautiful pre-
cision. "On the green, I fancy," he said complacently.

Wexford picked up his bag, sighed, and he strode
manfully up the fairway. He murmured under his
breath and with feeling towards the doctor's back,
" 'Thou shalt not kill but needs't not strive, officiously
to keep alive.' "

The aspect of the house which faced the road and in front of which Burden now parked his car was the back or, more properly, the garden front. There could be no doubt from this distance that Saltram House was a shell. He went up to one of the stone-faced windows and stared through it into the still, dim and silent depths. Elder trees and young oaks—for how old is a mature oak?—thrust their way up out of sand and rubble. The scars of the fire had long faded, their blackness washed away by fifty winters of rain. The leaves were golden now and rattling yellow, lying in their thousands on broken stone and massed rubble. The house had been like this when he and Jean had first come here and the only change was that the trees were taller, nature more rampant and more arrogant in her conquest, and yet it seemed to him that the ruin was personal, symbolic of his own.

He never read poetry. He seldom read anything. But like that of most people who don't read, his memory was good and sometimes he remembered the things Wexford had quoted to him. Under his breath, wonderingly, he whispered:

"Ruin hath taught me thus to ruminate
    That time will come and take my love away . . ."

He didn't know who had said it, but whoever it was knew all right. He swung away from the back of the house. There was no entering it this way. You entered by the front, clambering through what had once been an Italian garden.

To the right and left of him neglected parkland fell away. Whom did it belong to? Why did no one farm it? He didn't know the answers, only that this was a still and beautiful desert where grass grew long and wild and trees that man, not nature, had planted, cedars and ilexes and the tall slender *ginko biloba*, the Chinese maidenhair tree, raised proud trunks and prouder branches from an alien soil. It was a wilderness, desperately sad in that it should have been tended, was designed to be tended, but those who loved to tend it had been removed by ruining time. He thrust aside branches and brambles and came to the incomparably more beautiful front of Saltram House.

There was a great pediment crowning it with a frieze of classical figures and beneath this, above the front door, a vertical sun-dial, sky blue with figures of gold, which the wind and rain had scarred but not spoiled. From where he stood Burden could see the sky through the bones, as it were, of the house, pieces of sky as blue as the sun-dial.

It was no longer possible, and hadn't been for years, to walk into the Italian garden or up to the house without climbing. Burden scrambled over a five-foot-high wall of broken stone, through the cracks of which brambles and bryony had thrust their tendrils.

He had never seen the fountains playing, but he knew there had once been fountains here. Twelve years ago, when he and Jean had first penetrated as far as this, two bronze figures holding vases aloft had stood on either side of the overgrown drive. But vandals had come since then and torn the statues from their plinths, greedy perhaps for the lead from which the fountain pipes were made.

One figure had been that of a boy, the other of a girl in delicate drapery. The boy had disappeared, but the girl lay among the weeds, and the long-leaved gray mullion with its yellow flowers pushed its stalks between her arm and the curve of her body. Burden bent down and lifted the statue. It was broken and half-eaten away by verdegris and underneath it the ground was quite bare, a blank area of earth oddly and unpleasantly in the shape of a small human body.

He replaced the mass of metal which had once been a fountain and climbed the broken steps that led up to the door. But as soon as he stood on the threshold, at the point where in the past guests had entered and given their cloaks to a servant, he saw that there was no concealing a body here, not even the small body of a five-year-old.

For everything in Saltram House, cupboards, doors,

staircase, even to a great extent dividing walls, was gone. There remained scarcely anything of the works of man. True, the towering and somewhat sinister walls of the house soared above him, but even these, which had once been painted and adorned with frescoes, were now hung everywhere with ivy, and they sheltered from the wind a young forest of rich growth. Elders and oaks, birch and beech saplings had forced their way from the rich burnt soil and some of them now rivalled the walls themselves in height. Burden was looking down into a copse which the breeze, entering by the window holes, ruffled gently. He could see the roots of these trees and see too that nothing lay amongst them.

He gazed and then he turned away. Down the steps he went and back into the Italian garden, remembering with a sudden pang how they had once eaten their tea on this very spot, and Pat, a little girl of six or so, had asked him why he couldn't make the fountains play. Because they were broken, because there was no water, he had said. He had never thought of it again, never wondered about it till now.

But those fountains had played once. Where had the water come from? Not directly from the main, surely, even if main water had ever reached Saltram House. For things like this, fountains and any ornamental water gadgets, you always had tanks. And whether there was main water or not at the time the house was burnt, there certainly wouldn't have been when the fountains were set up in seventeen something or other.

Therefore the water must have been stored somewhere. Burden felt a little thrill of dread. It was a stupid idea, he told himself. Fantastic. The searchers had been all over these grounds twice. Surely a notion like this would have occurred to one of them? Not if they didn't know the place like I do, he thought, not if they didn't know that statue was once a fountain.

He knew he wouldn't rest or have a moment's peace if he went now. He dropped down off the steps and stood kneedeep in weeds and brambles. The cisterns, if cisterns there were, wouldn't be up here by the house but as near as possible to the fountain plinths.

In the first place, these plinths were hard to find. Burden cut himself an elder branch with his penknife and pruned off its twigs. Then he began lifting away the dead and dying growth. In places the tangle seemed immovable and he had almost decided this was an impossible task when his stick struck something metallic and gave off a dull ring. Using his bare hands now, he tore away first ivy and under it a tenacious healthy plant to reveal a bronze disc with a hole in its centre. He closed his eyes, thought back and remembered that the boy had stood here, the girl in a similar position on the other side of the drive.

Now where would the cistern be? Not surely between the plinth and the drive, but on the other side. Again he used his stick. It hadn't rained for two or three weeks and the ground beneath the jungle of weeds was as hard as stone. No use going by feel, unless he felt with his feet. Accordingly, he shuffled slowly along the not very clear passage his stick was making.

He was looking down all the time, but still he stumbled when his left toe struck what felt like a stone ridge or step. Probing with the stick, he found the ridge and then traced a rectangular outline. He squatted down and worked with his hands until he had cleared away all the growth and revealed a slate slab the size and shape of a gravestone. Just as he had thought, the fountain cistern. Would it be possible to raise that slab? He tried and it came up easily before he had time to brace himself against the shock of what he might find inside.

The cistern was quite empty. Dry, he thought, for half a century. Not even a spider or a woodlouse had penetrated its stone fastness.

Well, there was another one, wasn't there? Another cistern to feed the fountain on the opposite side? No difficulty, at any rate, about finding it. He paced out the distance and cleared the second slab. Was it his imagination or did the growth seem newer here? There were no dense brambles, anyway, only the soft sappy weeds that die away entirely in winter. The slab looked just like its fellow, silvery black and here and there greened with lichen.

Burden's fingers were torn and bleeding. He wiped them on his handkerchief, raised the slab and, with a rasping intake of breath, looked down at the body in the cistern.

8

Harry Wild knocked out his pipe into the ashtray on Camb's counter. "Well, are you going to tell me?"

"I don't know anything, Harry, and that's a fact. They sent for Mr. Wexford off the golf course and he just about tore in here. You'll have to wait till he's got a moment to spare. We're all at sixes and sevens. I don't remember a Sunday like it all my time in the force."

The phone rang. Camb lifted the receiver and said, "You've seen John Lawrence in Brighton, madam? One moment while I put you through to the officers who are dealing with this information." He sighed. "That," he said to Wild, "makes thirty calls today from people who claim to have seen that kid."

"He's dead. My informant who's very reliable says he's dead. Burden found his body this morning and that's why I'm working on a Sunday." Wild watched to see how this affected Camb, and then added, "I just want confirmation from Wexford and then I'm off to interview the mother."

"Rather you than me," said Camb. "By gum, I wouldn't have your job for all the tea in China."

Not at all abashed, Wild re-lit his pipe. "Talking of tea, I don't suppose there's any going?"

Camb didn't answer him. His phone was ringing again. When he had dealt with a man who claimed to have found a blue sweater answering to the description of the one John Lawrence had been wearing he looked up and saw the lift doors open. "Here's Mr. Wexford now," he said, "and Mr. Burden. On their way to the mortuary to see what Dr. Crocker's come up with, I daresay."

"Ah, Mr. Burden," Wild said, "the very man I want to see. What's all this about finding the body of the lost kid?"

Burden gave him an icy stare, then turned on his heel, but Wexford snapped, "What d'you want to know for, anyway? That rag of yours doesn't go to press till Thursday."

"Excuse me, sir," said Camb, "but Mr. Wild wants to send the stories to the London papers."

"Oh, linage. I see. Well, far be it from me to keep a journalist from earning an honest penny on the Sabbath. Mr. Burden did find a body this morning, in one of the fountain cisterns at Saltram House. You can say foul play is suspected. The body is that . . ." He paused and then went on more quickly, "of a female child, aged about twelve, so far unidentified."

"It's Stella Rivers, isn't it?" said Wild greedily. "Come on, give a working man a break. This could be the biggest story of my career. Missing child found dead in ruins. No clue yet to lost boy. Is Kingsmarkham another Cannock Chase? I can see it all, I can . . ."

Wexford had great self-control. He also had two daughters and a grandson. He loved children with a passionate tenderness and his self-control broke down.

"Get out of here!" he roared. "You back-street death reporter! You revolting ghoulish hack! Get out!"

Wild got out.

A gloom settles on policemen and on their police station when the body of a child has been found. Later they hunt for a child's killer with zeal, but at first, when the crime is discovered, they are aghast and sick at heart. For this is the crime most against nature, most life-denying and least forgivable.

Not at all ashamed of his castigation of Harry Wild, Wexford made his way to the mortuary where Dr. Crocker and Burden stood on either side of the sheeted body.

"I've sent Loring to fetch Ivor Swan, sir," said Burden. "Better have him do it than the mother."

Wexford nodded. "How did she die?"

"The body's been there for God knows how many months," said Crocker. "The path experts will have to get working on it. I'd say, at a guess, asphyxiation. Violent pressure on the windpipe. There are no wounds or anything like that and she wasn't strangled. No sexual interference."

"We knew," said Wexford quietly, "that she must have been dead. It oughtn't to seem so horrible. It oughtn't to be such a shock. I hope she wasn't too frightened, that's all." He turned away. "I hope it was quick," he said.

"That," said Crocker, "is the kind of thing you'd expect her parents to say, not a tough old nut like you, Reg."

"Oh, shut up. Maybe it's because I know her parents won't say it that I'm saying it. Look at you, you bloody half-baked quack, you don't even *care*."

"Now, steady on . . ."

"Here's Mr. Swan," said Burden.

He came in with Loring. Dr. Crocker lifted the sheet. Swan looked and went white. "That's Stella," he said. "The hair, the clothes . . . God, how horrible!"

"You're sure."

"Oh, yes. I'd like to sit down. I've never seen a dead person before."

Wexford took him into one of the interview rooms on the ground floor.

Swan asked for a glass of water and didn't speak again until he had drunk it.

"What a ghastly sight! I'm glad Roz didn't see it. I thought I was going to pass out in there." He wiped his face with his handkerchief and sat staring at nothing but as if he were still seeing the child's body. Wexford thought his horror was occasioned only by the sight of what eight months underground had done to Stella Rivers and not by personal grief, an impression that wasn't much weakened when Swan said, "I was fond of her, you know. I mean, it wasn't as if she was my own but I'd got quite attached to her."

"We've been into all that before, Mr. Swan. How well do you know the grounds of Saltram House?"

"That's where she was found, isn't it? I don't even know where it is."

"And yet you must have passed the house every time you drove Stella to Equita."

"D'you mean that ruin you can see from the road?" Wexford nodded, watching the other man carefully. Swan looked at the walls, the floor, anywhere but at the chief inspector. Then he said in the tone a man uses when his car keeps breaking down, "I don't know why this sort of thing has to happen to me."

"What d'you mean, 'this sort of thing?' "

"Oh, nothing. Can I go now?"

"Nobody's detaining you, Mr. Swan," said Wexford.

Half an hour later he and Burden were sitting on the crumbling wall watching half a dozen men at work in the cistern, photographing, measuring, examining. The sun was still hot and its brilliance gave to the place an air of classical antiquity. Broken columns showed here and there among the long grass and the investigations had turned up fragments of pottery.

It might have been an archaeological dig they were supervising rather than a hunt for clues in a murder case. They had failed to find any trace of the male statue, but the figure of the girl lay as Burden had left her, lay like a dead thing, her faced buried in ivy, her sculpted metal hair gleaming in the sun as gold as the hair of Stella Rivers in life.

"You'll think me a fanciful old fool," said Wexford musingly, "but I can't help seeing the analogy. It's like an omen." He pointed to the statue and looked quizzically at Burden. "The girl's dead. The boy has disappeared, someone has taken him away." He shrugged "In life," he said. "In bronze. And somewhere maybe the thief has set the boy up in pleasant surroundings, taken care of him. I mean the statue, of course."

"Well, sure, what else? More likely used what was useful and chucked the rest out."

"Christ . . ." Wexford saw the inspector had no idea what he had meant and gave up. He ought to have known, he reflected, that it was no use going into flights of fancy with Mike. "Whoever put her in there," he said more practically, "knew the place better than you do. You didn't even know there were any cisterns."

"I've only been here in summer. The slabs wouldn't be so overgrown in wintertime."

"I wonder?" Wexford called Peach over. "You were with the search parties in February, Peach. Did you notice the cisterns?"

"We covered this ground the day after Stella went missing, sir. The Friday, it was. It poured with rain all the previous night and it was raining hard when we were here. The whole of this area was a sea of mud. I don't reckon you could have guessed the cistern slabs were there."

"I think we'll go and have a word with Mrs. Fenn."

She was a small fair woman, anxious to help, appalled at the discovery which had been made less than a quarter of a mile from her home.

"She was the most promising pupil I had," she said in a quiet voice with an edge of horror to it. "I used to boast about her to my friends. Stella Rivers, I used to say—or Stella Swan, you never knew which was her right name—Stella Rivers will be a first-class show jumper one day. She won't, will she? God, it's so *awful*. I'll never forgive myself for letting her go off on her own that day. I should have phoned Mr. Swan. I knew he was a bit absent-minded. That wasn't the first time he'd let her down and forgotten to come."

"You mustn't blame yourself," said Wexford. "Tell me, did you know those fountains had cisterns? If you knew, it means other local people would know."

"Of course I knew." Mrs. Fenn looked puzzled. "Oh you mean they get overgrown in summer?" Her brow cleared. "I often ride up there in dry weather and take my guests for walks or on picnics. I know I've pointed out the fountains to people because the statues are so pretty, aren't they?" With a little tremor in her voice she said, "I shan't feel like going there ever again." She shook her head with a kind of shudder. "After heavy rain the slabs might get covered, especially if a lot of earth got washed down from the side of the house."

They were carrying the slab out to the waiting van now. It would go to the lab for extensive tests.

"If he left any prints," said Wexford, "all the mud and water will have got rid of them. The weather was on his side, wasn't it? What's the matter? Had an idea?"

"I'm afraid not." Burden contemplated the quiet lane and the surrounding meadows. He didn't look back at the house but he felt its blind empty eyes on him. "I was wondering about Mrs. Lawrence," he said. "I mean, ought I to go and . . ."

Wexford snapped off the sentence in his scissors voice. "Martin's been. I sent him to Fontaine Road as soon as we heard what you'd found. It wouldn't do for her to hear we'd found a body and not know whose."

"That's what I thought."

"So you needn't bother with her tonight. She won't want coppers hanging around her place all the time. Let her have a bit of peace. Besides, she said she'd got a friend coming down from London."

He needn't bother with her tonight . . . Burden wondered who the friend was. Man or woman? Actress? Artist? Maybe someone who would listen avidly while Gemma told her about the kiss she had received from a sex-starved policeman. No, he needn't go there again tonight or any other night come to that. The Stella Rivers case would take up all his time and it would be better that way. Far better, said Burden firmly to himself.

The national press had arrived in force on Sunday evening, and Wexford, most unwillingly, had held a conference. He didn't like reporters, but they had their uses. On the whole, he supposed, the publicity they gave to pain and horror did more good than harm. Their stories would be inaccurate, with most of the names spelt wrong—a national daily had once repeatedly referred to him as Police Chief Waterford— but the public would be alerted, someone might come up with something helpful. Certainly there would be hundreds of phone calls and, no doubt, more anonymous letters of the kind that this morning had sent Martin, Gates and Loring to keep a date in Cheriton Forest.

Wexford had left home before his morning paper arrived, and now, at nine, he entered Braddon's to buy all the dailies. The shop had only just opened, but there was someone ahead of him. Wexford sighed. He knew that round grizzled head, that short spare figure. Even now, when innocently purchasing sixty Number Six, the man had an air of lurking.

"Good morning, Monkey," said Wexford softly.

Monkey Matthews didn't jump. He froze briefly and then turned round. It was easy to see when you regarded him full-face how he had acquired his nickname. He stuck out his prognathous jaw, wrinkled up his nose and said glumly, "Small world. I come in here with Rube, just for the bus ride, minding my own business, and before I get me first fag on I've got the fuzz on me tail."

"Don't be like that," said Wexford pleasantly. He bought his papers and shepherded Monkey out on to the pavement.

"I haven't done nothing."

Monkey always made this remark to policemen, even when he encountered one by chance, as on this present occasion. And Burden had once replied, "Two negatives make an affirmative, so we know where we are, don't we?"

"Long time no see." Wexford abhorred the expression, but Monkey would understand it and find it irritating.

He did. To cover a slight confusion he lit a cigarette and inhaled voraciously. "Been up north," he said vaguely. "Had a spell in the rag trade. Liverpool."

Later, Wexford decided, he would check. For the present he made an inspired guess. "You've been in Walton."

At the name of the prison, Monkey removed the cigarette from his lip and spat. "Me and my partner," he said, "as straight a feller as you'd wish to meet, we had this stall like and a dirty little bastard of a fuzz cadet planted fifty dozen pair of fishnet tights on us. Seconds, they were supposed to be, but half of them hadn't got no crotch. Bleeding little agent provoker."

"I don't want to hear that sort of talk," said Wexford, and then less severely, "Back with Ruby, are you? Isn't it about time you made an honest woman of her?"

"Me with a wife living?" Unconsciously, Monkey echoed the Lear Limerick. "Bigamy, sir, is a crime," he said. "Pardon me, but that's my bus coming. I can't stand about nattering all day."

Grinning broadly, Wexford watched him scuttle off to the bus stop on the Kingsbrook bridge. He scanned the front page of the first of his papers, saw that Stella had been found by a Sergeant Burton in a cave not far from the tiny hamlet of Stowerton, and changed his grin to a scowl.

9

Monkey Matthews had been born during the First War in the East End of London and had been educated for the most part in Borstal institutions. His marriage at the age of twenty to a Kingsmarkham girl had brought him to her home town where he had lived—when not in gaol—with his wife in her parents' house. Violence was foreign to him, but only perhaps because he was a coward, not from principle. He stole mostly. He stole from private houses, from his own wife and her aged parents and from those few people who were foolish enough to employ him.

The second war absorbed him into the Army, where he stole stores, officers' uniforms and small electrical equipment. He went to Germany with the army of occupation; he became an expert in the black market and, on his return home, was probably Kingsmarkham's first spiv. Patiently, his wife took him back each time he came out of prison.

In spite of his looks, he was attractive to women. He met Ruby Branch in Kingsmarkham magistrates' court as she was leaving it after being put on probation and he entering between two policemen. They didn't, of course, speak. But Monkey sought her out when he was free again and became a frequent visitor to her house in Charteris Road, Stowerton, especially when Mr. Branch was on night work. He suggested to her that she wasn't getting the most out of her job at the underwear factory and soon, on his advice, she was clocking out most Fridays wearing three bras, six slips and six suspender belts under her dress. An ardent lover, Monkey was waiting for her when she came back from Holloway.

Since those days Wexford had put Monkey away for shopbreaking, larceny as a servant, attempting to blow up one of Ruby's rivals with a home-made bomb, and stealing by finding. Monkey was nearly as old as Wexford, but there was as much life left in him as in the chief inspector, although he smoked sixty cigarettes a day, had no legitimate means of support and, since his wife had finally thrown him out, no fixed abode.

Returning to his office, Wexford wondered about him. Monkey could never be free for long without getting into trouble. Busy as he was, Wexford decided to do the checking he had resolved on outside the newsagent's.

His notion that Monkey had been in Walton was soon confirmed. He had been released in September. The conviction had been for receiving, knowing it to have been stolen, so huge a quantity of tights, nylon briefs, body stockings and other frippery which, had it ever been sold, would surely have supplied the entire female teenage population of Liverpool for months to come.

Shaking his head, but smiling rather wryly, Wexford dismissed Monkey from his mind and concentrated on the pile of reports that awaited his attention. He had read through three of them when Sergeant Martin came in.

"No one turned up, of course?" he said, looking up.

"I'm afraid not, sir. We separated, according to instructions. It's out of the question we could have been spotted, the forest's so thick there. The only person to come along the road was the receptionist at the Cheriton Forest Hotel. No one came down the ride. We stayed there till ten."

"I knew it would be a dead loss," said Wexford.

Burden shared his chief's antipathy to Ivor and Rosalind Swan but he found it impossible to view them with Wexford's cynicism. They had something, those two, the special relationship of two people who love each other almost exclusively and who mean their

love to survive until death parts them. Would he ever
again find a love like that for himself? Or was to have
it once all that any man could expect, knowing that
few ever found it at all? Rosalind Swan had lost her
only child in a hideous way but she could bear that
loss without too much pain while she had her husband. He felt that she would have sacrificed a dozen
children to keep Swan. How had Stella fitted into
this honeymoon life? Had either or both of them felt
her a hindrance, a shadowy and undesired third?

Wexford had been questioning them for half an
hour and Mrs. Swan looked tired and pale, but she
seemed to feel the enormity of her husband's interro-
gation more keenly than its cause. "Ivor loved Stella,"
she kept saying, "and Stella loved him."

"Come, Mr. Swan," Wexford said, ignoring this,
"you must often since then have thought about that
ride of yours and yet you can't name to me a single
person, apart from Mr. Blain, who might have seen
you."

"I haven't thought about it much," Swan said, holding his wife's hand closely in both his own. "I wanted
to forget it. Anyway, I do remember people, only not
what they looked like or their car numbers. Why
should I go about taking car numbers? I didn't know
I'd have to give anyone an alibi."

"I'll get you a drink, my lover." She took as much
trouble over it as another woman might over the
preparation of her baby's feed. The glass was polished
on a table napkin, Gudrun was applied to for ice.
"There. Have I put too much soda in?"

"You're good to me, Rozzy. I ought to be looking
after you."

Burden saw her grow pink with pleasure. She lifted
Swan's hand and kissed it as if there was no one
there to see. "We'll go away somewhere," she said.
"We'll go away tomorrow and forget all this beastli-
ness."

The little scene which had brought a pang of envy
to Burden's heart had no softening effect on Wexford.
"I'd rather you didn't go anywhere until we've got a

much clearer picture of this case," he said. "Besides, there will be an inquest which you must attend and, presumably," he added with stiff sarcasm, "a funeral."

"An inquest?" Swan looked aghast.

"Naturally. What did you expect?"

"An inquest," Swan said again. "Will I have to attend it?"

Wexford shrugged impatiently. "That's a matter for the coroner, but I should say, yes, certainly you will."

"Drink up your drink, my lover. It won't be so bad if we're together, will it?"

"There's a mother for you!" Wexford exploded.

Burden said nothing for a moment. He was wondering if most of the ideas he held on mother love were perhaps fallacious. Until now he had supposed that to a woman the death of her child would be an insupportable grief. But maybe it wouldn't. People were very resilient. They recovered fast from tragedy, especially when they had someone to love, especially when they were young. Rosalind Swan had her husband. Whom would Gemma Lawrence have when she was fetched away to view a body in a mortuary?

It was three days since he had seen her, but hardly an hour had passed without his thinking of her. He relived that kiss and each time he experienced it again in retrospect he felt a shivering thrill of excitement. Telling himself to stop dwelling on it and on her was useless, and there was no question for him of out of sight, out of mind. She was almost more vivid to him in her absence than her presence, her body softer and fuller, her hair more thick and brilliant, her childlike sweetness sweeter. But while he kept away he felt that he was safe. Time would dull the memory if only he had the strength to stay away.

In the back of the car Wexford's probing eyes were on him. He had to say something.

"What about the father, Rivers?" he managed at last. "You must have got on to him way back in February."

"We did. Immediately after the divorce he married again and his airline sent him to San Francisco. We did more than get on to him. We checked him very closely. There was always the chance that he had popped over and smuggled the child into the States."

"What, just like that? Hopped on a plane, grabbed her and flown off again? He can't be a rich man."

"Of course he isn't," Wexford retorted, "but he could have done it just as easily as if he were a millionaire with a private aircraft. Don't forget he works for an airline and like any of their employees travels at only a small surcharge. The same applies within reason to any dependent he might take with him. Also he'd have access to any aircraft, provided there was a vacant seat. Gatwick's only about thirty miles from here, Mike. If he had found out the girl's movements, fiddled a passport and a ticket, he could have done it all right."

"Only he didn't."

"No, he didn't. He was at work in San Francisco all day on February 25th. Naturally, he came over when he was told Stella had disappeared and, no doubt, he'll be over again now."

Detailed reports from forensics had come in during Wexford's absence. They confirmed Crocker's diagnosis and, for all the expertise of those who had compiled them, added little to it. Eight months had elapsed since the child's death, but the conclusion was that she had died from manual pressure on her throat and mouth. Her mildewed and tattered clothes afforded no clues and neither did the slab which had covered the cistern.

More phone calls had come in from people who claimed to have seen John, to have seen Stella alive and well in September, to have seen them alive and well and together. A woman holidaying in the Isle of Mull wrote to say a girl answering Stella's description had spoken to her on a beach and asked to be shown the road to Tobermory. The little boy with her had fair hair and the girl said his name was John.

"I wish they wouldn't waste our time," said Wexford, knowing it would have to be followed up, picking up the next envelope. "What's this, then? Another communication from our rabbit-keeper, I think."

"I warned you not to wait for me. Did you think I would not know what was in your minds? I know everything. Your men are not very skilful at hiding. John was disappointed at not going home on Monday. He cried all night. I will return him only to his mother. She must be waiting *alone* on Friday at twelve noon at the same place. Remember what I did to Stella Rivers and do not try any more tricks. I am sending a copy of this letter to John's mother."

"She won't see it, that's one blessing. Martin's collecting all her mail unopened. If we don't catch this joker before Friday we'll have to dress one of the policewomen up in a red wig."

The idea of this travesty of Gemma waiting for a boy who wouldn't come made Burden feel rather sick. "I don't like that bit about Stella Rivers," he muttered.

"Doesn't mean a thing. He's just read the papers, that's all. My God, don't say you're going to fall for his line. He's just a hoaxer. Here's Martin now with Mrs. Lawrence's mail. I'll take those, thank you, Sergeant. Ah, here's our joker's effusion in duplicate."

Burden couldn't stop himself. "How is she?" he said quickly.

"Mrs. Lawrence, sir? She was a bit the worse for wear."

Blood came into Burden's cheeks. "What d'you mean, worse for wear?"

"Well, she'd been drinking, sir." Martin hesitated, letting his face show as much exasperation as he dared. The inspector's eyes were cold, his face set, a prudish blush on his cheeks. Why did he always have to be so darned straitlaced? Surely a bit of sorrow-drowning was permitted in a woman as mad with anxiety as Mrs. Lawrence? "You can understand it. I mean to say . . ."

"I often wonder what you do mean to say, Martin," Burden snapped. "Believe me, it's not clear from your words."

"I'm sorry, sir."

"I suppose she's got someone with her?" Wexford raised his eyes from the letter and its copy which he had been perusing.

"The friend didn't turn up," said Martin. "Apparently, she took offence because the Met had been on to her, asking if she or some boy friend of hers had seen John lately. I gather they weren't too tactful, sir. The boy friend's got a record and he's out of work. This girl who was coming to stay with Mrs. Lawrence teaches at drama school and acts a bit. She said that if it got about, the police questioning her, it wouldn't do her any good in her profession. I did offer to fetch a neighbour to be with Mrs. Lawrence but she wouldn't have any. Shall I pop back and . . .?"

"Pop anywhere as long as you get out of here!"

"Break it up," said Wexford mildly. "Thank you, Sergeant." He turned to Burden when Martin had gone. "You've been in a state, Mike, ever since we left Hall Farm. Why bite his head off? What's he done?"

If Burden had realised how haggard his own face was, how it mirrored all his pain and his turbulent feelings, he wouldn't have lifted it numbly to stare at the chief inspector. Thoughtfully, Wexford returned his gaze, but for a moment neither man spoke. Why don't you get yourself a woman? Wexford was thinking. D'you want to drive yourself into a nervous collapse? He couldn't say those things aloud, not to Mike Burden.

"I'm going out," Burden muttered. "See if they need any help searching the forest."

Wexford let him go. He shook his head gloomily. Burden knew as well as he did that they had completed their search of Cheriton Forest on Monday afternoon.

10

The inquest on Stella Rivers was opened and adjourned until further evidence should come to light. Swan and his wife were there and Swan stumbled brokenly through his evidence, impressing the coroner as a shattered parent. This was the first sign Wexford had seen of any real grief in Stella's stepfather and he wondered why it had taken the inquest to bring it out. Swan had heard the news of Burden's discovery stoically and had identified Stella's body with no more physical nausea. Why break down now? For he had broken down. Leaving the court, Wexford saw that Swan was weeping, a lost soul, clinging to his wife's arm.

Now, if ever, was the time to verify Rosalind Swan's statement that she couldn't drive. Wexford watched eagerly as they got into the shooting brake. And it was she, he saw, who got into the driving seat. But after a while, when they had whispered together and Rosalind had briefly laid her cheek against her husband's, they changed places. Odd that, Wexford thought.

Swan took the wheel wearily and they drove off in the direction of the Myfleet road.

She would get him home and comfort him with her drinks and her kisses and her love, Wexford thought. "Come, come, come, come, give me your hand," he said to himself. "What's done cannot be undone. To bed, to bed, to bed." But Rosalind Swan was no Lady Macbeth to counsel murder or even connive at it. As far as he knew. Certainly she would cover up any crime Swan might commit, even the killing of her own child, for the sake of keeping him with her.

The fine weather had broken. It was raining now, a fine drizzle dispersing the fog which had settled on Kingsmarkham since early morning. Pulling up his raincoat collar, Wexford walked the few yards that separated the court from the police station. No one at the inquest had mentioned John Lawrence, but the knowledge that a second child was missing had underlain, he felt, everything that was said. There was not a soul in Kingsmarkham or Stowerton who didn't connect the two cases, not a parent who doubted that a child killer stalked their countryside. Even the policemen who stood about the entrances to the court wore the grave aspect of men who believed a madman, a pathological criminal who killed children simply because they were children, went free and might attack again. He couldn't recall any inquest at which these hardened men had looked so dour and so downcast.

He stopped in his tracks and viewed the length of the High Street. The primary school's half-term was over and all the younger children back at work. The big ones hadn't yet broken up. But was it imagination or fact that he could hardly see a single four-year-old out with its mother this morning, scarcely a toddler or a baby in its pram? Then he spotted a pram which its owner was parking outside the supermarket. He watched her lift out the baby and its older sister, take the one in her arms and propel the other, who could only just walk, ahead of her into the shop. That such care should have to be exercised in the town whose guardian he was brought him a deep depression.

Why not Ivor Swan? Why not? It meant nothing that the man had no record. He had no record perhaps because no one had ever found him out. Wexford decided that he would again review Swan's life with particular reference to the districts he had lived in since he left Oxford. He would find out if any children had disappeared while Swan was in their vicinity. If Swan had done this, he swore to himself, he would get Swan.

But before making further investigations into the

antecedents of her stepfather he had to see Stella's father. Their appointment was for twelve and when Wexford reached his office Peter Rivers had already been shown in.

A woman is often attracted by the same type of man and Rivers was not unlike his supplanter. Here was the same dapper quality, the same groomed look, neat small head, finely cut, almost polished, features and womanish tapering hands. But Rivers lacked Ivor Swan's indolent air, the impression he gave that sexually he would be far from indolent. There was something bustling about him, a fussy restiveness combined with a nervous manner, that might not endear itself to a silly romantic woman like Rosalind Swan.

He jumped up when Wexford came into the room and embarked on a long explanation of why he hadn't attended the inquest followed by an account of the tiresomeness of his journey from America. Wexford cut him short.

"Will you be seeing your former wife while you are here?"

"I guess so." Sponge-like, Rivers, although domiciled for less than a year in America, had already picked up a transatlantic phraseology. "I guess I'll have to. Needless to say, I can't stand that Swan. I should never have let Stell go to him."

"Surely you had no choice, Mr. Rivers?"

"Where did you get that idea? I never opposed her mother's application for custody, that's all, on account of Lois—that's the present Mrs. Rivers—not wanting to be lumbered with a big kid like that. Rosie wasn't keen on getting custody either, come to that. Swan egged her on. I can tell you why, if you want to know."

Sickened by all this, Wexford merely looked his assent.

"Swan knew he wouldn't have a bean after he'd paid the costs, nowhere to live, nothing. The three of them were pigging it in a crummy furnished place in Paddington. His uncle told him he'd let him have that

Hall Farm place if Rosie kept Stell. I know it for a fact. Rosie told me."

"But why? Why should his uncle care?"

"He wanted Swan to settle down, raise a family and do a bit of good for himself. Some hopes! Swan was supposed to take an agricultural course at the college here so that he could farm the land. As soon as he got here he let the whole lot off to a farmer who had his eye on it. I don't know why the uncle doesn't kick them both out. He's got pots of money and no one to leave it to but Swan."

"You seem to know a lot about it, Mr. Rivers."

"I made it my business to. Yes, sir! Rosie and me have corresponded regularly since Stell went missing. I'll tell you another thing. Before he came out to Karachi and messed up my married life Mr. Ivor Swan was living with his uncle *and* the aunt. Only she died while he was there. You'll know what I mean when I say she died very suddenly."

"Will I?"

"You're a detective. I'd have thought that'd make you sit up. Swan thought he was coming in for some money, but it all went to uncle."

"I don't think I need detain you any longer, Mr. Rivers," said Wexford, who was beginning to think Rosalind Swan had decidedly bad taste in men. The dislike he felt for Swan was nothing to the loathing this man aroused in him. He watched Rivers buttoning his raincoat and waited for him to say something to the effect that he mourned the child whom nobody seemed to have wanted. The words came at last and in curious form.

"It was a bit of a shock hearing she was dead," Rivers said briskly, "but she'd been dead to me for a couple of years, anyway, in a manner of speaking. I guess I'd never have seen her again." He made for the door, not at all abashed by Wexford's scowl. "A newspaper's offered me two thousand for my exclusive story."

"Oh, I should take it," said Wexford in a level voice. "It will be some recompense for your tragic loss."

He went to the window. It was still raining. The children who went home to lunch were issuing from Queen Street where the primary school was. Usually on wet days they managed the journey as best they could. Today, the first day of the second half of term, not one went unaccompanied, not one lacked the shelter of an umbrella, which seemed to Wexford to have a deeper significance than that of protecting small heads from the drizzle.

Routine checking occupied Burden's afternoon. It was only just after six when he got home. For almost the first time since Jean's death he was anxious to be at home and with his children, particularly with his daughter. All day long he had been thinking of her, her image driving away Gemma's, and as he made himself more and more familiar with the circumstances of Stella's life and death, he kept seeing Pat alone and frightened and cruelly overpowered and—dead.

It was she who rushed to let him in almost before his key was in the lock. And Burden, thinking he saw in her eyes some special alarm, some unusual need for comfort, bent swiftly and put his arms round her. Had he only known it, Pat had quarrelled with her aunt and natural ally and was turning for support to the only other available grown-up.

"What is it, darling?" He saw a car stopping, a hand beckoning, a figure stepping out into the wet dusk. "Tell me what's happened?"

"You've got to tell Auntie Grace she's not to meet me from school. I'm at the high school, I'm not an infant. I was *humiliated*."

"Oh, is that all?" With relief came gratitude. He laughed at Pat's rebelliously pouting lower lip, tugged at her ponytail, and went out to the kitchen to thank Grace for her forethought. What a fool he had been to worry when he had such a guardian!

But he felt a need to stay close by his daughter that evening. All through their meal and afterwards, while he was helping John with his geometry—Pythagoras' theorem which "old Mintface" insisted on the third form knowing by the next day—his thoughts and his eyes wandered to Pat. He had failed in his duty to her, failed, through the indulgence of selfish grief, to watch over her and interest himself in her activities as he should have done. Suppose she were taken from him as Stella Rivers, her contemporary, had been taken?

"In a right-angled triangle," he said mechanically, "the square on the hypotenuse is equal to the sum of the squares on the other two sides."

Grace hadn't failed. He watched her covertly while John drew his diagram. She was sitting in a dark corner of the room, a table lamp throwing a small pool of light on to the letter she was writing. Suddenly it occurred to him that she must thousands of times have sat in just that attitude, at a lamplit desk in a long quiet hospital ward, writing the night's report and, while all the time aware that she was surrounded by people who depended on her, yet at the same time detached from them and contained. She wrote—indeed she did everything—with a beautiful economy of movement, an absence of fuss or flutter. Her training had taught her this efficiency, this almost awe-inspiring reliability, but instead of spoiling her delicate feminine quality, had somehow enhanced it. They had had wisdom and prevision, he thought, those parents-in-law of his, when they named her Grace.

And now his gaze encompassed both his daughter and his sister-in-law, the child moving up to her aunt and standing beside her within the same circle of light. They were very alike, he saw, with the same strong gentle face and the same light gauzy hair. They were both like Jean. The image of Gemma Lawrence coarsened beside them, became harsh-coloured, red and white and strained. Then it dwindled away, leaving a vacant space for his daughter and her aunt to fill with the wholesome beauty he understood.

Grace, he realised, was just the type of woman he most admired. There was the delicate prettiness he loved combined with the competence he needed. Couldn't she, he asked himself, be Jean all over again? Why not? Couldn't she be his Rosalind Swan, as loving, as devoted, as all-in-all to him, without the other woman's silly affectations? Usually, when they parted for the night, Grace simply got up out of her chair, picked up her book and said, "Well, good night, Mike. Sleep well," and he said, "Good night, Grace. I'll see that everything's locked up." That was all. They never even touched hands, never stood close beside each other or let their eyes meet.

But tonight, when the time came for them to separate, why shouldn't he take her hand and, saying something of what her goodness had meant to him, take her gently in his arms and kiss her? He glanced at her again and this time both Grace and Pat turned to him and smiled. His heart seemed to swell with an easy warm happiness, very different from the storm of feelings Gemma Lawrence aroused in him. That had been a kind of madness, nothing more than lust brought about by frustration. How unimportant it seemed now!

Pat loved her aunt. If he married Grace she would return to him entirely. He put out his hand to his daughter and she, her earlier annoyance with him forgotten, skipped over to the sofa where he was sitting and snuggled close against him, her arms hard around his neck.

"Shall I show you my scrapbook?"

"What have you got in it?" said John, his eyes on the proof of his theorem. "Pictures of caterpillars?"

"Caterpillars are my summer hobby." Pat spoke with great dignity. "You're so ignorant you wouldn't know, but in the winter they go into their chrysalises."

"And even you couldn't collect pictures of chrysalises. Here, let's see."

"You shan't! You're not to! It's mine!"

"Leave her alone, John. Put that book down."

John said in disgust, "It's only dancers, old ballet dancers."

"Come and show me, love."

Pat resumed her semi-suffocation of her father. "Can I have ballet lessons, Daddy? I do want to. It's the great ambition of my life."

"I don't see why not."

Grace was smiling at him, her letter completed. They smiled at each other like fond parents, happy in conspiracy, in contemplation of what they would do for their children.

"You see," said Pat, "it'll be too late if I don't start now. I know I should have to work and work, but I don't mind that because it's my great ambition, and perhaps I could get a scholarship and be in the Bolshoi and be a *prima ballerina assoluta* like Leonie West."

"I thought," said her brother, "you were going to be a research scientist."

"Oh, *that*. That was ages ago, when I was a child."

A cold shadow had touched Burden. "Who did you say?"

"Leonie West. She's gone to live in *absolute retirement* in her flat and her house at the seaside. She broke her leg skiing and couldn't dance any more, but she was the most wonderful dancer *in the world*." Pat considered. "Anyway, I think so," she said. "I've got masses and masses of pictures of her. Shall I show you?"

"Yes, darling, if you like."

There were indeed masses and masses of pictures. Pat had cut them out of magazines and newspapers. Not all of them were of Leonie West, but most were.

In the distant shots she was a beautiful woman, but time and perhaps too the exigencies of continual strenuous dancing showed the toll they had taken in close-ups. For Burden that heavily painted heart-shaped face with its smoothly parted black hair held no magic, but he made appreciative comments to please his daughter as he turned the pages.

There were stills of ballet films, shots of the star at home, at social functions, dancing all the great classical roles. He was nearly at the end now.

He said, "They're very nicely arranged, dear," to Pat, and turned to the last photograph.

A fan of Leonie West would have seen only her, a magnificent figure in a floor-length cloak stiff with gold embroidery. Burden hardly noticed her. He was looking, his heart knocking dully, at the crowd of friends from which she had emerged. Just behind the dancer, holding a man's arm and smiling listlessly with a kind of shy anxiety, was a red-haired woman swathed in a black-and-gold shawl.

He didn't need the caption to tell him anything, but he read it. "Pictured at the first night of *La Fille Mal Gardee* at Covent Garden is Miss Leonie West with (right) actor Matthew Lawrence and his wife Gemma, 23." He said nothing, but closed the book quickly and leaned back, shutting his eyes, as if he had felt a sudden pain.

No one took any notice of him. John was repeating the proof of his theorem, learning it by heart. Pat had taken her book away to restore it to some secret treasure chest. It was nine o'clock.

Grace said, "Come along, my dears. Bed."

The usual argument ensued. Burden put in the stern words which were expected of him, but he felt no enthusiasm, no real care whether his children got the required amount of sleep or not. He picked up the evening paper which he hadn't yet read. The words were just a black-and-white pattern, hiero-glyphics as meaningless as they would be to someone who has never learned to read.

Grace came back from kissing Pat good night. She had combed her hair and put on fresh lipstick. He noticed and he felt a shrinking distaste. This was the same woman that, half an hour before, he had con-sidered wooing with a view to making her his second wife. He must have been mad. Suddenly he saw clear-ly that all his imaginings of the evening had been madness, a fantasy of his own conjuring, and what they had made to appear as madness was his reality.

He could never marry Grace, for in gazing at her, studying and admiring her, he had forgotten what

any happy marriage must have, what Rosalind Swan
so evidently had. He liked Grace, was at ease with
her. She was his ideal of what a woman should be,
but he hadn't a particle of desire for her. The thought
of attempting to kiss her, of going further than a kiss,
caused a shrivelling in his flesh.

She had brought her chair closer to the sofa where
he sat and, laying aside her book, looked expectantly
at him, waiting for the conversation, the adult exchange of views, which all day long she was denied.
His feeling for her was so slight, his acceptance of
her as someone content with the world he had provided for her so great, that it hardly occurred to him
she would be hurt by anything he did.

"I'm going out," he said.

"What, *now?*"

"I've got to go out, Grace."

He saw it now. Am I so boring? her eyes said. I
have done everything for you, kept your house, cared
for your children, borne with your moods. Am I so
boring that you can't sit quietly with me for one single evening?

"Please yourself," she said aloud.

11

The rain had stopped and a thick mist settled on the countryside. Water clung to the trees in heavy drops and fell dully and regularly so that it seemed as if it were still raining. Burden swung the car into Fontaine Road and immediately made a U-turn out again. He was suddenly loth to let his car be seen outside her house at night. All the street would be on watch, ready to spread rumours and tell tales.

Finally he parked at the bottom of Chiltern Avenue. A footpath, skirting the swings field, joined this cul-de-sac with its neighbour, Fontaine Road. Burden left the car under a street lamp whose light the fog had dimmed to a faintly glowing nimbus and walked slowly towards the path. Tonight its entrance looked like the opening to a black tunnel. There were no lights on in the adjacent houses, no sound in the darkness but that of water dripping.

He walked along between bushes whose branches with their wet dying leaves splashed his face and dragged softly at his clothes. Half-way through he found the torch he always carried and switched it on. Then, just as he reached the point where a gate in Mrs. Mitchell's fence opened into the path, he heard pounding feet behind him. He swung round, directing his torch beam back the way he had come and on to a white face framed in flying wet hair.

"What is it? What's the matter?"

The girl must have recognised him, for she almost threw herself into his arms. He recognised her too. It was Mrs. Crantock's daughter, a child of about fourteen.

"Did something frighten you?" he asked.

"A man," she said breathlessly. "Standing by a car. He spoke to me. I got in a panic."

"You shouldn't be out alone at night." He shepherded her into Fontaine Road, then thought better of it. "Come with me," he said. She hesitated. "You're all right with me."

Back through the black tunnel. Her teeth were chattering. He raised his torch and brought it like a searchlight on to the figure of a man who stood beside the bonnet of Burden's parked car. The duffel coat he wore with its raised hood gave him enough of a sinister air to alarm any child.

"Oh, it's Mr. Rushworth." She sounded shamefaced.

Burden had already recognised the man and saw he was recognised too. Frowning a little, he walked towards the husband of the woman who had failed to notify the police after Mrs. Mitchell's warning.

"You gave this young lady a bit of a scare."

Rushworth blinked in the glare of the torch. "I said hallo to her and something about it being an awful night. She scooted off like all the devils in hell were after her. God knows why. She knows me by sight, at any rate."

"Everyone round here is a bit nervous at present, sir," said Burden. "It's wiser not to speak to people you don't really know. Good night."

"I suppose he was taking his dog out," the girl said as they came into Fontaine Road. "I didn't see his dog, though. Did you?"

Burden hadn't seen a dog. "You shouldn't be out alone at this time of night."

"I've been round to my friends. We were playing records. My friend's father said he'd see me home, but I wouldn't let him. It's only a couple of minutes' walk. Nothing could happen to me."

"But something did, or you thought it did."

She digested this in silence. Then she said, "Are you going to see Mrs. Lawrence?"

Burden nodded, and, realising she couldn't see his nod, said a bald, "Yes."

"She's in an awful state. My father says he wouldn't be surprised if she did something silly."

"What does that mean?"

"Well, *you* know. Committed suicide. I saw her after school in the supermarket. She was just standing in the middle of the shop, crying." A true daughter of the *bourgeoisie*, she added with some disapproval, "Everyone was looking at her."

Burden opened the gate to the Crantocks' garden. "Good night," he said. "Don't go out alone after dark any more."

There were no lights in Gemma's house and for once the front door was shut. Very likely she had taken one of Lomax's sleeping tablets and gone to bed. He peered through the stained glass and made out a faint gleam of light coming from the kitchen. She was still up, then. He rang the bell.

When the gleam grew no brighter and still she didn't come, he rang the bell again and banged the lion's-head door knocker. Behind him, from the branches of the untended trees, came the incessant drip drip of water. He remembered what Martin had said about her drinking and then what the Crantock girl had said and, having rung the bell once more in vain, he made for the side entrance.

The path was nearly as overgrown as the gardens of Saltram House. He pushed away wet holly and slimy creeper, soaking his hair and his raincoat. His hands were so wet that he could hardly turn the handle on the back door, but the door wasn't locked and at last he got it open.

She was slumped at the kitchen table, her head on her outflung arms, and in front of her was an un-opened bottle, labelled: "Chianti-type wine, produce of Spain. This week's offer, 7p off." He went up to her slowly and laid his hand on her shoulder.

"Gemma . . ."

She said nothing. She didn't move. He pulled up another chair, pulled it close to her, and took her gently in his arms. She rested against him, not resist-ing, breathing shallowly and fast, and Burden forgot all his agony of the past week, his battling against temptation, in an overwhelming selfish happiness. He could hold her like this for ever, he thought, warmly and wordlessly, without passion or desire or the need for any change.

She lifted her head. Her face was almost unrecognisable, it was so swollen with crying. "You didn't come," she said. "For days and days I waited for you and you didn't come." Her voice was thick and strange. "Why didn't you?"

"I don't know." It was true. He didn't know, for now his resistance seemed the height of pointless folly.

"Your hair's all wet." She touched his hair and the raindrops on his face. "I'm not drunk," she said, "but I have been. That stuff is very nasty but it deadens you for a bit. I went out this afternoon to buy some food —I haven't eaten for days—but I didn't buy any, I couldn't. When I came to the sweet counter I kept thinking of how John used to beg me to buy chocolate and I wouldn't because it was bad for his teeth. And I wished I'd let him have it, all he wanted, because it wouldn't have made any difference now, would it?"

She stared at him blankly, the tears pouring down her face.

"You mustn't say that."

"Why not? He's dead. You know he's dead. I keep thinking that sometimes I got cross with him and I smacked him and I wouldn't let him have the sweets he wanted . . . Oh, Mike! What shall I do? Shall I drink that wine and take all Dr. Lomax's tablets? Or shall I go out in the rain and just walk and walk till I die? What's the use of living? I've got no one, no one."

"You've got me," said Burden.

For answer she clung to him again, but this time more tightly. "Don't leave me. Promise you won't leave me."

"You ought to go to bed," he said. There was, he

thought, a sickening irony here. Wasn't that what he had intended when he left the car in the next street? That he and she should go to bed? He had really imagined that this demented grief-stricken woman would welcome his love-making. You fool, he whispered harshly to himself. But he managed to say calmly, "Go to bed. I'll make you a hot drink and you can take a tablet and I'll sit with you till you go to sleep."

She nodded. He wiped her eyes on a handkerchief Grace had ironed as carefully as Rosalind Swan ironed her husband's shirts. "Don't leave me," she said again, and then she went, dragging her feet a little.

The kitchen was in a hideous mess. Nothing had been washed up or put away for days and there was a stale sweetish smell. He found some cocoa and some dried milk and did his best with these unsatisfactory ingredients, mixing them and heating them on a cooker that was black with burned-on fat.

She was sitting up in bed, the black-and-gold shawl around her shoulders, and that magic exotic quality, compounded of colour and strangeness and lack of inhibition, had to some extent returned to her. Her face was calm again, the large still eyes staring. The room was untidy, chaotic even, but its chaos was powerfully feminine, the scattered clothes giving off mingled sweet scents.

He tipped a sleeping pill out of the bottle and handed it to her with her drink. She gave him a wan smile and took his hand, lifting it first to her lips and then holding it tight.

"You won't ever stay away from me like that again?"

"I am a poor substitute, Gemma," he said.

"I need," she said softly, "another kind of loving to make me forget."

He guessed at what she meant but didn't know what reply to make, so he sat silently with her, holding her hand, until at last her hand grew limp and she sank back against the pillows. He switched off the bed lamp and stretched himself beside her but on top of the covers. Presently her steady regular breathing told him that she was asleep.

The luminous dial of his watch showed half past ten. It seemed much later, as if a lifetime had passed since he left Grace and drove out here through the damp, rain-filled mist. The room was cold, perfumed and thick-aired and cold. Her hand lay loosely in his. He slid his hand away and edged across the bed to get up and leave.

Wary, even in sleep, she murmured, "Don't leave me, Mike." Thick with sleep, her voice held a note of terror, of dread that she might again be abandoned.

"I won't leave you." He made up his mind quickly and decisively. "I'll stay all night."

Shivering, he stripped off his clothes and got into bed beside her. It seemed quite natural to lie as he had lain beside Jean, his body curled about hers, his left arm around her waist, clasping the hand which again had grown possessive and demanding. Although cold to him, his body must have felt warm to her, for she sighed with a kind of happiness and relaxed against him.

He thought he would never sleep or, if he did, that he would fall immediately into one of those dreams of his. But the way they were lying, side by side, was what he had been used to in his happy years and had missed bitterly in the last wretched one. It brought him desire, but at the same time it lulled him. While wondering how he could bear this continuing continence, he fell asleep.

It was just beginning to get light when he awoke to find the other half of the bed empty but still warm. She was sitting by the window, wrapped in her shawl, a big album with gilt clasps open on her lap. He guessed that she was looking, in the first light of dawn, at pictures of her son, and he felt a powerful black jealousy.

For what seemed a long time he watched her,
almost hating the child who came between them and
drew his mother away with a ghostly subtle hand.
She was slowly turning the pages, pausing sometimes
to stare downwards with a passionate intensity. A resentment which he knew was totally unjust made him
will her to look at him, to forget the child and remember the man who longed to be her lover.

At last she lifted her head and their eyes met. She
said nothing and Burden didn't speak, for he knew
that if he did it would be to say cruel indefensible
things. They gazed at each other in the pale grey
morning light, and then, getting up silently, she drew
the curtains. They were of brocade, old and frayed
but still retaining their rich plum colour and, filtering
through them, the light in the room looked purplish.
She dropped the shawl and stood still in this coloured
shadow-light so that he might look at her.

Her red hair seemed to have grown purple, but the
colour hardly touched her body, which was dazzling
white. He gazed at her in a kind of wonder, content
for the moment to do nothing but gaze. This ivory
woman, still and smiling now, was nothing like his
lascivious dream woman, or did she resemble the dis-
traught and weary creature he had comforted to
sleep. The child had almost vanished from his
jealousy and, he believed, from her thoughts. It was
hardly possible to imagine that this exquisite firm
body had ever borne a child.

Only a little stabbing doubt remained.

"Not out of gratitude, Gemma," he said. "Not to reward me."

She moved then and came close to him. "I never
even thought of that. That would be to cheat."

"To forget, then? Is that what you want?"

"Isn't all love about forgetting?" she said. "Isn't it
always a lovely escape from—from hatefulness?"

"I don't know." He put out his arms to her. "I don't
care." Gasping at the feel of her, here the slenderness
and there the swell of flesh, he said breathlessly, "I

shall hurt you. I can't help it, it's been so long for me."

"And for me," she said. "It will be like the first time. Oh, Mike, kiss me, make me happy. Make me happy for a little while. . . ."

12

"Not bad news?" said Dr. Crocker. "About the Lawrence boy, I mean?"

Morosely eyeing the pile of papers on his desk, Wexford said, "I don't know what you're on about."

"You haven't got a lead, then? I was sure there must be something when I passed Mike driving out of Chiltern Avenue at seven-thirty this morning." He breathed heavily on one of Wexford's window-panes and began drawing one of his recurrent diagrams. "I wonder what he was doing?" he said thoughtfully.

"Why ask me? I'm not his keeper." Wexford glared at the doctor and at his drawing of a human pancreas. "I might ask you what you were doing, come to that."

"A patient. Doctors always have an excuse."

"So do policemen," Wexford retorted.

"I doubt if Mike was ministering to a fellow who'd been struck down with stroke. Worst case I've come across since they called me out to that poor old boy who collapsed on Stowerton station platform back in February. Did I ever tell you about that? Chap had been staying here on holiday, got to the station and then found he'd left one of his cases behind in this hotel or whatever it was. Went back for it, got in a bit of a flutter and the next thing . . ."

Wexford let out an angry bellow. "So what? Why tell me? I thought you were supposed to treat your patients in confidence. I'll have a stroke myself if you go on like that."

"It was just that possibility," said Crocker sweetly, "that inspired my little narrative." He dotted in the Islets of Langerhans with his little finger. "Want a fresh prescription for those tablets of yours?"

"No, I don't. I've got hundreds of the damned things left."

"Well, you shouldn't have," said Crocker, pointing a damp finger at him. "You can't have been taking them regularly."

"Go away. Get lost. Haven't you anything better to do than deface my windows with your nasty anatomical studies?"

"Just going." The doctor made a dancing exit, pausing in the doorway to favour the chief inspector with what seemed to Wexford a meaningless wink.

"Silly fool," Wexford remarked to the empty room. But Crocker's visit had left him with an uneasy feeling. To rid himself of it, he began to read the reports the Metropolitan Police had sent him on Gemma Lawrence's friends.

For the most part they appeared to be in the theatrical profession or on its fringes, but hardly a name was familiar to him. His younger daughter had just left drama school and through her Wexford had heard of many actors and actresses whose names had never been in lights or the print of the *Radio Times*. None of them appeared in this list and he was aware of what they did only because "actor" or "assistant stage manager" or "model" was written after almost every name.

They were an itinerant crowd, mostly—in Wexford's own official terminology—of no fixed abode. Half a dozen had been convicted on charges of possessing drugs or of allowing cannabis to be smoked on their premises; a further two or three fined for conduct likely to lead to a breach of the peace. Demonstrating or taking their clothes off in the Albert Hall, Wexford supposed. None were harbouring John Lawrence; none showed by their past histories or their present tendencies a propensity to violence or perverted inclination. From reading between the lines, he gathered that, rather than desire the company of a child, they would go to almost any lengths to avoid having one.

Only two names on the list meant anything to him. One was a ballet dancer, her name at one time a household word, the other a television character actor whose face appeared so monotonously on Wexford's screen that he was sick of the sight of him. He was called Gregory Devaux and he had been a friend of Gemma Lawrence's parents. Particular interest had been taken in him because once, five years ago, he had attempted to smuggle out of the country, and the care of his estranged wife, their six-year-old son. The report promised that a watch would be kept on Gregory Devaux.

According to the porter of the Kensington block where she had a flat, Leonie West, the dancer, had been in the South of France since August.

Nothing there. No hint of any of them taking more than a casual friendly interest in Mrs. Lawrence and her son; no hint of a connection between any of them and Ivor Swan.

At ten Martin came in with Policewoman Polly Davies whom Wexford scarcely recognised under the red wig she wore.

"You look terrible," he said. "Where in God's name did you dig that up? A jumble sale?"

"Woolworth's, sir," said Martin, rather offended. "You're always telling us to go easy on expenses."

"No doubt it would look better if Polly hadn't got black eyes and such a—well, Welsh complexion. Never mind. You'll have to cover it, anyway. It's pouring with rain."

Sergeant Martin always took an old-womanish interest in the weather and its vagaries. Having first wiped off the doctor's pancreas diagram, he opened the window and stuck out one hand. "I think it'll stop, sir. I see a gleam of light."

"I only wish you did," said Wexford. "Pray cover your dismay as best you can. I've decided to come with you. I get sick of all this vicarious living."

They went down the corridor in single file, to be stopped by Burden who opened the door of his own office. Wexford looked him up and down, looked him all over, hard.

"What's got into you? Your Ernie bonds come up?"

Burden smiled.

"I am glad," said Wexford sarcastically, "that some-one sees fit to spread a little sunshine in this deluge, in this—er—town of terror. What d'you want, any-way?"

"I thought you might not have seen today's paper. There's an interesting story on the front page."

Wexford took the paper from him and read the story as he went down in the lift. Under the headline, *Landowner Offers £2,000 reward. New Move in Stella Hunt,* he read: "Group Captain Percival Swan, wealthy landowner and uncle of Mr. Ivor Swan, Stella Rivers' stepfather, told me last night that he was offering a reward of £2,000 for information lead-ing to the discovery of Stella's killer. 'This is a devilish thing,' he said as we chatted in the drawing room of his centuries-old mansion near Tunbridge Wells. 'I was fond of Stella, though I had seen little of her. Two thousand pounds is a large sum, but not too large to sacrifice for the sake of seeing justice done.' "

There was a good deal more in the same vein. Not so very interesting, Wexford thought, as he got into his car.

True to Sergeant Martin's prediction, the rain soon left off. Cheriton Forest was shrouded in thick white mist.

"You may as well take that thing off," said Wexford to Polly Davies. "He won't be able to see you if he does come."

But nobody came. No car passed along the road and no one came down the Myfleet Ride which joined it. Only the mist moved sluggishly and the water which dripped from the boughs of the closely planted fir trees. Wexford sat on a damp log among the trees, thinking of Ivor Swan who rode in this forest and knew it well, who had ridden here on the day his step-daughter died. Did he really suppose Swan would ap-pear, walking on the wet sandy ride or mounted on the chestnut horse? With the child perched beside him or holding his hand? A hoax, a hoax, a cruel nonsense, he kept saying to himself, and at one, when the appointed time was an hour behind him and he was shivering with cold, he came out of his hiding place and whistled up the other two.

If Burden remained in his early mood he would, at any rate, have a cheerful lunch companion. There was no one behind the desk in the police-station foyer, an unheard-of dereliction of duty. With mounting rage Wexford stared at the empty stool on which Sergeant Camb should have been perched and was about to press a bell that had never, in all its years of existence, needed to be pressed before, when the Sergeant appeared, scuttling from the lift, the inevitable teacup in his hand.

"Sorry, sir. We're so short-handed what with all these crazy calls coming in that I had to fetch my own tea. I've only been away half a tick. You know me, sir, I perish without my tea."

"Next time," said Wexford, "you perish. Remember, Sergeant, that the guard dies but it never surrenders."

He went upstairs and looked for Burden.

"Mr. Burden went to lunch ten minutes ago, sir," said Loring.

Wexford cursed. He badly wanted to engage with Burden in one of those acrimonious but rewarding conferences which both cemented their friendship and contributed to their work. Lunch alone at the Carousel would be a dismal affair. He opened the door of his own office and stopped dead on the threshold.

Seated in the chief inspector's swivel chair at the chief inspector's rosewood desk, the cigarette in his fingers scattering ash all over the lemon-coloured carpet, was Monkey Matthews.

"They might have told me," said Wexford distantly, "that I'd been deposed. This kind of thing smacks of goings-on behind the Iron Curtain. What am I to do? Manage a power station?"

Monkey grinned. He had the grace to get up out of Wexford's chair. "I'd never have believed," he said, "it was so easy to get into a nick. I reckon that old geezer Camb must have dropped dead at last and they've all gone off to bury him. Got in without a soul the wiser, I did. Bloody sight easier," he added, "to get in this nick than get out of it."

"You won't find it hard today. You can get out now. And fast, before I do you for being found on enclosed premises for an unlawful purpose."

"Ah, but my purpose *is* lawful." Monkey stubbed out his cigarette in Wexford's inkwell and surveyed the room with a pleased expression. "This is the first time I've ever been in a nick of what you might call my own accord." A dreamy smile spread across his face and was abruptly quenched by a fit of coughing.

Wexford stood half in the office, half in the corridor, waiting unsympathetically.

"You may as well shut the door," said Monkey when he had recovered. "We don't want the whole place to hear, do we? I've got some info. The Lawrence case."

Wexford closed the door but gave no other sign that Monkey's remark had interested him. "*You* have?" he said.

"Friend of mine has."

"I didn't know you had any friends, Monkey, bar poor old Ruby."

"You don't want to judge everybody by yourself," said Monkey, stung. He coughed and stubbed out his cigarette, immediately lighting another and regarding the discarded stub with resentment, as if some peculiarity of its construction or fault in its make-up were responsible for his choking attack, rather than the tobacco it contained. "I've got a lot of friends, picked up in me travels."

"Picked up in cells, you mean," said Wexford.

Monkey had long ago forgotten how to blush, but the wary look which crossed his face told Wexford the shot had gone home. "My friend," he said, "come down here yesterday for a bit of a holiday with me and Rube. A bit of a rest, like. He's an old feller and his health's not what it was."

"All those damp exercise yards, I daresay."

"Oh, give over, will you? My friend has got some

info as'll open your eyes all right, re the antecedents of Mr. Ivor Bloody Swan."

If Wexford was surprised, he didn't show it. "He has no antecedents," he said coldly, "or not what you mean by the term."

"Not wrote down, I daresay. Not all our misdemeanours is recorded, Mr. Wexford, not by a long chalk. I've heard it said there's more murderers walking the streets free as ever got topped on account of them as they murdered being thought to have died natural."

Wexford rubbed his chin and looked thoughtfully at Monkey. "Let's see your friend," he said, "and hear what he's got to say. It might be worth a few bob."

"He would want paying."

"I'm sure he would."

"He made a point of that," said Monkey conversationally.

Wexford got up and opened a window to let some of the smoke out. "I'm a busy man, Monkey. I can't hang about fencing with you all day. How much?"

"A monkey," said Monkey succinctly.

In a pleasant but distant voice, tinged with incredulous outrage, Wexford said, "You must be off your nut if you seriously think the government is going to pay five hundred pounds to a clapped-out old lag for information it can get for nothing out of a file."

"Five hundred," Monkey repeated, "and if it all works out nice, the two thou reward the uncle's putting up." He coughed thickly but with no sign of distress. "If you don't want nothing to do with it," he said sweetly, "my friend can always go to the chief constable. He's called Griswold, isn't he?"

"Don't you bloody threaten me!" said Wexford.

"Threaten? Who's threatening? This info's in the public interest, that's what it is."

Wexford said firmly, "You can bring your friend along here and then we'll see. Might be worth a couple of nicker."

"He won't come here. He wouldn't go voluntary like into a fuzz box. Different to me, he is. But him and me, we'll be in the Pony six sharp tonight and I daresay he'd accept a friendly overture in the form of liquor."

Was it possible that there was something in this story? Wexford wondered after Monkey had gone. And immediately he recalled Rivers' hints as to the death of Swan's aunt. Suppose, after all, that Swan *had* hastened the old lady's departure? Poison, maybe. That would be in Swan's line, a lazy, slow way of killing. And suppose this friend of Monkey's had been in service in the house, an odd-job man or even a butler? He might have seen something, extracted something, kept it hidden for years in his bosom . . .

Wexford came down to earth and, laughing, quoted to himself a favourite passage from Jane Austen: "Consult your own understanding, your own sense of the probable, your own observation of what is passing around you. Does our education prepare us for such atrocities? Do our laws connive at them? Could they be perpetrated without being known in a country like this where social and literary intercourse is on such a footing; where every man is surrounded by a neighbourhood of voluntary spies and where roads and newspapers lay everything open?"

Long ago he had learned these lines by heart. They had been of constant service to him and, when inclined to sail away on flights of fancy, kept his feet firmly on the ground.

It was much too late now to go out for lunch. The staff of the Carousel looked askance at you if you arrived for your midday meal after one-thirty. Wexford sent to the canteen for sandwiches and had eaten the first half-round when the report on the lock of hair came in from the lab. The hair, Wexford read, was a child's but not John Lawrence's. Comparison had been made with the strands taken from John's hairbrush. Understanding only about twenty-five per cent of the the technical jargon, Wexford did his best to follow just how they could be so certain the hairs in the brush differed from the hairs in the cut lock, and finally had to be content to know that they did differ.

His phone rang. It was Loring from the room where all the calls connected with the Lawrence and Rivers cases were received and checked.

"I think you'll want to take this one, sir."

Immediately Wexford thought of Monkey Matthews and just as quickly dismissed the thought. Monkey had never been known to use a telephone.

"Record it, Loring," he said, and then, "Is it from a call box?"

"I'm afraid not, sir. We can't trace it."

"Put him on," said Wexford.

As soon as he heard the voice he knew an attempt was being made to disguise it. A couple of pebbles in the man's mouth, he decided. But some quality, the pitch perhaps, couldn't be disguised. Wexford recognised the voice. Not its owner, nor could he recall where he had seen the speaker, what he had said or anything about him. But he was sure he recognised the voice.

"I'm not prepared to give my name," it said. "I've written to you twice."

"Your letters were received." Wexford had stood up to take the call and from where he stood he could see the High Street and see a woman tenderly lifting a baby from a pram to take it with her into a shop. His anger was immense and he could feel the dangerous blood pounding in his head.

"You played around with me this morning. That's not going to happen tomorrow."

"Tomorrow?" Wexford said evenly.

"I shall be in the grounds of Saltram House tomorrow by the fountains. I'll be there at six p.m. with John. And I want the mother to come for him. *Alone.*"

"Where are you speaking from?"

"My farm," said the voice, growing squeaky. "I've got a three-hundred-acre farm not so far from here. It's a fur farm, mink, rabbits, chinchillas, the lot. John doesn't know I keep them for their fur. That would only upset him, wouldn't it?"

Wexford caught the authentic note of derangement. He didn't know whether this comforted or distressed

him. He was thinking about the voice which he had
heard before, a thin high voice, its possessor quick to
take offence, looking for insult where none existed.

"You haven't got John," he said. "That hair you sent
me wasn't John's." Scorn and rage made him forget
caution. "You are an ignorant man. Hair can be as precisely identified as blood these days."

Heavy breathing at the other end of the line succeeded this statement. Wexford felt that he had
scored. He drew breath to let loose vituperation, but
before he could speak the voice said coldly:

"D'you think I don't know that? I cut that hair from
Stella Rivers."

13

The Piebald Pony is not the kind of pub connoisseurs of rural England normally associate with her countryside. Indeed, if you approach it from the direction of Sparta Grove, and if you keep your eyes down so that you cannot see the green surrounding hills, you would not suppose yourself in the country at all. Sparta Grove and Charteris Road which it joins at a right angle—on this corner stands the Piebald Pony—resemble the back streets of an industrial city. A few of the houses have narrow front gardens, but most doors open directly on to the pavement, as do the entrances to the Pony's public and saloon bars.

One of these rooms fronts Sparta Grove, the other Charteris Road. They are the same shape and size and the saloon bar is distinguished from the public only in that drinks cost more in the former, about a third of its stone floor is covered with a square of brown Axminster and its seating includes a couple of settees, upholstered in battered black, of the kind that used to be seen in railway waiting rooms.

On one of the settees, under a poster recommending the Costa del Sol and displaying a photograph of a girl in a wet-look bikini leering at a bull in its death throes, sat Monkey Matthews with an old man. He looked, Wexford thought, very much by time's fell hand defaced and in nearly as bad case as the bull. It wasn't that he was thin or pale—in fact his squarish toad's face was purple—but there was an air about him of one who has been physically ruined by years of bad feeding, damp dwellings and nasty indulgences whose nature Wexford preferred not to dwell on.

Each man had an almost empty half-pint glass of the cheapest obtainable bitter and Monkey was smoking a minuscule cigarette.

" 'Evening," said Wexford.

Monkey didn't get up but indicated this companion with an airy wave. "This is Mr. Casaubon."

Wexford gave a tiny sigh, the outward and audible sign of an inward and outrageous scream. "I don't believe it," he said thinly. "Just enlighten me to which one of you two intellectuals is acquainted with George Eliot."

Far from living up to Monkey's image of a man intimidated by the police, Mr. Casaubon had brightened as soon as Wexford spoke and now rejoined in thick hideous cockney, "I see him once. Strangeways it was, 1929. They done him for a big bullion job."

"I fear," Wexford said distantly, "that we cannot be thinking of the same person. Now what are you gentlemen drinking?"

"Port and brandy," said Mr. Casaubon almost before the words were out, but Monkey, to whom what could be inhaled always took priority over what could merely be imbibed, pushed forward his empty bitter glass and remarked that he would appreciate twenty Dunhill International.

Wexford bought the drinks and tossed the crimson and gold package into Monkey's lap. "I may as well open the proceedings," he said, "by telling you two jokers you can forget about five hundred pounds or anything like it. Is that clear?"

Mr. Casaubon received this in the manner of one used to frequent disappointment. The liveliness which had briefly appeared in his watery eyes died away and, making a low humming sound that might have been a long-drawn murmur of assent or just an attempt at a tune, he reached for his port and brandy. Monkey said, "When all's said and done, me and my friend would settle for the reward."

"That's very handsome of you," said Wexford sarcastically. "I suppose you realise that money will be paid only for information leading directly to the arrest of the murderer of Stella Rivers?"

"We wasn't born yesterday," said Monkey. This remark was so obviously true, particularly in the case of Mr. Casaubon, who looked as if he had been born in 1890, that the old man broke off from his humming to emit a cackle of laughter, showing Wexford the most hideous, dilapidated and rotting set of teeth he had ever seen in a human mouth. "We can read what's in the papers as well as you," Monkey went on. "Now then, cards on the table. If my friend tells you what he knows and what he's got papers to *prove*, are you going to do fair by us and see we get what's our right when Swan's under lock and key?"

"I can get a witness, if that's what you want. Mr. Burden perhaps?"

Monkey puffed smoke out through his nostrils. "I can't stomach that sarcastic devil," he said. "No, your word's good enough for me. When folks run down the fuzz I always say, Mr. Wexford's hounded me, God knows, but he . . "

"Monkey," Wexford interrupted, "are you going to tell me or aren't you?"

"Not here," said Monkey, shocked. "What, give you a load of info that'll put a man away for life here in what you might call the market place?"

"I'll drive you back to the station, then."

"Mr. Casaubon wouldn't like that." Monkey stared at the old man, perhaps willing him to show some sign of terror, but Mr. Casaubon, his eyelids drooping, simply continued to hum monotonously. "We'll go to Rube's place. She's out babysitting."

Wexford shrugged his agreement. Pleased, Monkey gave Mr. Casaubon a poke. "Come on, mate, wakey-wakey."

It took Mr. Casaubon quite a long time to get on to his legs. Wexford walked impatiently to the door, but Monkey, not usually renowned for his considerate manners, hovered with some solicitude at his friend's side, and then, giving him an arm, helped him tenderly out into the street.

Burden had never phoned her before. His heart palpitated lightly and fast as he listened to the ringing tone and imagined her running to answer, her heart beating quickly too because she would guess who it was.

The steadiness of her voice took the edge off his excitement. He spoke her name softly, on a note of enquiry.

"Yes, speaking," she said. "Who is it?"

"Mike." She hadn't recognised his voice and his disappointment was profound.

But immediately he had identified himself she gasped and said quickly, "You've got some news for me? Something's happened at last?"

He closed his eyes momentarily. She could only think of that child. Even his voice, her lover's voice, was to her just the voice of someone who might have found her child. "No, Gemma, no, there's nothing."

"It was the first time you ever phoned me, you see," she said quietly.

"Last night was a first time too."

She said nothing. Burden felt that he had never known so long a silence, aeons of silence, time for twenty cars to drone past the phone box, time for the lights to change to green and back again to red, time for a dozen people to enter the Olive and leave the door swinging, swinging, behind them until it lapsed into stillness. Then at last she said, "Come to me now, Mike. I need you so."

There was another woman he had to have speech with first.

"I'm just going out on a job, Grace," said Burden, too straitlaced, too innocent perhaps, to see a *double entendre* which would have had Wexford in stitches. "I may be hours."

They were given to pregnant, throbbing silences, his women. Grace broke the one she had created with a sharp ward sister's snap. "Don't lie to me, Mike. I just phoned the station and they said you had a free evening."

"You had no business to do that," Burden flared. "Even Jean never did that and she had the right, she was my wife."

"I'm sorry, but the children asked and I thought . . . As a matter of fact, there's something special I want to discuss with you."

"Can't it wait till tomorrow?" Burden thought he knew these discussions of Grace's. They were always about the children, more precisely about the children's psychological problems or what Grace imagined those problems to be: Pat's supposedly butterfly mind and John's mental block over his mathematics. As if all children didn't have their difficulties which were a part of growing up and which he in his day, and surely Grace in hers, had faced satisfactorily without daily analysis. "I'll try to be in tomorrow night," he said weakly.

"That," said Grace, "is what you always say."

His conscience troubled him for about five minutes. It had long ceased to do so before he reached the outskirts of Stowerton. Burden had yet to learn that the anticipation of sexual pleasure is the most powerful of all the crushers of conscience. He wondered why he felt so little guilt, why Grace's reproach had only momentarily stung him. Her words—or what he could recall of them—had become like the meaningless and automatic admonition of some schoolteacher spoken years ago. Grace was no longer anything to him but an impediment, an irritating force which conspired with work and other useless time-wasters to keep him from Gemma.

Tonight she came to the door to meet him. He was prepared for her to speak of the child and her anxieties and her loneliness, and he was ready with the gentle words and the tenderness which would come so easily to him after an hour in bed with her but which now his excitement must make strained and abrupt. She said nothing. He kissed her experimentally, unable to guess her mood from those large blank eyes.

She took his hands and put them against her waist

which was naked when she lifted the shirt she wore.
Her skin was hot and dry, quivering against his own
trembling hands. Then he knew that the need she
had spoken of on the phone was not for words or reassurance or searching of the heart but the same need
as his own.

If Mr. Casaubon had been capable of inspiring the
slightest sentimentality, Wexford reflected, it would
have been impossible to witness Monkey's extravagant
care of him without disgust. But the old man—his
real name would have to be ferreted out from some
file or other—was so obviously a villain and a parasite
who took every advantage of his age and an infirmity
that was probably assumed that Wexford could only
chuckle sardonically to himself as he watched Monkey
settle him into one of Ruby Branch's armchairs and
place a cushion behind his head. No doubt it was obvious to the receiver of these attentions as it was to
the chief inspector that Monkey was merely cosseting
the goose that would lay a golden egg. Presumably
Mr. Casaubon had already come to some financial
agreement with his partner of impresario and knew
there was no question of affection or reverence for
old age in all this fussing with cushions. Humming
with contentment in the fashion of an aged purring
cat, he allowed Monkey to pour him a treble whisky,
but when the water jug appeared the hum rose a
semitone and a gnarled purple hand was placed over
the glass.

Monkey drew the curtains and placed a table lamp
on the end of the mantelpiece so that its radiance fell
like a spotlight on the bunchy rag-bag figure of Mr.
Casaubon, and Wexford was aware of the dramatic
effect. It was almost as if Monkey's protégé was one
of those character actors who delight to appear solo
on the London stage and for two hours or more en-
tertain an audience to a monologue or to readings
from some great novelist or diarist. And Mr. Casaubon's repetitive nodding and humming rather enhanced this impression. Wexford felt that at any mo-

ment the play would begin, a witticism would issue from those claret-coloured lips or the humming would give place to a speech from *Our Mutual Friend*. But because he knew that this was all fantasy, deliberately achieved by that crafty little con-man Monkey Matthews, he said sharply: "Get on with it, can't you?"

Mr. Casaubon broke the silence he had maintained since leaving the Piebald Pony. "Monk can do the talking," he said. "He's got more the gift of the gab than me."

Monkey smiled appreciatively at this flattery and lit a cigarette. "Me and Mr. Casaubon," he began, "made each other's acquaintance up north about twelve months back." In Walton gaol, Wexford thought, but he didn't say it aloud. "So when Mr. Casaubon was glancing through his morning paper the other day and saw about Mr. Ivor Swan and him living in Kingsmarkham and all that, his thoughts naturally flew to me."

"Yes, yes, I get all that. In plain English he saw the chance to make a little packet and thought you could help him to it. God knows why he didn't come straight to us instead of getting involved with a shark like you. Your gift of the gab, I suppose." A thought struck Wexford. "Knowing you, I wonder you didn't try putting the black on Swan first."

"If you're going to insult me," said Monkey, snorting out smoke indignantly, "we may as well have done, and me and my friend'll go to Mr. Griswold. I'm doing this as a favour to you, like to advance you in your profession."

Mr. Casaubon nodded sagely and made a noise like a bluebottle drowsing over a joint of beef. But Monkey was seriously put out. Temporarily forgetting the respect due to age and golden geese, he snapped in the tone usually reserved for Mrs. Branch, "Give over that buzzing, will you? You're getting senile. Now you can see," he said to Wexford, "why the silly old git needs me to prop him up."

"Go on, Monkey. I won't interrupt again."

"To get to the guts of the business," said Monkey, "Mr. Casaubon told me—and showed me his paper to prove it—that fourteen years back your Ivor Bloody Swan—listening, are you? Ready for a shock?—your Ivor Swan killed a kid. Or, to put it more accurate, caused her death by drowning her in a lake. There, I thought that'd make you sit up."

Rather than sitting up, Wexford had slumped into his chair. "Sorry, Monkey," he said, "but that's not possible. Mr. Swan hasn't a stain on his character."

"Hasn't paid the penalty, you mean. I'm telling you, this is fact, it's gospel. Mr. Casaubon's own niece, his sister's girl, was a witness. Swan drowned the kid and he was up in court, but the judge acquitted him for lack of evidence."

"He can't have been more than nineteen or twenty," Wexford said ruminatively. "Look here, I'll have to know more than that. What's this paper you keep on about?"

"Give it here, mate," said Monkey.

Mr. Casaubon fumbled among his layers of clothing, finally bringing out from some deep recess beneath mackintosh, coat and matted wool a very dirty envelope inside which was a single sheet of paper. He held it lovingly for a moment and then handed it to his go-between who passed it on to Wexford.

The paper was a letter with neither address nor date.

"Before you read it," said Monkey, "you'd best know that this young lady as wrote it was chambermaid in this hotel in the Lake District. She had a very good position, lot of girls under her. I don't know exactly what she was but she was the head one."

"You make her sound like the madame in a brothel," said Wexford nastily, and cut short Monkey's expostulation with a quick, "Shut up and let me read."

The letter had been written by a semi-literate person. It was ill-spelt, almost totally lacking in punctuation. While Mr. Casaubon hummed with the complacency of a man showing off to an acquaintance the prize-winning essay of some young relative, Wexford read the following.

"Dear Uncle Charly.

"We have had a fine old fuss up hear that you will want to know of there is a young Colledge feller staying in the Hotel and what do you think he as done he as drowned a little girl swimmin in the Lake in the morning befor her Mum and Dad was up and they have had him up in Court for it Lily that you have herd me speak of had to go to the Court and tell what she new and she tell me the Judge give it to him hot and strong but could not put him away on account of Nobody saw him do the deed the young fellers name is IVOR LIONEL FAIRFAX SWAN i got it down on paper when Lily said it gettin it from the Judge on account i new you would wish to know it in ful.

"Well Uncle that it all for now i will keep in touch as ever hoping the news may be of use and that your Leg is better Your Affect. Niece

"Elsie"

The pair of them were staring eagerly at him now. Wexford read the letter again—the lack of commas and stops made it difficult to follow—and then he said to Mr. Casaubon, "What made you keep this for fourteen years? You didn't know Swan, did you? Why keep this letter in particular?"

Mr. Casaubon made no reply. He smiled vaguely as people do when addressed in a foreign language and then he held out his glass to Monkey, who promptly refilled it and, once more taking on the task of interpreter, said, "He kept all her letters. Very devoted to Elsie is Mr. Casaubon, being as he never had no kiddies of his own."

"I see," said Wexford, and suddenly he did. He felt his features mould themselves into a scowl of rage as the whole racket worked by Mr. Casaubon and his niece grew clear to him. Without looking again at the letter he recalled certain significant phrases. "A fine old fuss that you will want to know of" and "hoping the news may be of use" sprang to mind. A chambermaid, he thought, a chiel among us taking notes . . . How many adulterous wives had Elsie spotted? Into how many bedrooms had she blundered by the merest chance? How many homosexual in-

trigues had she discovered when homosexual practice
was still a crime? Not to mention the other secrets to
which she would have had access, the papers and
letters left in drawers, the whispered confidences between women, freely given at night after one gin too
many. The information about Swan, Wexford was
sure, was just one of many such pieces of news re-
tailed to Uncle Charly in the knowledge that he
would use them for the extortion of money of which
Elsie, in due course, would claim her share. A clever
racket, though one which, to look at him now, had
not finally worked to Mr. Casaubon's advantage.

"Where was this Elsie working at the time?" he
snapped.

"He don't remember that," said Monkey. "Somewhere up in the Lakes. She had a lot of jobs one way
and another."

"Oh, no. It was all one way and a dirty way at
that. Where is she now?"

"South Africa," mumbled Mr. Casaubon, showing
his first sign of nervousness. "Married a rich yid and
went out to the Cape."

"You can hang on to the letter." Monkey smiled in-
gratiatingly. "You'll want to do a bit of checking up.
I mean, when all's said and done, we're only a couple
of ignorant fellers, let's face it, and we wouldn't know
how to go about getting hold of this judge and all
that." He edged his chair towards Wexford's. "All we
want is our rightful dues for setting you on the track.
We don't ask for no more than the reward, we don't
want no thanks nor nothing. . . ." His voice faltered
and Wexford's baleful face finally silenced him. He
drew in a deep lungful of smoke and appeared to
decide that at last it was time to offer hospitality to
his other guest. "Have a drop of Scotch before you go?"

"I wouldn't dream of it," Wexford said pleasantly.
He eyed Mr. Casaubon. "When I drink I'm choosey
about my company."

14

Nervous bliss, Wexford decided, best described Inspector Burden's current state of mind. He was preoccupied, often to be found idle and staring distantly into space, jumping out of his skin over nothing, but at least it was a change from that bleak irritable misery everyone had come to associate with him. Very likely the cause of the change was a woman, and Wexford, encountering his friend and assistant in the lift on the following morning, remembered Dr. Crocker's words.

"How's Miss Woodville these days?"

He was rewarded, and somewhat gratified, by the uneven burning blush that spread across Burden's face. It confirmed his suspicion that recently there had been something going on between those two and something a good deal more exciting than discussions about whether young Pat ought to have a new blazer for the autumn term.

"My wife," he went on, pressing his point home, "was only saying yesterday what a tower of strength Miss Woodville has been to you." When this evoked no response, he added, "All the better when the tower of strength has an uncommonly pretty face, eh?"

Burden looked through him so intensely that Wexford suddenly felt quite transparent. The lift halted.

"I'll be in my office if you want me."

Wexford shrugged. Two can play at that game, he thought. You won't get any more friendly overtures from me, my lad. Stiff-necked prude. What did he care about Burden's dreary love life, anyway? He had other things on his mind and because of them he hadn't slept much. Most of the night he had lain awake thinking about that letter and Monkey Matthews and the old villain who was Monkey's guest, and he had pondered on what it all meant.

Elsie was as sharp as a needle but bone ignorant. To a woman like her any J.P. was a judge and she wouldn't know the difference between assizes and a magistrates' court. Was it possible that all those years ago the young Swan had appeared before a *magistrate*, charged with murder or manslaughter, and the case been dismissed? And if that was so had the facts of that hearing somehow escaped being included in Wexford's dossier of Swan?

Night is a time for conjecture, dreams, mad conclusions; morning a time for action. The hotel had been somewhere in the Lake District and as soon as he was inside his office Wexford put through calls to the Cumberland and Westmorland police. Next he did a little research into the antecedents of Mr. Casaubon, working on the assumption that he had been in Walton at the same time as Monkey, and this conclusion and the investigations it led to proved fruitful.

His name was Charles Albert Catch and he had been born in Limehouse in 1897. Pleased to discover that all his guesswork had been correct, Wexford learned that Catch had served three terms of imprisonment for demanding money with menaces but since reaching the age of sixty-five had fallen on evil days. His last conviction was for throwing a brick through the window of a police station, a ploy to secure—as it had done— a bed and shelter for the blackmailer who had become an impoverished vagrant.

Wexford wasted no sympathy on Charly Catch but he did wonder why Elsie's information had led her uncle to take no steps against Swan at the time. Because there really was no evidence? Because Swan had been innocent with nothing to hide or be ashamed of? Time would show. There was no point in further conjecture, no point in taking any steps in the matter until something came in from the Lakes.

With Martin and Bryant to keep watch from a discreet distance, he sent Polly Davis, red-wigged, off to her assignation at Saltram House. It was raining again and Polly got soaked to the skin, but nobody brought John Lawrence to the park of Saltram House or to the Italian garden. Determined not to speculate any further on the subject of Swan, Wexford racked his brains instead about the caller with the shrill voice but still he was unable to identify that voice or to remember any more about it but that he had heard it somewhere before.

Holding her in his arms in the dark, Burden said, "I want you to tell me that I've made you happier, that things aren't so bad because I love you."

Perhaps she was giving one of her wan smiles. He could see nothing of her face but a pale glow. The room smelt of the scent which she used to use when she was married and had, at any rate, a little money. Her clothes were impregnated with it, a stale musty sweetness. He thought that tomorrow he would buy her a bottle of scent.

"Gemma, you know I can't stay the night. I only wish to God I could, but I promised and . . ."

"Of course you must go," she said. "If I were going to my—to my children, nothing would keep me. Dear kind Mike, I won't keep you from your *children*."

"You'll sleep?"

"I shall take a couple of those things Dr. Lomax gave me."

A little chill touched his warm body. Wasn't satisfied love the best soporific? How happy it would have made him to know that his love-making alone could send her into sweet sleep, that thoughts of him would drive away every dread. Always the child, he thought, always the boy who had secured for himself all his mother's care and passion. And he imagined the miracle happening and the lost dead boy, restored to life and to home, running into the darkened bedroom now, bringing his own light with him, throwing himself into his mother's arms. He saw how she would forget her lover, forget that he had ever existed, in a little world made just for a woman and a child.

He got up and dressed. He kissed her in a way that was meant to be tender only but became passionate because he couldn't help himself. And he was rewarded with a kiss from her as long and desirous as his own. With that he had to be satisfied; with that and with the crumpled chiffon scarf he picked up as he left the room.

If only he would find his bungalow empty, he mused as he drove towards it. Just for tonight, he told himself guiltily. If only he could go into emptiness and solicitude, free of Grace's gentle brisk demands and Pat's castles in the air and John's mathematics. But if he were going home to an empty house he wouldn't be going home at all.

Grace had said she wanted to discuss something with him. The prospect was so dreary and so tedious that he forebore speculating about it. Why endure an agony twice over? He held the scented chiffon against his face for comfort before entering the house but instead of comfort it brought him only longing.

His son was hunched over the table, ineptly grasping a compass. "Old Mint Face," he said when he saw his father, "told us that 'mathema' means knowledge and 'pathema' means suffering, so I said they ought to call it pathematics."

Grace laughed a little too shrilly. She was flushed, Burden noticed, as if with excitement or perhaps trepidation. He sat down at the table, neatly drew the diagram for John and sent him off to bed. "May as well have an early night myself," he said hopefully.

"Spare me just ten minutes, Mike. I want—there's something I want to say to you. I've had a letter from a friend of mine, a girl—a woman—I trained with." Grace sounded extremely nervous now, so unlike herself that Burden felt a small disquiet. She was holding the letter and seemed about to show it to him, but she changed her mind and stood clutching it. "She's come into some money and she wants to start a nursing home and she . . ." The words tumbled out in a rush, ". . . she wants me to come in with her."

Burden was beginning on a bored, "Oh, yes, that's nice," when suddenly he did a double-take and what she was actually saying came home to him. The shock was too great for thought or politeness or caution. "What about the children?" he said.

She didn't answer that directly. She sat down heavily like a tired old woman. "How long did you think I would stay with them?"

"I don't know." He made a helpless gesture with his hands. "Till they're able to look after themselves, I suppose."

"And when will that be?" She was hot now and angry, her nervousness swamped by indignation. "When Pat's seventeen, eighteen? I'll be forty."

"Forty's not old," said her brother-in-law feebly.

"Maybe not for a woman with a profession, a career she's always worked at. If I stay here for another six years I won't have any career, I'd be lucky to get a job as a staff nurse in a country hospital."

"But the children," he said again.

"Send them to boarding school," she said in a hard voice. "Physically, they'll be just as well looked after there as here, and as for the other side of their lives —what good do I do them alone? Pat's coming to an age when she'll turn against her mother or any mother substitute. John's never cared much for me. If you don't like the idea of boarding school, get a transfer and go to Eastbourne. You could all live there with Mother."

"You've sprung this on me, all right, haven't you, Grace?"

She was almost in tears. "I only had Mary's letter yesterday. I wanted to talk to you yesterday, I begged you to come home."

"My God," he said, "what a thing to happen. I thought you liked it here, I thought you loved the kids."

"No, you didn't," she said fiercely, and her face was
suddenly Jean's, passionate and indignant, during one
of their rare quarrels. "You never thought about me
at all. You—you asked me to come and help you and
when I came you turned me into a sort of house-
mother and you were the lofty superintendent who
condescended to visit the poor orphans a couple of
times a week."

He wasn't going to answer that. He knew it was
true. "You must do as you please, of course," he said.

"It isn't what I please, it's what you've driven me to.
Oh, Mike, it could have been so different! Don't you
see? If you'd been with us and pulled your weight
and made me feel we were doing something worth
while *together*. Even now if you . . . I'm trying to
say . . . Mike, this is very hard for me. If I thought
you might come in time to . . . Mike, won't you help
me?"

She had turned to him and put out her hands, not
impulsively and yearningly as Gemma did, but with
a kind of modest diffidence, as if she were ashamed.
He remembered what Wexford had said to him that
morning in the lift and he recoiled away from her.
That it was almost Jean's face looking at him, Jean's
voice pleading with him, about to say things which
to his old-fashioned mind no woman should ever say
to a man, only made things worse.

"No, no, no!" he said, not shouting but whispering
the words with a kind of hiss.

He had never seen a woman blush so fierily. Her
face was crimson, and then the colour receded, leaving it chalk white. She got up and walked away,
scuttling rather, for on a sudden she had lost all her
precise controlled gracefulness. She left him and
closed the door without another word.

That night he slept very badly. Three hundred
nights had been insufficient to teach him how to sleep
without a woman and, after them, two of bliss had
brought back with savagery all the loneliness of a single bed. Like a green adolescent he held, pressed

against his face so that he could smell it, the scarf of the woman he loved. He lay like that for hours, listening through the wall to the muffled crying of the woman he had rejected.

15

The lock of hair did not belong to Stella Rivers either. Enough of her own blond curls remained on what remained of her for them to make comparison. "A bracelet of bright hair about the bone," Wexford thought, shuddering.

That proved nothing, of course. It was only to be expected, it was known, that the fur man—Wexford thought of his correspondent and his caller as the "fur man" now—was a liar. There was nothing for him to do but wait for news from the Lakes, and his temper grew sour. Burden had been unbearable for the last couple of days, hardly answering when you spoke to him and not to be found when most he was wanted. The rain fell unceasingly too. Everyone in the police station was irritable and the men, depressed by the weather, snapped at each other like wet, ill-tempered dogs. The black-and-white foyer floor was blotched all day by muddy footmarks and trickles from sodden raincapes.

Marching briskly past the desk to avoid an encounter with Harry Wild, Wexford almost crashed into a red-faced Sergeant Martin who was waiting for the lift.

"I don't know what the world's coming to, sir, I really don't. That young Peach, usually won't say boo to a goose, flares up at me because I tell him he should be wearing a stouter pair of boots. Mind your own business, he has the nerve to say to me. What's up, sir? What have I said?"

"You've solved something for me," Wexford said, and then more soberly, because this was only the beginning of an investigation, not a solution: "Sergeant, the night we were searching for John Lawrence you told a man in the search party to put on thicker shoes —you must have a thing about it—and he too told you to mind your own business. Remember?"

"I can't say I do, sir."

"I spoke to him too," Wexford said wonderingly. "He tried to stroke the dogs." Fur, he thought, fur and rabbits. He had tried to stroke the alsatian, his hand seemingly impelled towards that soft thick coat. "God, I can't remember what he looked like! But I remember that voice. That voice! Sergeant, the man you spoke to, the man who tried to stroke the dogs, is the writer of those letters."

"I just don't recall him, sir."

"Never mind. It should be easy to find him now."

But it wasn't.

Wexford went first to Mr. Crantock, the husband of Gemma Lawrence's neighbour, who was head cashier at the Kingsmarkham branch of Lloyd's Bank. Certain that this man would know every member of the search parties by sight if not by name, Wexford was disappointed to learn that not every searcher had been drawn from the three streets, Fontaine Road, Wincanton Road and Chiltern Avenue.

"There were a lot of chaps I'd never seen before," said Crantock. "Heaven knows where they came from or how they got to know the kid was missing that early. But we were glad of anyone we could get, weren't we? I remember there was one character came on a bike."

"News of that kind travels fast," Wexford said. "It's a mystery how it does, but people get to know of things before there's time for them to be on television or radio or in the papers."

"You could try Dr. Lomax. He led one of the parties until he had to go back on a call. Doctors always know everybody, don't they?"

The supplier of Gemma Lawrence's sleeping pills practised from his own home, a Victorian Gothic house of considerable dimensions that was superior to

its neighbours in Chiltern Avenue. Wexford arrived in
time to catch the doctor at the end of his afternoon
surgery.

Lomax was a busy harassed little man who spoke
with a shrill voice, but it wasn't the shrillness Wexford was listening for and, besides, the doctor had a
faint Scottish accent. It seemed that he too was unlikely to be of much help.

"Mr. Crantock, Mr. Rushworth, Mr. Dean . . ." He
enumerated a long list of men, counting them on his
fingers, though of what use this was Wexford didn't
know, as the search parties had never been counted.
Lomax, however, seemed certain when he reached the
end of his list that there had been three strangers,
one the cyclist.

"How they even knew about it beats me," he said,
echoing Crantock. "I only knew myself because my
wife came in and told me while I was holding surgery.
She acts as my nurse, you see, and she'd overheard
someone talking in the street while she was helping
an elderly patient out of a car. She came straight in
here and told me and when my last patient had gone
I went outside to see what I could do and saw all
your cars."

"What time would that have been?"

"When my wife told me or when I went outside?
It would have been something after six when I went
out, but my wife told me at twenty past five. I can
be sure of that because the old lady she helped from
the car always comes at five twenty on the dot on
Thursdays. Why?"

"Were you alone when your wife told you?"

"No, of course not. I had a patient with me."

Wexford's interest quickened. "Did your wife come
up to you and whisper the news? Or did she say it
aloud so that the patient could have heard?"

"She said it aloud," said Lomax rather stiffly. "Why
not? I told you she acts as my nurse."

"You will remember who the patient was, naturally, Doctor?"

"I don't know about naturally. I have a great many patients." Lomax reflected in silence for a moment. "It wasn't Mrs. Ross, the old lady. She was still in the waiting room. It must have been either Mrs. Foster or Miss Garrett. My wife will know, she has a better memory than I."

Mrs. Lomax was called in.

"It was Mrs. Foster. She's got four children of her own and I remember she was very upset."

"But her husband didn't come in the search party," said Lomax, who seemed now to be following Wexford's own line of reasoning. "I don't know him, he's not my patient, but he couldn't have. Mrs. Foster had just been telling me he'd broken one of his big toes."

Except to say in an embarrassed low tone, "Of course, I'll stay till you've made other arrangements," Grace had scarcely spoken to Burden since telling him of her plans. At table—the only time they were together —they kept up a thin polite pretence of conversation for the sake of the children. Burden spent his evenings and his nights with Gemma.

He had told her, but no one else, that Grace was deserting him, and wondered, not understanding at all, when her great wistful eyes widened and she said how lucky he was to have his children all to himself with no one to come between or try to share their love. Then she fell into one of her terrible storms of weeping, beating with her hands on the dusty old furniture, sobbing until her eyes were swollen and half-closed.

Afterwards she let him make love to her, but "let" was the wrong word. In bed with him she seemed briefly to forget that she was a mother and bereaved and became a young sensual girl. He knew that sex was a forgetting for her, a therapy—she had said as much—but he told himself that no woman could show so much passion if her involvement was solely physical. Women, he had always believed, were not made that way. And when she told him sweetly and almost

shyly that she loved him, when she hadn't mentioned
John for two hours, his happiness was boundless, all
his load of cares nothing.

He had had a wonderful idea. He thought he had
found the solution to the sorrows of both of them. She
wanted a child and he a mother for his children.
Why shouldn't he marry her? He could give her another child, he thought, proud in his virility, in the
potency that gave her so much pleasure. She might
even be pregnant already, he had done nothing to
avoid it. Had she? He was afraid to ask her, afraid
to speak of any of this yet. But he turned to her,
made strong and urgent by his dreams, anxious for
quick possession. Even now they might be making a
child, the two of them. He hoped for it, for then she
would have to marry him. . . .

The Fosters lived in Sparta Grove, a stone's throw
from the Piebald Pony, in a little house that was one
of a row of twelve.

"I didn't tell a soul about that poor kid," said Mrs.
Foster to Wexford, "except my husband. He was sitting in a deckchair, resting his poor toe, and I rushed
out to tell him the good news."

"The *good* news?"

"Oh dear, what must you think of me? I don't mean
the poor little boy. I did mention that, but only in
passing. No, I wanted to tell him what the doctor said.
Poor man, he'd been going up the wall and so had I,
for that matter. My husband, I mean not the doctor.
We thought we was going to have another one you
see, thought I'd fallen again and me with four already.
But the doctor said it was the onset of the change.
The relief! You've no idea. I give the kids their tea
and then my husband took me up the Pony to cele-
brate. I did mention the poor little boy when we was
in there. I mean, you like to have a bit of a natter,
don't you, especially when you're on top of the world.
But it was well gone seven before we got there, that
I do know."

It had looked like a promising lead, had proved a dead end.

It was still half-light and Sparta Grove full of children, playing on the pavements. No one seemed to be supervising them, no one peeping from behind a curtain to keep an eye on that angelic-looking boy with the golden curls or guarding the coffee-skinned, sloe-eyed girl on her tricycle. No doubt the mothers were there, though, observing while themselves remaining unobserved.

The Pony was opening and, as sure as the sun rises, Monkey Matthews, supporting Charly Catch alias Mr. Casaubon, appeared from the direction of Charteris Road. Wexford hurried off before they spotted him.

Find the three strangers in the search party was next morning's order of the day, made the more urgent by the printed letter which awaited Wexford among his mail. It was repetitious and Wexford hardly glanced at it, for awaiting him also was a report compiled and signed by an Inspector Daneforth of the Westmorland Constabulary.

Strict orders having been given that he was not to be disturbed, Wexford read:

"On August 5th, 1957, the body of a child, Bridget Melinda Scott, aged 11, was recovered from Fieldenwater lake, Westmorland. The child was found to have met her death by drowning and on August 9th an inquest was held by the Mid-Westmorland Coroner, Dr. Augustine Forbes."

An inquest. Of course! Why hadn't he thought of that? Elsie would call an inquest a court and a coroner a judge. Vaguely disheartened, Wexford read on.

"Evidence was given by:

"1) Lilian Potts, chambermaid, employed at the Lakeside Hotel where Bridget Scott with her parents, Mr. and Mrs. Ralph Scott, was a guest. Miss Potts told the coroner that she had met Bridget in one of the first floor passages of the hotel at 8 a.m. on the morning of August 5th. Bridget had said she was going swimming in the lake and was wearing a bathing costume with a beach robe over it. She was alone. Miss Potts advised her not to go out of her depth. Bridget made no reply and Miss Potts saw her go down the stairs.

"2) Ralph Edward Scott, plumbing engineer, of 28 Barrington Gardens, Colchester, Essex. Mr. Scott said he was the father of Bridget Scott. He and his wife and daughter had been spending a fortnight's holiday at the Lakeside Hotel, Fieldenwater. By August 5th they had been there for ten days. Bridget was a keen swimmer and used to swim in the lake regularly before breakfast. On August 5th, before he and his wife were up, Bridget came into their bedroom to say she was going for a swim. He warned her to stay close to the shore. He never saw her alive again.

"3) Ada Margaret Patten, widow, aged 72, of 4 Blenheim Cottages, Water Street, Fieldenwater Village. She said she had been exercising her dog, as was her habit, at 8:15 a.m. on the north shore of Fieldenwater, the opposite shore to that on which the hotel is situated. She heard a cry for help and noticed that there was a bather in difficulties. Herself unable to swim, Mrs. Patten observed two men bathing at the eastern end of the lake and another man fishing from a rowing boat a short distance from the bather who had called for help. Asked by the coroner to explain what she meant by a short distance, Mrs. Patten said she would calculate the distance was about twenty yards. Mrs. Patten was carrying a walking stick which she waved in the direction of the boat. She also tried to attract the attention of the other two bathers. The men at the eastern end of the lake eventually heard her and began to swim northwards. Her shouts had no apparent effect on the fisherman in the boat. Finally, she saw the boat moving towards the distressed swimmer but before it reached that part of the lake the swimmer had disappeared. She did not understand how the boatman could have failed to hear her as sound carries over water. She had often been in boats on the lake herself and knew that sounds from the shore were clearly audible in its centre.

"4) George Baleham, agricultural worker, of 7, Bulmer Way, New Estate, Fieldenwater Village. Mr. Baleham told the coroner that he and his brother had gone for a swim in Fieldenwater at 7:30 a.m. on August 5th. He saw a child enter the lake from the Lakeside Hotel towards 8:10. Five minutes later he heard cries from across the water and heard Mrs. Patten shouting. Immediately he and his brother began swimming towards the child who was two hundred yards from them. There was a boat in the vicinity of the child and he saw a man fishing from it. He shouted to the man in the boat, "There's a kid drowning. You are nearer than us," but the boat did not move. Mr. Baleham said the boat did not begin to move until he was ten yards from it. By this time the child had disappeared. In his opinion, the man in the boat could easily have reached the child before she sank. From where he was he could not have failed to see the child or hear her cries.

"5) Ivor Lionel Fairfax Swan . . ."

Here it was then, what he had been waiting for. The name in cold type gave Wexford a strange little cold thrill. He felt like a man who for months has stalked a particular stag and now, groping through the brush and undergrowth of a bleak moor, sees his quarry standing aloof and unsuspecting, near him, oh, so near! on a crag. Stealthily and silently he reaches for his gun.

"5) Ivor Lionel Fairfax Swan, student, aged 19, of Carien Hall, Carien Magna, Bedfordshire, and Christ's College, Oxford. Mr. Swan said he was on holiday at the Lakeside Hotel with two friends. Bridget Scott had occasionally spoken to him in the hotel lounge and on the lake beach. Apart from that he did not know her and had never spoken to her parents. He enjoyed fishing and sometimes hired a boat to take out on to the lake in the early morning.

"On August 5th he took the boat out at 7 a.m. He was alone on the lake. He noticed two men swimming from the eastern shore at about 7:40, then, soon after eight, Bridget Scott came down the steps from the hotel and entered the water. He did not know whether she was a strong swimmer or not. He knew very little about her.

"She called something out to him but he did not answer. He thought she would make a nuisance of herself and disturb the fish. Some minutes later he heard her call again and again he took no notice. Several times in the previous week she had done things to draw his attention to herself and he though it wiser not to encourage her. He heard Mrs. Patten shouting, but thought she was calling her dog.

"Very soon after that two swimmers attracted his attention and then he saw that Bridget was in genuine difficulty. At once he began to draw in his line and make towards where he had last seen her. By then she had disappeared.

"In answer to the coroner's questions, Mr. Swan said he had not thought of diving overboard and swimming. His line was an expensive one and he did not wish to spoil it. He could not dive and was not a strong swimmer. Up until the moment Bridget sank he had never believed her to be in genuine distress. No, he would not say he disliked the child. He had hardly known her. It was true he had not liked her attempts to intrude on himself and his friends. He was sorry she was dead and wished now that he had made efforts to save her. He was, however, sure in his own mind, that under the circumstances, he had acted as would any other man in his position.

"6) Bernard Varney Frensham, aged 19, student, of 16 Paisley Court, London, S.W.7 and Christ's College, Oxford. Mr. Frensham said he was a friend of Mr. Swan and had been on holiday with him and his (Mr. Frensham's) fiancée at the Lakeside Hotel. Bridget Scott had taken an immediate liking to Mr. Swan, a 'crush' he supposed it would be called, and had tended to pester him. He said he had never been in a boat on Fieldenwater. Fishing did not interest him. When asked by the coroner if Mr. Swan was a good swimmer, Mr. Frensham said, 'Must I answer that?' Dr. Forbes insisted and Mr. Frensham said he did not know anything about Mr. Swan's style as a swimmer. He had never swum for his college. Pressed further, Mr. Frensham said that he had once been shown a life-saving certificate with Mr. Swan's name on it."

At this point there was a note explaining that medical and police evidence had been omitted. The report ended:

"The coroner commended Mr. George Baleham and Mr. Arthur Baleham for their prompt action in attempting to save the child.

"He then reprimanded Mr. Swan. He said this was the worst case of callousness towards a child who was obviously drowning that he had ever come across. He took a serious view of what he could only call deliberate and cowardly lying on Mr. Swan's part. Far from being an indifferent swimmer, he was an expert at life-saving. There was no doubt in his mind that Mr. Swan had refused to listen to the child because he believed, or said he believed, she was pestering him. If he had jumped overboard when he first heard her cry out, Bridget Scott would be alive today. He could not be excused on the ground of his youth as he was a man of intelligence, an Oxford undergraduate and a man of privileged background. The coroner said he was only sorry the law permitted him to take no further steps. He then expressed sympathy for Mr. and Mrs. Scott.

"A verdict was returned of death by misadventure."

16

When giving Burden a résumé of Swan's life, Wexford had remarked on the series of disasters he had left in his wake. Here, then, was another instance of that catastrophe-causing faculty of his, that gift, or propensity, of leaving a trail of trouble and distress and disturbance. A true catalyst was Swan, Wexford reflected, a possessor of the power to hurt who yet did—nothing.

It wasn't difficult to picture that morning on the lake, Swan's line cast, the sun shining on the flat brown water, and Swan off in one of his daydreams that nothing must be allowed to disturb. Had he even caught a fish? Did he ever actually *do* anything? Shoot a rabbit? Choose a dog? Buy a pony?

And that was the crux of it. Clearly, Swan had let a child die. But the operative word there was "let." Would he actively force death on a child? Had he the nerve, the impulse, the *energy?*

Wexford would have liked to chew the whole thing over with Burden. They were illuminating and fruitful, those long discussions of theirs, examining motive, analysing character. But Burden was no longer fit to participate in such conversations. As soon expect percipience and intelligent speculation from Martin as from him. Each day he seemed to go a little more downhill, to grow more irritable and more distracted until Wexford began to wonder with dread how long it could go on. At present he daily covered up for Burden, did his work, smoothed his path. There was a limit to that, for soon the crack-up would come, the error that couldn't be overlooked or the hysterical scene in public. And then what? The embarrassed re-

144

quest for Burden's resignation before he was forced out?

Wexford shook himself out of these miserable reflections to concentrate on the report. One mystery, at any rate, was cleared up. He need no longer wonder why Swan had baulked at attending an inquest, particularly an inquest on another dead little girl.

The next step was to find Frensham, and this proved easy. Fourteen years had changed him from an undergraduate into a stock jobber, moved him from his parents' flat but not from Kensington, and maintained him in his bachelor state. What had happened to that fiancée who had accompanied him on that Lake holiday?

Hardly a question which need concern him, Wexford decided. He made the requisite polite phone call to the Metropolitan Police and then prepared to set off for London. In the foyer he met Burden.

"Any lead on the missing men from the search party?"

Burden lifted troubled eyes and muttered, "Martin's got it in hand, hasn't he?"

Wexford went out into the rain, not looking back.

He alighted at Gloucester Road Tube station, got lost, and had to ask a policeman the way to Veronica Grove. At last he found it, a narrow little tree-lined lane which threaded its way from Stanhope Gardens down behind Queen's Gate. Water dripped softly from the branches overhead, and, except that the trees were planes and not oaks, he felt that he might have been at home in Kingsmarkham. The environs of the Piebald Pony were much more his idea of what London should be.

Meditating on such anomalies, he came within a few minutes to Bernard Frensham's house. It was tiny, a mews cottage, with neat but empty window boxes, and it looked very modest unless you happened to know that such properties were sold for twenty-five thousand pounds.

A manservant, small, lithe and dark, admitted

him and showed him into the single living room the
house contained. It was, however, a large room on
three different levels and the furnishing gave an impression of varying textures, satiny polish, smooth
velvet, delicate filigree work and highlighted china,
rather than of solid masses. Much money had been
spent on it. The years Swan had wasted had been
turned to good account by his friend.

Frensham, who had risen from his chair at the far
end of the room when Wexford entered it, had received prior warning of his coming. And "warning"
rather than "notice" seemed the appropriate word, for
it was very apparent that he had been drinking. Because the coming interview caused him disquiet? Wexford was forced to suppose so. A stock jobber could
hardly be so successful as Frensham surely was if
seven o'clock always saw him as drunk as he was
tonight.

Not that he didn't hold it well. It was only the
brandy smell and the strangeness of Frensham's eyes
that told Wexford of his condition.

He was thirty-three and he looked forty, the black
hair already thinning and the face marked with dark
patches. On the other hand, Swan, his contemporary,
looked twenty-seven. Slothfulness and placidity pre-
serve youth; hard work and anxiety accelerate its
passing.

Frensham wore a beautiful suit of charcoal grey
with a coppery sheen to it, a black-and-copper tie,
and, on the little finger of his left hand, an opal ring.
What an impression of civilised distinction the man
would have made, Wexford thought, but for the
brandy on his breath which struck you full-blast in the
face.

"Let me give you a drink, Chief Inspector."

Wexford would have refused, was on the point of
refusing, but there was so much subdued urgency in
Frensham's added, "Please do," that he felt bound to
consent.

Frensham opened the door and called a name that
sounded like "Haysus." Brandy was brought and vari-

ous other bottles and decanters. When the manservant had gone, Frensham said, "Odd, aren't they, the Spanish? Calling a boy Jesus." He gave a short disconcerting giggle. "Most inappropriate, I can tell you. His parents are Maria and Joseph or so he says."

Taking a gulp of his drink, he pursued this theme, but Wexford decided he wouldn't be sidetracked by Iberian nomenclature. It was impossible not to feel that Frensham was trying to postpone their discussion for as long as possible.

"May we talk about Mr. Ivor Swan, sir?"

Frensham left the subject of Spanish names abruptly and said in a clipped voice, "I haven't seen Ivor for years, not since we both came down from Oxford."

"That doesn't matter. I have. Perhaps you can't remember much about him?"

"I remember all right," said Frensham. "I shall never forget." He got up and walked across the room. At first Wexford thought he had gone to fetch a photograph or some document and then he realised that Frensham was in the grip of a powerful emotion. His back was towards the chief inspector and for some minutes he didn't move. Wexford sat watching him in silence. He wasn't easily embarrassed, but he wasn't prepared for Frensham's next words either. Wheeling round suddenly, staring oddly at Wexford, he said, "Has he vine leaves in his hair?"

"I beg your pardon?"

"You have never seen or read *Hedda Gabler?* It doesn't matter. It's the kind of question I feel natural to ask about Ivor." The man was very drunk, with the intoxication that rids the tongue of inhibition without slurring speech. He came back to his chair and rested his elbows against the back of it. "Ivor was remarkably beautiful then, a pale golden-brown Antinous. I was very fond of him. No, that isn't true. I loved him with—with all my heart. He was very lazy and—well, tranquil. He never seemed to know what the time was or to take any account of time at all." Frensham spoke as if he had forgotten Wexford was there or forgotten what he was. He reached for his brandy

standing up. "That kind of indifference to time, that
sublime idleness, is very attractive. I often think it
was this quality in her, rather than her religious zeal,
that made Christ praise Mary and condemn Martha,
the bustling busy worker."

Wexford had not come to hear about the character
of Ivor Swan, which he thought he already understood, but he was no more willing to interrupt Frensham in the midst of his discourse than a spiritualist
would have been to cut short the outpourings of a
medium in a trance. He felt somehow, as might the
spiritualist also, that it would be dangerous to do so.

"He was always pursued by droves of girls," Frensham went on. "Some of them were beautiful and all
of them were intelligent. I am speaking, of course, of
Oxford girls. He slept with some of them but he never
took them out, not even for a drink. He couldn't be
bothered. He used to say he didn't like clever women
because they tried to make him talk.

"Once I told him the sort of woman he would
marry, a feather-brained idiot who would adore him
and fuss about him and demand only his presence.
He wouldn't marry her, she would marry him, drag
him to the altar against all odds. I saw in the paper he
is married. Is she like that?"

"Yes, she is," said Wexford. "Exactly like that."

Frensham sat down heavily. He looked ravaged
now, as if overcome by painful memories. Wexford
wondered if he and Swan had really been lovers, but
decided against it. The willingness would have been
there on Frensham's part all right, but Swan just
wouldn't have been "bothered."

"I never married," said Frensham. "I was engaged
to that girl, Adelaide Turner, but it never came to
anything. I remember Ivor didn't want her to go on
holiday with us and I didn't either, not really, not by
then. He said she would get in the way." He refilled
his glass and said, "I can't stop drinking, I'm afraid. I
don't drink much usually but once I start I can't stop.
I promise you I won't make a fool of myself."

Some would say he was doing that already. Wexford was less harsh. He felt sorry for Frensham, sorrier when he said suddenly:

"I don't know whether I'm giving you a true picture of Ivor's character or not. You see, although I haven't seen him for twelve years, I dream about him a great deal, as much as three times a week. It must sound very silly, I haven't ever told anyone before. I mention it now because I don't know any more what is the real Ivor and the Ivor my own dreams have created. The two images are so confused they have run into each other and become one."

Wexford said gently, "Tell me about the holiday. Tell me about Bridget Scott."

"She was only eleven," Frensham said, and his voice was saner and more even when he wasn't speaking of Swan. "But she looked much older, at least fourteen. It sounds very absurd to say she fell in love with him at first sight, but she did. And, of course, at that age she hadn't learned to hide her feelings. She used to pester Ivor all the time, ask him to go swimming with her, wanted him to sit next to her in the lounge. She even asked her mother in our hearing if he could go up and say good night to her when she was in bed."

"And how did Swan deal with all that?"

"Simply by taking no notice. He treated Adelaide in the same way. He used to answer Adelaide if she spoke to him, but most of the time he didn't speak to Bridget at all. He said she got in the way, and once, I remember, he told her so."

Frensham leaned back and gave a heavy sigh. His eyes closed momentarily and he opened them as if with a great effort. "The coroner," he said, "was an old man like a vulture. I didn't want to betray Ivor. They made me tell them about his swimming. I hadn't any choice." The heavy lids fell again. "I felt like Judas," he said.

"What happened that morning when Bridget was drowned?"

Still Frensham kept his eyes closed and now his speech had begun to thicken. "I never went out fish-

ing with Ivor. I've never been an early riser. Ivor was.
You'd think a man like—a man like him, would go to
bed late and get up late. Ivor always used to be up by
six. He'd sleep in the day, or course, if he got the
chance. He could sleep anywhere. It was the early
morning he liked and the countryside, the peace of it
and the light." Frensham made a funny little noise
like a sob. "He used to quote those lines of W. H.
Davies. 'What is this life, if full of care, we have
no time to stand and stare?' "

"Go on about that morning."

Frensham sat up, and half-toppled forward, resting
his elbows on his knees, his chin in his hands. "I don't
know. I wasn't there. I woke up to hear people shouting in the corridor outside my room, running up and
down and shouting. You can imagine. I went outside.
The mother was there, screaming, and that poor old
man, Scott."

"Old? Bridget's father?"

"Not really old, I suppose. About sixty. The mother
was younger. They had older children, someone told
me. Does it matter? I found Ivor in the dining room,
drinking coffee. He was very white. He said, 'It was
nothing to do with me. Why involve me?' and that
was all he ever said about it."

"You mean he never again mentioned the subject
of Bridget Scott's drowning to you? Not when you
both had to attend the inquest?"

"He didn't like it because we had to stay on over
the end of our holiday," remembered Frensham, and
now a glaze had come across his eyes. Weariness?
Tears? Or only the effect of the drink? "After—after
the inquest he wouldn't let me speak of it. I don't
know what he felt." Very softly now, Frensham said,
"It may have been callousness or that he was upset or
just wanted to forget. There wasn't much about the
inquest in the daily papers and when we went up no
one knew until—until Adelaide told them."

"Why do you think he let her drown?" said Wexford.

"She got in his way," said Frensham, and then he

began to cry weakly. "When people annoyed him or began to—to bore him he just—just—just . . ." There was a sob between each word. ". . . Just—ignored— them — pretended — they — weren't — there — didn't — talk — didn't — see — them — did — that — to — me — after — later . . ." He threw out a hand and the brandy glass went over, spreading a stain across the thick pale carpet.

Wexford opened the door and called, "Here, Jesus, or whatever your name is, your master wants you. You'd better get him to bed."

The man came in, sidling and smiling. He put his arms under Frensham's shoulders and whispered to him. Frensham lifted his head and said to Wexford in a normal clear tone, "Vine leaves in his hair . . ." Then he closed his eyes and slid into unconsciousness.

17

Friday's edition of the *Kingsmarkham Courier* carried on its front page a double-column spread asking for the three missing men from the search party to come forward. Much good that would do, Wexford thought, as he read it. Hadn't it occurred to Martin, when he asked Harry Wild for publicity, that an appeal of this kind would fetch forth only the innocents? And where was Burden in all this, Burden who was supposed to rule the place in Wexford's absence, yet who seemed as much surprised by the newspaper appeal as he was?

When he got back from London he had phoned Burden's house. He needed to discuss that interview with someone and he thought too that this might be a way of reawakening Burden's interest. But Grace Woodville had told him her brother-in-law was out, she didn't know where.

"I think he may just be sitting somewhere in his car, brooding about Jean and—and everything."

"He's supposed to leave a number where he can be found."

"Cheriton Forest doesn't have a number," said Grace.

On Saturday afternoon two men walked into Kingsmarkham police station to say that they had read the *Courier* and believed they were two of the three missing men. They were brothers, Thomas and William Thetford, who lived in adjoining houses in Bury Lane, a half-slum, half-country road on the far side of Stowerton, not far from Sparta Grove. News of John Lawrence's disappearance had been brought to them by William's wife who cleaned for Mrs. Dean and who had reached home at five-thirty. The Thetford brothers were on shift work, had both finished for that day. Guessing a search party might be got up —hoping for a bit of excitement to brighten up their day, Wexford thought—they had got into William's car and driven to Fontaine Road.

Neither man had a squeaky voice or even a voice Wexford could remember hearing before. They denied having passed the news on to anyone and said they had discussed it only with each other. Wexford supposed that routine demanded an interview with Mrs. Thetford. Monday would be time enough for that.

"Golf in the morning?" said Dr. Crocker, bouncing in after the Thetfords had gone.

"Can't. I'm going to Colchester."

"Whatever for?" Crocker said crossly, and then, without waiting for an answer, "I wanted to have a little chat with you about Mike."

"I'd really rather you didn't. I'd rather you saw him. You're his doctor."

"I think he's found a better doctor than I," said Crocker slyly. "I saw his car again last night."

"Don't tell me. In Cheriton Forest. And he was in it, brooding."

"It wasn't and he wasn't. It was parked at the bottom of Chiltern Avenue at midnight."

"You're ubiquitous, you are," Wexford grumbled. "You're like the Holy Ghost."

"It was at the bottom of *Chiltern Avenue*, next to *Fontaine Road* at *midnight*. Come on, Reg. I knew you were thick round the middle but not . . ." The doctor tapped his head ". . . not up here."

"That's not possible," said Wexford sharply. His voice faltered. "I mean . . . Mike wouldn't . . . I don't want to talk about it." And he cast upon the doctor a fierce glare. "If I don't know about it," he said with none of his usual logic, "it isn't happening."

"I know it would be like a miracle," said Gemma, "but if—if John is ever found and comes back to me,

I shall sell this house, even if I only get what the land's worth, and go back to London. I could live in one room, I shouldn't mind. I hate it here. I hate being in here and I hate going out and seeing them all look at me."

"You talk like a child," said Burden. "Why talk about what you know can't happen? I asked you to marry me."

She got up, still without answering, and began to dress, but not in the clothes she had taken off when she and Burden had come into the bedroom. He watched her hungrily, but puzzled as he always was by nearly every facet of her behaviour. She had pulled over her head a long black dress, very sleek and tight. Burden didn't know whether it was old, a garment of her aunt's, or the latest fashion. You couldn't tell these days. Over her shoulders and around her waist she wrapped a long scarf of orange and blue and green, so stiff and encrusted with embroidery that it crackled as she handled it.

"We used to dress up a lot, John and I," she said, "dress up and be characters from the *Red Fairy Book*. He would have grown up to be a great actor." Now she was hanging jewellery all over herself, long strings of beads draped from her neck and wound about her arms. "That sometimes happens when one of your parents, or both of them, has been a second-rate artist. Mozart's father was a minor musician." She swayed in the soft red light, extending her arms. There was a ring on every finger to weigh down her thin hands. She shook down her hair and it fell in a flood of fire, the light catching it as it caught all the stones in the cheap rings and made them flash.

Burden was dazzled and fascinated and appalled. She danced across the room, drawing out the scarf and holding it above her head. The jewels rang like little bells. Then she stopped, gave a short abrupt laugh, and ran to him, kneeling at his feet.

" 'I will dance for you, Tetrarch,' " she said. " 'I am awaiting until my slaves bring perfumes to me and the seven veils and take off my sandals.' "

Wexford would have recognised the words of Salome. To Burden they were just another instance of her eccentricity. Very distressed and embarrassed, he said, "Oh, Gemma . . .!"

In the same voice she said, "I will marry you if . . . if life is to go on like this with nothing, I'll marry you."

"Stop play-acting."

She got up. "I wasn't acting."

"I wish you'd take those things off," he said.

"You take them off."

Her huge staring eyes made him shiver. He reached out both hands and lifted the bunch of chains from her neck, not speaking, hardly breathing. She lifted her right arm, curving it in a slow sweep and then holding it poised. Very slowly he slid the bracelets down over her wrist and let them fall, pulled the rings from her fingers one by one. All the time they stared into each other's eyes. He thought that he had never in his life done anything as exciting, as overpoweringly erotic, as this stripping a woman of cheap glittering jewellery, although in doing so he had not once touched her skin.

Never . . . He hadn't even dreamed that such a thing might be possible for him. She stretched out her left arm and he made no other move towards her until her last ring had joined the others in a heap on the floor.

It wasn't until he awoke in the night that he realised fully what had happened, that he had proposed and been accepted. He told himself that he ought to be elated, in a seventh heaven of happiness, for he had got what he wanted and there would be no more agony or struggling or loneliness or dying small daily deaths.

The room was too dark for him to see anything at all, but he knew exactly what the first light would show him here and downstairs. Yesterday it hadn't mattered much, the mess and the chaos, but it mattered now. He tried to see her installed in his own

house as its mistress, caring for his children and cooking meals, tending on them all as Grace did, but it
was impossible to conjure up such a picture, he hadn't
enough imagination. What if Wexford were to call
one night for a chat and a drink as he sometimes did
and Gemma appear in her strange dress and her shawl
and her long beads? And would she expect him to
have her friends there, those itinerant subactors with
their drugs? And his children, his Pat . . . !

But all that would change, he told himself, once
they were married. She would settle down and be a
housewife. Perhaps he could persuade her to have that
mane of hair cut, that hair which, at one and the
same time, was so beautiful and so evocative of desire and yet so unbecoming in a policeman's wife.
They would have a child of their own, she would
make new suitable friends, she would change . . .

He did not allow himself to dwell on the notion
that such changes as he envisaged would destroy her
personality and dull all the strangeness that had first
attracted him, but it touched the edges of his mind.
He pushed it away almost angrily. Why make difficulties where none existed? Why seek always to find flaws
in perfect happiness?

Gemma and he would have love, a nightly orgy for
two, an endless honeymoon. He turned towards her,
pressing his lips against the mass of hair of which he
planned to deprive her. Within minutes he was asleep
and dreaming that he had found her child, restoring
him to her and seeing her, by that gift, transformed
into everything he wanted her to be.

"Kingsmarkham?" said Mrs. Scott, smiling comfortably
at Wexford. "Oh, yes, we know Kingsmarkham, don't
we, dear?" Expressionless, her husband gave a tiny
nod. "We've got a niece lives in ever such a nice little
house near Kingsmarkham, built back in the seventeen
hundreds, it was, and we used to go there regularly
for our holidays right up till this year. But now . . ."

Wexford, who while she was speaking had been taking stock of the room and looking particularly at the

framed photographs of those older Scott children who had survived, middle-aged now and with teenage children of their own, followed her gaze towards their progenitor.

No need to ask why they wouldn't go back to Kingsmarkham or to question the implication that they would take no more holidays. Scott was a little old man, nearing eighty, whose face was badly twisted, especially about the mouth. Two sticks hung from the wings of his chair. Wexford supposed that he was unable to walk without their aid and, from his silence, was beginning to suppose that Ralph Scott had also lost the power of speech. It was something of a shock when the distorted mouth opened and a harsh voice said:

"What about a cup of tea, Ena?"

"I'll have it ready in a jiffy, dear."

Mrs. Scott jumped up and mouthed something to Wexford, indicating that he should join her in the kitchen. This was a sterile-looking place full of gadgets, and it was modern enough to gladden the heart of any house-proud woman, but Mrs. Scott seemed to think it needed apology.

"Mr. Scott had a stroke back in the winter," she said as she plugged in an electric kettle, "and it's really aged him. He's not at all the man he was. That's why we moved out here from Colchester. But if he was himself I'd have had everything automatic here, he'd have done the lot himself, not left it to those builders. I wish you could have seen my house in Colchester. The central heating was *too* hot. You had to have the windows open night and day. Mr. Scott did all that himself. Of course, him being in the trade all his life, there's nothing he doesn't know about heating and pipes and all that." She stopped, stared at the kettle which was making whining noises, and said in a voice that seemed to be suppressing something explosive, "We saw in the papers about that man Swan and you digging all that up again about his little girl. It made Mr. Scott ill, just seeing his name."

"The child died back in the winter."

"Mr. Scott never saw the papers then. He was too ill. We never knew Swan lived near our niece. We wouldn't have gone if we had. Well, he was living there the last time we went but we didn't know." She sat down on a plastic-upholstered contemporary version of a settle and sighed. "It's preyed on Mr. Scott's mind all these years, poor little Bridget. I reckon it would have killed him to have come face to face with that Swan."

"Mrs. Scott, I'm sorry to have to ask you, but in your opinion, is it possible he let your daughter drown? I mean, is it possible he knew she was drowning and let it happen?"

She was silent. Wexford saw an old grief cross her face, travel into her eyes and pass away. The kettle boiled with a blast and switched itself off.

Mrs. Scott got up and began making the tea. She was quite collected, sorrowful but with an old dry sadness. The fingers on the kettle handle, the hand on the teapot, were quite steady. A great grief had come to her, the only grief, Aristotle says, which is insupportable, but she had borne it, had gone on making tea, gone on exulting in central heating. So would it be one day for Mrs. Lawrence, Wexford mused. Aristotle didn't know everything, didn't know perhaps that time heals all pain, grinds all things to dust and leaves only a little occasional melancholy.

"Mr. Scott loved her best," Bridget's mother said at last. "It's been different for me. I had my sons. You know how it is for a man and his little girl, his youngest."

Wexford nodded, thinking of his Sheila, his ewe lamb, the apple of his eye.

"I never took on about it like he did. Women are stronger, I always say. They get to accept things. But I was in a bad way at the time. She was my only girl, you see, and I had her late in life. In fact, we never would have had another one, only Mr. Scott was mad on getting a girl." She looked as if she were trying to remember, not the facts, but the emotions of the time, trying and failing. "It was a mistake going to that hotel," she said. "Boarding houses were more in our line. But Mr. Scott was doing so well and it wasn't for me to argue when he said he was as good as the next man and why not a hotel when we could afford it? It made me feel uncomfortable, I can tell you, when I saw the class of people we had to mix with, Oxford boys and a barrister and a Sir. Of course, Bridget didn't know any different, they were just people to her and she took a fancy to that Swan. If I've wished it once I've wished it a thousand times that she'd never set eyes on him.

"Once we were in the lounge and she was hanging about him—I couldn't stop her. I did try—and he gave her such a push, not saying anything, you know, not talking to her, that she fell over and hurt her arm. Mr. Scott went right over and had a go at him, told him he was a snob and Bridget was as good as him any day. I'll never forget what he said. 'I don't care whose daughter she is,' he said. 'I don't care if her father's a duke or a dustman. I don't want her around. She gets in my way.' But that didn't stop Bridget. She wouldn't leave him alone. I've often thought since then that Bridget swam out to that boat so as she could be alone with him and no one else there."

Mrs. Scott picked up her tray, but made no other move to return to the sitting room. She seemed to be listening and then she said:

"She couldn't swim very far. We'd told her over and over again not to go out too far. Swan knew, he'd heard us. He let her drown because he just didn't *care*, and if that's killing, he killed her. She was only a child. Of course he killed her."

"A strong accusation to make, Mrs. Scott."

"It's no more than the coroner said. When I saw in the paper about his own little girl I didn't feel sorry for him, I didn't think he'd got his desserts. He's done the same to her, I thought."

"The circumstances were hardly the same," said Wexford. "Stella Rivers died from suffocation."

"I know. I read about it. I'm not saying he did it deliberately any more than I'm saying he actually pushed Bridget under the water. It's my belief she got in his way too—stands to reason she would, a step-daughter and him newly married—and maybe she said something he didn't like or got too fond of him like Bridget, so he got hold of her, squeezed her neck or something and—and she died. We'd better to go back to Mr. Scott now."

He was sitting as they had left him, his almost sight-less eyes still staring. His wife put a teacup into his hands and stirred the tea for him.

"There you are, dear. Sorry I was so long. Would you like a bit of cake if I cut it up small?"

Mr. Scott made no reply. He was concentrating on Wexford and the chief inspector realised that no ex-planation of his visit had been given to the old man. True, there had been a passing reference to Kings-markham and a cousin, but Wexford had not been identified by name or rank.

Perhaps it was the look in his wife's eyes or perhaps something that he had overheard while they were in the kitchen that made him say suddenly in his harsh monotone:

"You a policeman?"

Wexford hesitated. Scott was a very sick man. It was possible that the only real contact he had ever had with the police was when his beloved daughter died. Would it be wise or kind or even necessary to bring memories back to that exhausted, fuddled brain?

Before he could make up his mind, Mrs. Scott said brightly. "Oh, no dear. Whatever gave you that idea? This gentleman's just a friend of Eileen's from over Kingsmarkham way."

"That's right," said Wexford heartily.

The old man's hand trembled and the cup rattled in its saucer. "Shan't go there any more, not in my state. Shan't last much longer."

"What a way to talk!" Mrs. Scott's brisk manner did little to cover her distress. "Why, you're almost your old self again." She mouthed incomprehensible things to Wexford and followed them up with a louder, "You should have seen him last March, a couple of weeks after he had that stroke. More dead than alive he was, worse than a new-born baby. And look at him now."

But Wexford could hardly bear to look. As he left them, he reflected that the interview hadn't been entirely fruitless. At least it would spur him on to take Crocker's tablets with renewed zeal.

18

The impressions Swan made on other people had subtly altered Wexford's own image of him, investing him with a callous coldness and a magnetic beauty, making him godlike in appearance and power, so that when he came face to face with the man himself once more he felt a sense of letdown and almost of shock. For Swan was just Swan, still the idle good-looking young man leading his slow aimless existence. It was strange to reflect that the mere mention of his name might be enough to kill Mr. Scott and that, incubus-like, he lived a separate life as the haunter of Frensham's dreams.

"Does Roz have to know about this?" he asked, and went on when Wexford looked surprised, "I'd more or less forgotten it myself, except that going to that inquest brought it back. Do we have to talk about it?"

"I'm afraid we do."

Swan shrugged. "We won't be overheard. Roz is out and I got rid of Gudrun." Wexford's face showed the absurd effect this had on him and Swan gave a low ironical laugh. "Told her to go, sacked her, I mean. What did you think I'd done? Made away with her? In your eyes my path is strewn with corpses, isn't it? Roz and I love to be alone and Gudrun got in our way, that's all."

That phrase again. "She got in his way . . ." Wexford was beginning to get the shivers every time he heard it.

"D'you want a drink? It'll have to be something out of a bottle. Making tea and coffee is Roz's province

162

and, anyway, I don't know where she keeps the things."

"I don't want a drink. I want to hear about Bridget Scott."

"Oh God, it was such a hell of a long time ago, ancient history. I suppose you've already had a splendid selection of biassed accounts." Swan sat down and rested his chin in his hands. "I don't know what you want me to say. I went to this hotel with another man and a girl. If you'll give me a minute I'll try and remember their names."

"Bernard Frensham and Adelaide Turner." Poor Frensham, Wexford thought. Swan lived on in his dreams but he had no reciprocal place in Swan's memory.

"Why ask me if you've already talked to them?"

"I want your version."

"Of what happened on the lake? All right. I did let her drown, but I didn't know she was drowning." Swan's face was petulant. In the November light, fitful and fading, he might have been nineteen again, but Wexford could see no shadow of vine leaves in his hair. "She plagued the life out of me," he said, the sullen look deepening. "She hung about me and tried to get me to go swimming and walking with me and she staged scenes to attract my attention."

"What sort of scenes?"

"Once she was out in a rowing boat and I was swimming and she started shouting she'd dropped her purse overboard and would I dive for it. I didn't but what's-his-name—Frensham—did and after we'd all been messing about for about ten minutes she produced it from the bottom of the boat. It was all a ploy. Then she came into my room once in the afternoon when I was trying to sleep and said if I wouldn't speak to her she'd scream and when people came she'd tell them I'd done something to her. A kid of eleven!"

"So that when you heard her cry for help you thought it was another ruse to attract your attention?"

"Of course I did. That other time when she'd threatened to scream, I said, 'Scream away.' I can't be taken in by that kind of thing. Out in the boat, I *knew* she was putting on an act. I couldn't believe it when they said she'd drowned."

"Were you sorry?"

"I was a bit shattered," said Swan. "It made an impression on me, but it wasn't my fault. For quite a long time after that I didn't like having kids of that age around me. I don't now, come to that."

Had he realised what he had said? "Stella was just that age when you first saw her, Mr. Swan," said Wexford.

But Swan seemed unaware of the innuendo. He went on to make matters worse. "She used to try the same things on, as a matter of fact, always trying to get attention." The petulance returned, making him almost ugly. "Could she have a dog? Could she have a horse? Always trying to involve me. I sometimes think . . ." He directed at Wexford a gaze full of fierce dislike. "I sometimes think the whole world is trying to get between me and what I want."

"And that is?"

"To be left alone with Rosalind," said Swan simply. "I don't want children. All this has made me loathe children. I want to be in the country with Roz, just the two of us, in peace. She's the only person I've ever known who wants me for what I am. She hasn't made an image of me that's got to be lived up to, she doesn't want to jolly me along and encourage me. She loves *me*, she really knows me and I'm first with her, the centre of her universe. Once she'd seen me she didn't even care about Stella any more. We only kept her with us because I said we ought, that Roz might regret it later if she didn't. And she's jealous. Some men wouldn't like that, but I do. It gives me a wonderful feeling of happiness and security when Roz says if I so much as looked at another woman she'd do that woman the worst injury in her power. You don't know what that means to me."

I wonder what it means to me? Wexford thought. He said nothing but continued to keep his eyes fixed on Swan who suddenly flushed. "I haven't talked so much to anyone for years," he said, "except to Roz. That's her coming in now. You won't say anything about . . . ? If she began suspecting me I don't know what I'd do."

It was the sound of a car Swan had heard, the Ford shooting brake crunching on the gravel outside Hall Farm.

"I was under the impression you couldn't drive a car, Mrs. Swan," he said as she came in.

"Were you? I let my licence lapse while I was out in the East but I took a new test last month."

She had been shopping. In London perhaps, at any rate in some more sophisticated place than Kingsmarkham. Her packages were wrapped in black paper lettered with white, scarlet printed with gold. But she hadn't been buying for herself.

"A tie for you, my lover. Look at the label." Swan looked and so did Wexford. The label said Jacques Fath. "And some Russian cigarettes and a book and . . . It doesn't look very much now I've got it all home. Oh, how I wish we were rich!"

"So that you could spend it all on me?" said Swan.

"Who else? Did you remember to ring the electric people, darling?"

"I never got around to it," said Swan. "It went right out of my head."

"Never mind, my lover. I'll see to it. Now I'm going to make you some nice tea. Were you lonely without me?"

"Yes, I was. Very."

She had hardly noticed Wexford. He was investigating the murder of her only child but she had hardly noticed him. Her eyes, her attention, were solely for her husband. It was he who, now there was someone to prepare it, rather grudgingly suggested that Wexford might care to stay and share their tea.

"No, thank you," said the chief inspector. "I wouldn't want to be in your way."

The lock of hair had belonged neither to John Lawrence nor to Stella Rivers, but it was a child's hair. Someone had cut it from a child's head. That meant whoever had written the letters had access to a golden-headed child. And more than just access. No one could go up to a child in the street and chop off a piece of his or her hair without getting into trouble. Technically, it would be assault. Therefore, the letter-writer, the "fur man," must be in such close association with a golden-headed child as to be able to cut off a lock of its hair either while it was asleep or with its permission.

But how far did that get him? Wexford pondered. He couldn't interview every golden-haired child in Sussex. He couldn't even ask for such children to come forward, for the person "in close association"—father? uncle?—would prevent the one significant child from answering his appeal.

Although it wasn't the prescribed time, Wexford swallowed two of his blood-pressure tablets, washing them down with the dregs of his coffee. He'd need them if he was going to spend the rest of the day scouring Stowerton. Mrs. Thetford first, to see if there was any chance she had broadcast the news of John's disappearance around the town. Then perhaps Rushworth. Sit down with Rushworth for hours if necessary, make him remember, make him describe his fellow searchers, get to the bottom of it *today.*

The climate in which Burden and his sister-in-law now lived wasn't conducive to confidences. It was nearly a week since she had smiled at him or said any more than "Colder today" or "Pass the butter, please." But he would have to tell her about his forthcoming marriage, and tell the children too, perhaps even ask their permission.

He thought his opportunity had come when, thawing a little, Grace said, "Aren't you having next weekend off?"

Guardedly, he said, "Supposed to be. We're very busy."

"Mother's asked all four of us down for the week-end."

"I don't think . . ." Burden began. "I mean, I couldn't manage it. Look here, Grace, there's something . . ."

Grace jumped up. "There's always something. Don't bother to make excuses. I'll go alone with the children, if you've no objection."

"Of course I've no objection," said Burden, and he went off to work, or what would have been work if he had been able to concentrate.

He had half-promised to have his lunch in Fontaine Road. Bread and cheese, he supposed it would be, in that loathsome kitchen. Much as he longed to be with Gemma in the night, the meals she prepared had no attraction for him. The police-station canteen was almost preferable. And suddenly it occurred to him that soon every meal he ate at home would be prepared by Gemma.

Wexford had gone out somewhere. Time was when the chief inspector would never have gone out without leaving a message for him, but all that was changed now. He had changed it and the change in him had lost him Wexford's esteem.

Descending in the lift, he hoped he wouldn't encounter Wexford, and when the door opened he saw that there was no one in the foyer but Camb and Harry Wild, who these days had become almost a fixture, as much a part of the furnishings as the counter and the little red chairs. Burden treated him like a chair, accepting his presence but otherwise ignoring him. He was nearly at the swing doors when they burst open and Wexford appeared.

Except when he was with Gemma, muttering had become Burden's normal mode of speech. He muttered a greeting and would have gone on his way. Wexford stopped him with the "Mr. Burden!" he habitually used in the presence of such as Camb and Wild.

"Sir?" said Burden with equal formality.

Speaking in a lower tone, Wexford said, "I've spent the morning with that fellow Rushworth, but I couldn't get a thing out of him. Strikes me as a bit of a fool."

With an effort, Burden tried to fix his mind on Rush-worth. "I don't know," he said. "I wouldn't have considered him as a possible suspect myself, but he does wear a duffel coat and there was that business when he nearly frightened the wits out of the Crantock girl."

"*He did what?*"

The words had been spoken in a sharp hiss. "I told you," Burden said. "It was in my report." Hesitating, muttering again, he recounted to the chief inspector his experience of the encounter in Chiltern Avenue. "I must have told you," he faltered. "I'm sure I . . ."

Wexford forgot about Wild and Camb. "You never did!" he shouted. "You never made any bloody report. D'you mean to tell me now—*now*—that Rush-worth molested a child?"

Burden had no words. He felt his face grow crimson. It was true—he remembered now—he had made no report, the whole thing had vanished from his mind. Love and involvement had driven it away, for that night, while Stowerton was wrapped in mist, had been his first night with Gemma.

Things might have come to a head then between him and Wexford but for the intervention of Harry Wild. Insensitive to atmosphere, quite incapable of ever supposing himself to be *de trop,* Wild turned round and said loudly:

"D'you mean to tell me you've got Bob Rushworth lined up for this job?"

"I don't mean to tell you anything," Wexford snapped.

"There's no need to be like that. Don't you want any help in your enquiries?"

"What do you know about it?"

"Well, I do know Rushworth," said Wild, pushing himself between the two policemen. "And I know he's a nasty customer. Friend of mine rents a cottage from him down in Mill Lane, but Rushworth keeps a key to it and pops in and out just whenever the fancy takes him. He went through all my friend's private

papers one day without so much as by your leave and
his boy goes in and takes apples out of the garden,
pinched a pint of milk once. I could tell you things
about Bob Rushworth as'd make . . ."

"I think you've told me enough, Harry," said Wexford. Without extending the usual invitation to lunch,
without even looking at Burden again, he swung out
of the police station the way he had come.

Because he was sure that if he went to the Carousel
Burden would only follow him and ruin his lunch with
mealy-mouthed excuses, Wexford drove home and surprised his wife, who seldom saw him between nine
and six, with a peremptory demand for food. He
couldn't remember when he had last been in such a
bad temper. Angry-looking black veins were standing
out on his temples and this alarmed him so that he
took two anti-coagulant tablets with the beer Mrs.
Wexford produced off the ice. Burden ought to know
better than to upset him like that. Fine thing if he
ended up like poor old Scott.

Somewhat calmer by three o'clock, he drove off to
see Mrs. Thetford. According to a neighbour, she was
out at her job of cleaning for Mrs. Dean. Wexford
hung about till she got back and saw no reason to re-
fuse her offer of a cup of tea and a piece of fruit
cake. The Rushworths were both out all day, anyway,
and he wanted to see them together rather than endure
another interview with Rushworth in his estate agent's
office, their conversation constantly interrupted by
phone calls from clients.

But tea and cake were all he got out of Mrs. Thetford. She repeated the story he had already heard
from her husband. Mrs. Dean had given her the news
about John Lawrence at five o'clock but she declared
she had passed it on to no one except her husband
and her brother-in-law.

He drove slowly up the lane and entered Sparta
Grove. Lomax's patient, Mrs. Foster, was his only hope
now. She must have told someone what she had overheard at the doctor's. Or been overheard herself? It
was a possibility, perhaps the only one remaining.

Number 14 was her house. Wexford parked outside it and then he saw the boy. He was swinging on the gate of the house next door, number 16, and his rather long hair was bright gold.

By now all the children were home from school and Sparta Grove was full of them. Wexford beckoned to a girl of about twelve and she approached the car suspiciously.

"I'm not supposed to talk to strange men."

"Very proper," said Wexford. "I'm a policeman."

"You don't look like one. Show me your warrant card."

"By gum, you'll go far if you don't come to a bad end." He produced his card and the child scrutinised it with huge delight. "Satisfied?"

"Mmm." She grinned. "I learnt how to do that off the telly."

"Very educational, the telly. I wonder they bother to keep the schools open. You see that boy with the fair hair? Where does he live?"

"Where he is. That house he's on the gate of."

Ungrammatical but explanatory. "You needn't tell him I was asking." Wexford produced a coin which he knew he wouldn't get back out of expenses.

"What shall I say, then?"

"Come, come. You're a resourceful girl. Say I was a strange man."

Now was not the time. He must wait until all the children were in bed. When the Piebald Pony opened he went into the saloon bar and ordered sandwiches and half a bitter. Any minute now, he thought, Monkey and Mr. Casaubon would come in. Delighted to see him in their local, they would try to ascertain how near they were to getting their hands on that two thousand, and it would give him much pleasure to tell them they had never been farther from it. He would even be indiscreet and reveal his innermost conviction, that Swan was guiltless of any crime but that of indifference.

But nobody came. It was seven when Wexford left

the Piebald Pony and walked three-quarters of the length of quiet, dimly-lit Sparta Grove.

He tapped on the door of number 16. No lights showed Every one of those children must now be safely in bed. In this house the golden-headed boy would be sleeping. From the look of the place—no blue-white glow of a television screen showed behind the drawn curtains his parents had gone out and left him alone. Wexford had a low opinion of parents who did that, especially now, especially here. He knocked again, harder this time.

To a sensitive astute person an empty house has a different feel from a house which simply appears to be empty but which, in reality, contains someone who is unwilling to answer a door. Wexford sensed that there was life somewhere in that darkness, conscious tingling life, not just a sleeping child. Someone was there, a tense someone, listening to the sound of the knocker and hoping the knocks would cease and the caller go away. He made his way carefully through the side entrance and round to the back. The Fosters' house next door was well lit but all the doors and windows were shut. A yellow radiance from Mrs. Foster's kitchen showed him that number 16 was a well-kept house, its path swept and its back doorstep polished red. The little boy's tricycle and a man's bike leaned against the wall and both were covered by a sheet of transparent plastic.

He hammered on the back door with his fist. Silence. Then he tried the handle very stealthily, but the door was locked. No getting in here without a warrant, he thought, and there was no hope of getting one on the meagre evidence he had.

Treading softly, he began to move round to the back of the house, feeling moist turf under his feet. Then, suddenly, a flare of light caught him from behind and he heard Mrs. Foster say, as audibly as if she were standing beside his ear, "You won't forget to put the bin out, will you, dear? We don't want to miss the dustmen two weeks running."

Just as he thought. Every word spoken in the garden of number 14 could be heard in this garden. Mrs. Foster hadn't seen him. He waited until she had retreated into her kitchen before moving on.

Then he saw it, a thin shaft of light, narrower than the beam from a pencil torch, stretching across the grass from a french window. Tiptoeing, he approached the source of this light, a tiny gap between drawn curtains.

It was difficult to see anything at all. Then he saw that right in the middle of the window the edge of the curtain had been caught up on a bolt. He squatted down but still he couldn't see in. There was nothing for it but to lie down flat. Thank God there was no one to see him or observe how hard he found it to perform what should have been one of man's most natural actions.

Flat on his belly now, he got one eye up against the uncurtained triangle. The room unfolded itself before him. It was small and neat and conventionally furnished by a house-proud wife with a red three-piece suite, a nest of tables, wax gladioli and carnations whose petals were wiped each day with a damp cloth.

The man who sat writing at a desk was quite relaxed now and intent on his task. The importunate caller had gone away at last and left him to the special peace and privacy he demanded. It would show in his face, Wexford thought, that concentration, that terrible solitary egotism, but he couldn't see his face, only the bare legs and feet, and sense the man's rapt absorption. He suspected that under the fur coat he wore he was quite naked.

Wexford watched him for some minutes, watched him pause occasionally in his writing and pass the thick furry sleeve across nose and mouth. It made him shiver, for he knew he was eavesdropping on something more private than secret speech or love-making or the confessional. This man was not alone with himself, but alone with his other self, a separate personality which perhaps no one else had ever seen until now.

To witness this phenomenon, this intense private fantasising in a room which epitomised conformity, seemed to Wexford an outrageous intrusion. Then he remembered those fruitless trysts in the forest and Gemma Lawrence's hope and despair. Anger drove out shame. He pulled himself on to his feet and rapped hard on the glass.

19

In his anxiety to reach the lift, Burden shoved Harry Wild out of the way.

"Manners," said the reporter. "There's no need to push. I've a right to come in here and ask questions if I..."

The sliding door cut off the rest of his remarks which would perhaps have been to the effect that, but for his modesty and fondness for the quiet life, he would have been exercising his rights in loftier portals than those of Kingsmarkham police station. Burden didn't want to hear. He only wanted Harry's statement, that they had found the boy, confirmed or denied.

"What's this about a special court?" he demanded, bursting into Wexford's office.

The chief inspector looked tired this morning. When he was tired his skin took on a grey mattness and his eyes looked smaller than ever, but still steel-bright, under the puffy lids.

"Last night," he said. "I found our letter-writer, a certain Arnold Charles Bishop."

"But not the boy?" Burden said breathlessly.

"Of course not the boy." Burden didn't like it when Wexford sneered like that. His eyes seemed to be drilling two neat holes into the inspector's already aching head. "He's never even seen the boy. I found him at his home in Sparta Grove where he was occupied in writing another letter to me. His wife was out at her evening class, his children were in bed. Oh, yes, he has children, two boys. It was from the head of one of them that he cut the hair while the kid was asleep."

"Oh God," said Burden.

"He's a fur fetishist. Want me to read his statement?"

Burden nodded.

" 'I have never seen John Lawrence or his mother. I did not take him away from the care of his mother, his legal guardian. On October 16, at about 6 p.m., I overheard my neighbour, Mrs. Foster, tell her husband that John Lawrence was missing and that search parties would probably be arranged. I went to Fontaine Road on my bicycle and joined one of these search parties.

" 'On three subsequent occasions in October and November I wrote three letters to Chief Inspector Wexford. I did not sign them. I made one telephone call to him. I do not know why I did these things. Something came over me and I had to do them. I am a happily married man with two children of my own. I would never harm a child and I do not own a car. When I wrote about the rabbits I did this because I like fur. I have three fur coats but my wife does not know this. She knows nothing of what I have done. When she goes out and the children are asleep I often put one of my coats on and feel the fur.

" 'I read in the paper that Mrs. Lawrence had red hair and John Lawrence fair fair. I cut a piece of hair from the head of my my son Raymond and sent it to the police. I cannot explain why I did this or any of it except by saying that I had to do it.' "

Burden said hoarsely, "The maximum he can get is six months for obstructing the police."

"Well, what would you charge him with? Mental torture? The man's sick. I was angry too last night, but not any more. Unless you're a brute or a moron you can't be angry with a man who's going through life with a sickness as grotesque as Bishop's."

Burden muttered something about it being all right for those who weren't personally involved, but Wexford ignored it. "Coming over to the court in about half an hour?"

"To go through all that muck again?"

"A great deal of our work consists of muck, as you call it. Clearing muck, cleaning up, learning what muck is and where it lives." Wexford rose and leaned heavily on his desk. "If you don't come, what are you going to do? Sit here mooning all day? Delegating? Passing the buck? Mike, I have to say this. It's time I said it. I'm tired. I'm trying to solve this case all on my own because I can't count on you any more. I can't talk to you. We used to thrash things out together, sift the muck, if you like. Talking to you now—well, it's like trying to have a rational conversation with a zombie."

Burden looked up at him. For a moment Wexford thought he wasn't going to answer or defend himself. He just stared, a dead empty stare, as if he had been interrogated for many days and many sleepless nights and could no longer sort out the painful twisted threads that contributed to his unhappiness. But he knew, for all that, that the time for fobbing Wexford off was long gone by, and he brought it all out in a series of clipped sentences.

"Grace is leaving me. I don't know what to do about the kids. My personal life's a mess. I can't do my job." A cry he hadn't meant to utter broke out. "Why did she have to die?" And then, because he couldn't help himself, because tears which no one must see were burning his eyelids, he sank his head into his hands.

The room was very still. Soon I must lift my head, Burden thought, and take away my hands and see his derision. He didn't move except to press his fingers harder against his eyes. Then he felt Wexford's heavy hand on his shoulder.

"Mike, my dear old friend . . ."

An emotional scene between two normally unemotional men usually has its aftermath of deep miserable embarrassment. When Burden had recovered he felt very embarrassed, but Wexford neither blustered heartily nor made one of those maladroit efforts to change the subject.

"You're due to be off this weekend, aren't you, Mike?"

"How can I take time off now?"

"Don't be a bloody fool. You're worse than useless the state you're in. Make it a long weekend, starting on Thursday."

"Grace is taking the children down to Eastbourne ..."

"Go with them. See if you can't make her change her mind about leaving. There are ways, Mike, aren't there? And now—my God, look at the time!—I'll be late for the court if I don't get cracking."

Burden opened the window and stood by it, letting the thin morning mist cool his face. It seemed to him that with the arrest of Bishop their last hope —or his last fear?—of finding John Lawrence had gone. He wouldn't disturb Gemma with it and she had never read the local papers. The mist, floating white and translucent, washed him gently and calmed him. He thought of the mist by the seaside and the long bare beaches, deserted in November. Once there, he would tell the children and Grace and his mother-in-law about Gemma, that he was to be married again.

He wondered why the idea of this chilled him more than the cold touch of the autumnal air. Because she was the strangest successor to Jean he could have picked in all his world? In the past he had marvelled at men who, in their selflessness or their temporary infatuation, marry crippled or blind women. Wasn't he contemplating doing just that, marrying a woman who was crippled in her heart and her personality? And that was the only way he knew her. How would she be if her deformity were healed?

Ludicrously, monstrous, to think of Gemma as deformed. Tenderly and with an ache of longing, he recalled her beauty and their lovemaking. Then, closing the window sharply, he knew he wouldn't be going down to Eastbourne with Grace.

Bishop was remanded for a medical report. The head-shrinkers would get to work on him, Wexford thought. Maybe that would do some good, more likely it wouldn't. If he had had any faith in psychiatrists he would have recommended Burden to attend one. Still, their recent confrontation had done something to clear the air. Wexford felt the better for it and he hoped Burden did too. Now, at any rate, he was out on his own. Single-handed he must find the children's killer—or fall back on the Yard.

The events of the past twenty-four hours had distracted his mind from Mr. and Mrs. Rushworth. Now he considered them again. Rushworth was in the habit of wearing a duffel coat, Rushworth was suspected of molesting a child, but surely, if he had been the loiterer in the swings field, Mrs. Mitchell would have recognised him as one of her neighbours? Moreover, at the time of John's disappearance, every man within a quarter-mile radius of Fontaine Road had been closely investigated, Rushworth included.

Wexford delved once more among the reports. On the afternoon of October 16th Rushworth claimed to have been in Sewingbury where he had a date to show a client over a house. The client, Wexford saw, hadn't turned up. Back in February Rushworth hadn't even been questioned. Why should he have been? Nothing pointed to a connection between him and Stella Rivers and no one knew then that he was the owner of the rented cottage in Mill Lane. At the time the ownership of that cottage had seemed irrelevant.

He wouldn't see Rushworth yet. First he needed enlightenment as to the man's character and veracity.

"To get away from this house!" Gemma said. "Just to get away for a little while." She put her arms round Burden's neck and clung to him. "Where shall we go?"

"You decide."

"I'd like London. You can lose yourself there, be just one in a lovely enormous crowd. And there are lights all night and things going on and . . ." She paused, biting her lip, perhaps at the look of horror on Burden's face. "No, you'd hate it. We aren't much alike, are we, Mike?"

He didn't answer that. He wasn't going to admit it aloud. "Why not somewhere on the coast?" he said.

"The sea?" She had been an actress, if not a very successful one, and she put all the loneliness and depth and vastness of the sea into those two words. He wondered why she had shivered. Then she said, "I don't mind if you'd like to. But not to a big resort where you might see—well, families, people with—with children."

"I thought of Eastover. It's November, so there won't be children."

"All right." She didn't point out to him that he had asked her to decide. "We'll go to Eastover." Her lips trembled. "It'll be fun," she said.

"Everyone will think I've gone to Eastbourne with Grace and the children. I'd rather it was that way."

"So that they can't get hold of you?" She nodded with a kind of sage innocence. "I see. You remind me of Leonie. She always tells people she's going to one place when really she's going somewhere else so that she won't be badgered with letters and phone calls."

"It wasn't that," Burden said. "It's just—well, I don't want anyone . . . Not until we're married, Gemma."

She smiled, wide-eyed and uncomprehending. He saw that she really didn't understand him at all, his need to be respectable, to put a good face on things. They didn't speak the same language.

It was Wednesday afternoon, and Mrs. Mitchell, that creature of routine, was cleaning her landing window. While she talked she clutched a pink duster in one hand and a bottle of pink cleaning fluid in the other and, because she refused to sit down, Wexford couldn't either.

"Of course I should have known if it was Mr. Rushworth," she said. "Why, his own little boy, his Andrew, was playing there with the others. Besides, Mr. Rushworth's quite a big man and the man I saw

was little, very small-made. I told the other officer
what little hands he had. Mr. Rushworth wouldn't
pick leaves."

"How many children has he?"

"Four. There's Paul—he's fifteen—and two little
girls and Andrew. I'm not saying they're my idea of
good parents, mind. Those children are allowed to do
just what they please, and Mrs. Rushworth didn't
take a blind bit of notice when I warned her about
that man, but do a thing like that . . .! No, you've got
the wrong end of the stick there."

Perhaps he had. Wexford left Mrs. Mitchell to her
window-cleaning and crossed the swings field. The
year was far too advanced now for any children to
play there and there would be no more freak sum-
mers. The roundabout looked as if it had never spun
on its scarlet axis and mould had begun to grow on
the seesaw. Hardly a leaf remained on the trees, oak
and ash and sycamore, which grew between the field
and Mill Lane. He touched the lower branches and
fancied that here and there he could see where a twig
had been snapped off. Then, in a more ungainly
fashion, he was sure, than the leaf-picker and his
young companion, he scrambled down the bank.

Briskly he walked the length of the lane, telling
himself it was as much for his health's sake as for
duty. He hadn't expected to find anyone at home in
the rented cottage but Harry Wild's friend was off
work with a cold. Leaving again after a quarter of an
hour, Wexford was afraid his visit had only served to
raise the man's temperature, so heated had he been
on the subject of Rushworth, a far from ideal land-
lord. Unless the tenant's account was exaggerated, it
appeared that the whole Rushworth family was in the
habit of entering the cottage, helping themselves to
garden produce and occasionally removing small
pieces of furniture for which they substituted pen-
cilled notes of explanation. They had retained a key
of their own and the tenant paid so low a rent that
he was afraid to expostulate. At any rate, Wexford

now knew the identity of the boy who had been seen leaving the cottage that February afternoon. Beyond a doubt, it had been Paul Rushworth.

The day had been dull and overcast and now evening was closing in, although it was scarcely five. Wexford felt a first few drops of rain. On just such a day and at much this time Stella had followed the road he was taking, quickening her steps perhaps, wishing she had more to protect her than a thin riding jacket. Or had she even come so far back towards Stowerton? Had her journey—and her life—taken her no further than the cottage he had just left?

He had immersed himself so much in Stella, mentally transmuting his own elderly, male and stout body into the slight form of a twelve-year-old girl, that when he heard the sounds ahead of him he stepped back on to the grass verge and listened with a kind of hope.

The sounds were of horse's hooves. A horse was coming round the bend in the lane.

He was Stella, not old Reg Wexford. He was alone and a bit frightened and it was beginning to rain, but Swan was coming . . . On a *horse?* One horse for two people? Why not in a car?

The horse and its rider came into sight. Wexford shook himself back into himself and called out. "Good afternoon, Mrs. Fenn."

The riding instructress reined in the big grey. "Isn't he lovely?" she said. "I wish he was mine, but I've got to take him back to Miss Williams at Equita. We've had such a nice afternoon out, haven't we, Silver?" She patted the animal's neck. "You haven't—er—caught anyone yet? The man who killed poor Stella Swan?"

Wexford shook his head.

"Stella *Rivers,* I should say. I don't know why I find it so confusing. After all, I've got two names myself and half my friends call me Margaret and half by my second name. I ought not to get mixed up. Must be getting old."

Wexford felt no inclination for gallantry and simply asked if she had ever seen Rushworth in the grounds of Saltram House.

"Bob Rushworth? Now you come to mention it, he and his wife were up here a lot last winter and she actually asked me if I thought it would be all right for them to take one of the statues away with them. The one that was lying down in the grass, you know."

"You said nothing about this before."

"Well, of *course* not," said Mrs. Fenn, bending over to coo into the horse's ear. "I *know* the Rushworths, I've known them for years. Paul calls me auntie. I suppose they wanted the statue for their garden. It's not my place to say whether you can have it or you can't, I said, and they didn't take it, did they?" She edged herself more comfortably into the saddle. "If you'll excuse me I must be on my way. Silver's very highly bred and he gets nervous when it's dark." The horse lifted its head and emitted a loud whinny of agreement. "Never mind, darling," said Mrs. Fenn. "Soon be home with Mother."

Wexford went on. The rain was falling thinly but steadily. He passed Saltram Lodge and entered that part of the lane which was most thickly overshadowed by trees. They thinned out after two or three hundred yards to disclose the celebrated view of the great house.

The parkland looked grey and the house itself, looming through mist, a black skeleton with empty eye-sockets. Wexford was glad he had never known the place or been in the habit of visiting it. To him it had become a graveyard.

20

He hadn't been able to bring himself to book a double room for Mr. and Mrs. Burden. One day Gemma would be Mrs. Burden and then it would be different. In the meantime the name was Jean's. Jean held the title like a champion whose honours cannot be taken from her by death.

Their hotel was Eastover village pub which had been extended since the war to accommodate half a dozen guests, and they had been given rooms side by side, both overlooking the wide grey sea. It was too cold for bathing, but there are always children on beaches. While Gemma unpacked, Burden watched the children, five of them, brought down there to play by their parents. The tide was far out and the beach a silvery ochre, the sand packed too tight and flattened too firmly by the sea to show footprints from this distance. The man and the woman walked far apart from each other, seeming entirely detached. Married for many years, Burden supposed—the eldest girl looked at least twelve—they had no need of contact or of reassurance. The children, running from one to the other, then wheeling towards the sea, were evidence enough of love. He saw the parents, separated now by a wide drift of shells and pebbles, glance casually at each other and in that glance he read a secret language of mutual trust and hope and profound understanding.

One day it would be like that for him and Gemma. They would bring their children, his and *theirs*, to such a beach as this and walk with them between the water and the sky and remember their nights and days and look forward to the night. He turned quickly to tell her what he was thinking but suddenly it came to him that he mustn't tell her, he couldn't because to do so would be to draw her attention to the children.

"What is it, Mike?"

"Nothing, I only wanted to say that I love you."

He closed the window and drew the curtains, but in the half-dark he could still see the children. He took her in his arms and closed his eyes and still he could see them. Then he made love to her violently and passionately to exorcise the children and, in particular, the little fair-haired boy whom he had never seen but who was more real to him than those he had watched on the seashore.

The weekenders' cottage was very ancient, built before the Civil War, before the departure of the *Mayflower*, perhaps even before the last of the Tudors. Rushworth's was newer, though still old, belonging, Wexford decided, to the same period as that of Saltram House and its lodge, about 1750. In Burden's absence he was spending much of his time in Mill Lane, viewing the three little houses, sometimes entering their gardens and walking thoughtfully around them.

Once he walked from Rushworth's cottage to the fountains at Saltram House and back again, timing himself. It took him half an hour. Then he did it again, pausing this time to play-act the lifting of the cistern slab and the insertion of a body. Forty minutes.

He drove to Sewingbury and saw the woman who had a date to meet Rushworth on that October afternoon and heard from her that she had been unable to keep the appointment. What of that other afternoon in Feburary?

One evening he made his way to Fontaine Road in search of the Crantocks and on an impulse knocked first at number 61. He had nothing to say to Mrs. Lawrence, no good news, but he was curious to see this forlorn woman people said was beautiful and he knew from past experience that his very presence, stolid and fatherly, could sometimes be a comfort. No one answered his knock and this time he sensed quite a different atmosphere from that he had felt outside Bishop's door. Nobody answered because there was nobody there to hear.

For some moments he stood thoughtfully in the quiet street, and then, discomfited now for personal reasons, he went next door to the Crantocks.

"If you wanted Gemma," said Mrs. Crantock, "she's away, gone down to the South Coast for the weekend."

"I really want to talk to you and your husband. About a man called Rushworth and your daughter."

"Oh, that? Your inspector kindly saw her home. We *were* grateful. Mind you, there was nothing in it. I know they say Mr. Rushworth chases the girls, but I expect that's just gossip, and they don't mean *little* girls. My daughter's only fourteen."

Crantock came into the hall to see who had called. He recognised Wexford immediately and shook hands. "As a matter of fact," he said, "Rushworth came round the next day to apologise. He said he'd only called out to Janet because he'd heard we'd got a piano we wanted to get rid of." Crantock grinned and turned up his eyes. "I told him *sell*, not get rid of, so, of course, he wasn't interested."

"Silly of Janet, really," said his wife, "to have got so worked up."

"I don't know." Crantock had stopped smiling. "We're all on edge, especially kids who are old enough to understand." He looked deep into Wexford's eyes. "And people with kids," he added.

Wexford walked into Chiltern Avenue by way of the shrub-shadowed alley. There he had to use his torch and as he went he thought, not by any means for the first time, on his great good fortune in having been born a man, and a big man at that, instead of a woman. Only in daylight and fine weather could a woman have walked there without fear, without turning her head and feeling her heart-beats quicken.

No wonder Janet Crantock had been frightened. And then he thought of John Lawrence whose youth had given him a woman's vulnerability and who would never grow up to be a man.

In the evenings when the tide was far out they walked along the sands in the dark or sat on the rocks at the entrance to a cave they had found. The rain held off, but it was November and cold at night. The first time they went there they wore thick coats but the heavy clothing separated and isolated them, so after that Burden brought the car rug. They cocooned themselves in it, their bodies pressed together, their hands tightly clasped, the thick woollen folds enclosing them and keeping out the salty sea wind. When he was alone with her in the darkness on the seashore he was very happy.

Even at this time of the year Eastbourne would be crowded and she was afraid of people. So they avoided the big resort and even the next village, Chine Warren. Gemma had visited the place before and wanted to walk there, but Burden prevented her. It was from there, he believed, that the children came. He tried all the time to keep children out of her sight. Sometimes, pitying her for her sorrow yet jealous of the cause of it, he found himself wishing a modern Pied Piper would come and whistle away all the little children of Sussex so that they might not be there to laugh and play and torment her and deprive him of joy.

"Would it be a quick death, the sea?" she said.

He shivered, watching the running tide. "I don't know. Nobody who has died in it has ever been able to tell us."

"I think it would be quick." Her voice was a child's, gravely considering. "Cold and clean and quick."

In the afternoons Burden made love to her—he had never been more conscious of and more satisfied with his manhood than when he saw how his love comforted her—and afterwards, while she slept, he walked down to the shore or over the cliff to Chine

Warren. There was still a little warmth left in the sunshine and the children came to build sandcastles. He had discovered that they were not a family, the couple not husband and wife, but that four of the children belonged to the man and the other one to the woman. How teasing and deceptive were first impressions! He looked back now with self-disgust on his romancing, his sentimental notion that this pair, known to each other perhaps only by sight, had an idyllic marriage. Illusion and disillusion, he reflected, what life is and what we think it is. Why, from this distance he couldn't even tell if the solitary child were a boy or a girl, for it was capped and trousered and booted like all the children.

The woman kept stooping down to collect shells and once she stumbled. When she stood up again he noticed that she dragged her leg and he wondered if he should go down the seaweedy steps and cross the sands to offer her his help. But perhaps that would mean bringing her back to the hotel while he fetched his car, and the sound of the child's voice would awaken Gemma. . . .

They rounded the foot of the cliff, going towards Chine Warren. Receding fast, the tide seemed to be drawing the sea back into the heart of the red sunset, a November sunset which is the most lovely of the whole year.

Now the great wide sweep of beach was deserted, but its young visitors had left evidence behind them. As sure as he could be that he was unobserved, Burden walked down the steps, pretending to stroll casually. The two sandcastles stood proudly erect, as if confident of their endurance until the sea conquered them, rushing them away when it returned at midnight. He hesitated, the rational sensible man momentarily intervening, and then he kicked over their turrets and stamped on their battlements until the sand they were made of was as flat as the surrounding shore.

Once more the beach belonged to him and Gemma. John or his deputies, his representatives, should not take her away from him. He was a man and any day a match for a lost dead child.

Rushworth came to the door in his duffel coat.

"Oh, it's you," he said. "I was just going to take the dog out."

"Postpone it for half an hour, will you?"

Not very willingly, Rushworth took off his coat, hung up the lead and led Wexford into a living room amid the cries of the disappointed terrier. Two teen-age children were watching television, a girl of about eight sat at the table doing a jigsaw puzzle, and on the floor, lying on his stomach, was the most junior member of the family, Andrew, who had been John Lawrence's friend.

"I'd like to talk to you alone," said Wexford.

It was a biggish house with what Rushworth, in one of his house agent's blurbs, would perhaps have described as three reception rooms. That evening none was fit for the reception of anyone except possibly a second-hand-furniture dealer. The Rushworths were apparently acquisitive creatures, snappers up of anything they could get for nothing, and Wexford, seating himself in this morning room-cum-study-cum-library, observed a set of Dickens he had surely last seen in Pomfret Grange before the Rogerses sold out and two stone urns whose design seemed very much in keeping with the other garden ornaments of Saltram House.

"I've racked my brains and I can't tell you another thing about the fellows in that search party."

"I've not come about that," said Wexford. "Did you pinch those urns from Saltram House?"

" 'Pinch' is a bit strong," said Rushworth, turning red. "They were lying about and no one wanted them."

"You had your eye on one of the statues too, didn't you?"

"What's this got to do with John Lawrence?"

Wexford shrugged. "I don't know. It might have something to do with Stella Rivers. To put it in a nutshell, I'm here to know where you were and what you were doing on February 25th."

"How can I remember that far back? I know what it is, it's Margaret Fenn putting you up to all this. Just because I complained my girl wasn't doing as well as she should at her riding lessons." Rushworth opened the door and shouted, "Eileen!"

When she wasn't at work, typing specifications for her husband, Mrs. Rushworth managed this sprawling household single-handed and it showed. She looked dowdy and harassed and her skirt hem was coming down at the back. Perhaps there was some foundation in the gossip that her husband chased the girls.

"Where were you that Thursday?" she enquired of him. "In the office, I suppose. I know where I was. I got it all sorted out in my mind when there was all that fuss about Stella Rivers being missing. It was half-term and I'd taken Andrew to work with me. He came with me in the car to pick Linda up from Equita and—oh, yes—Paul—that's my eldest—he came too and dropped off at the cottage. There was a little table there we thought we might as well have here. But we didn't see Stella. I didn't even know her by sight."

"Your husband was in the office when you got back?"

"Oh, yes. He waited for me to get back before he went out in the car."

"What kind of a car, Mr. Rushworth?"

"Jaguar. Maroon colour. Your people have already been all over my car on account of its being a Jaguar and a kind of red colour. Look, we didn't know Stella Rivers. As far as we know, we'd never even seen her. Until she disappeared I'd only heard of her through Margaret always going on about how marvellous she was on a horse."

Wexford favoured them with a hard, unsympathetic stare. He was thinking deeply, fitting in puzzle pieces, casting aside irrelevancies.

"You," he said to Rushworth, "were at work when Stella disappeared. When John disappeared you were in Sewingbury waiting for a client who never turned up." He turned to Mrs. Rushworth. "You were at work when John disappeared. When Stella vanished you were driving back from Equita along Mill Lane. Did you pass anyone?"

"Nobody," said Mrs. Rushworth firmly. "Paul was still in the cottage. I know that—he'd put a light on —and, well, I'd better be quite frank with you. He'd actually been in Margaret Fenn's place too. I'm sure he had because the front door was open, just a little bit ajar. I know he shouldn't, though she does always leave her back door unlocked and when he was little she used to say he could let himself in and see her whenever he liked. Of course, it's different now he's so old, and I've told him again and again . . ."

"Never mind," Wexford said suddenly. "It doesn't matter."

"If you wanted to talk to Paul . . . I mean, if it would clear the air . . . ?"

"I don't want to see him." Wexford got up abruptly. He didn't want to see anyone at all. He knew the answer. It had begun to come to him when Rushworth called out to his wife and now nothing remained but to sit down somewhere in utter silence and work it all out.

21

"Our last day," said Burden. "Where would you like to go? Shall we have a quiet drive somewhere and lunch in a pub?"

"I don't mind. Anything you say." She took his hand, held it against her face for a moment, and burst out, as if she had kept the words inside her, burning and corroding for many hours, "I've got a dreadful feeling, a sort of premonition, that when we get back we'll hear that they've found him."

"John?"

"And—and the man who killed him," she whispered.

"They'd let us know."

"They don't know where we are, Mike. No one knows."

Slowly and evenly he said, "It will be better for you when you know it for sure. Terrible pain is better than terrible anxiety." But was it? Was it better for him to know that Jean was dead than to fear she would die? Terrible anxiety always contains terrible hope. "Better for you," he said firmly. "And then, when it's behind you, you can start your new life."

"Let's go," she said. "Let's go out."

It was Saturday and still no one had been charged.

"There's an uneasy sort of lull about this place," said Harry Wild to Camb. "Quite a contrast to all the activity of yore."

"My what?" said Camb.

"Your nothing. Yore. Days gone by."

"No good asking me. Nobody ever tells me anything."

"Life," said Wild, "is passing us by, old man. Trouble with us is we've not been ambitious. We've been content to sport with Amaryllis in the shade."

Camb looked shocked. "Speak for yourself," he said, and then, softening, "Shall I see if there's any tea going?"

Late in the afternoon Dr. Crocker breezed into Wexford's office. "Very quiet, aren't we? I hope that means you'll be free for golf in the morning."

"Don't feel like golf," said Wexford. "Can't, anyway."

"Surely you're not going to Colchester *again?*"

"I've been. I went this morning. Scott's dead."

The doctor pranced over to the window and opened it. "You need some fresh air in here. Who's Scott?"

"You ought to know. He was your patient. He had a stroke and now he's had another. Want to hear about it?"

"Why would I? People are always having strokes. I've just come from an old boy down in Charteris Road who's had one. Why would I want to know about this Scott?" He came closer to Wexford and bent critically over him. "Reg?" he said. "Are you all right? My God, I'm more concerned that you *shouldn't* have one. You look rotten."

"It *is* rotten. But not for me. For me it's just a problem." Wexford got up suddenly. "Let's go down to the Olive."

There was no one else in the lush, rather over-decorated cocktail bar.

"I'd like a double Scotch."

"And you shall have one," said Crocker. "For once I'll go so far as to prescribe it."

Briefly Wexford thought of that other humbler hostelry where Monkey and Mr. Casaubon had both disgusted him and whetted his appetite. He pushed them from his mind as the doctor returned with their drinks.

"Thanks. I wish your tablets came in such a palatable form. Cheers."

"Good health," said Crocker meaningfully.

Wexford leaned back against the red-velvet upholstery of the settle. "All the time," he began, "I thought it must be Swan, although there didn't seem to be any motive. And then, when I got all that stuff from Monkey and Mr. Casaubon and the more accurate stuff about the inquest, I thought I could see a motive, simply that Swan got rid of people who got in his way. That would imply madness, of course. So what? The world is full of ordinary people with lunacy underlying their ordinariness. Look at Bishop."

"What inquest?" Crocker asked.

Wexford explained. "But I was looking at it from the wrong way round," he said, "and it took me a long time to look at it the right way."

"Let's have the right way, then."

"First things first. When a child disappears one of the first things we consider is that he or she was picked up by a car. Another disservice done to the world by the inventor of the internal-combustion engine, or did kids once get abducted in carriages? But I mustn't digress. Now we knew it was very unlikely Stella accepted a lift in a car because she had *already refused the lift we knew had been offered to her.* Therefore it was probable that she was either met and taken somewhere by someone she knew, such as her mother, her stepfather or Mrs. Fenn, or that she went into one of the houses in Mill Lane."

The doctor sipped his sherry austerely. "There are only three," he said.

"Four, if you count Saltram House. Swan had no real alibi. He could have ridden to Mill Lane, taken Stella into the grounds of Saltram House on some pretext, and killed her. Mrs. Swan had no alibi. Contrary to my former belief, she *can* drive. She could have driven to Mill Lane. Monstrous as it is to think of a woman killing her own child, I had to consider Rosalind Swan. She worships her husband obsessively. Was it possible, in her mind, that Stella, who also worshipped Swan—little girls seem to— would in a few years' time grow into a rival?"

"And Mrs. Fenn?"

"Tidying up at Equita, she *said*. We had only her word for it. But even my inventive mind, twisted mind, if you like, couldn't see a motive there. Finally, I dismissed all those theories and considered the four houses." Wexford lowered his voice slightly as a man and a girl entered the bar. "Stella left Equita at twenty-five minutes to five. The first house she passed was the weekenders' cottage, but it was a Thursday and the cottage was empty. Besides, it dated from about 1550."

Crocker looked astonished. "What's that got to do with it?"

"You'll see in a minute. She went on and it began to rain. At twenty to five the Forby bank manager stopped and offered her a lift. She refused. For once it would have been wise for a child to have accepted a lift from a strange man." The newcomers had found seats by a far window and Wexford resumed his normal voice. "The next cottage she came to is owned, though not occupied, by a man called Robert Rushworth who lives in Chiltern Avenue. Now Rushworth interested me very much. He knew John Lawrence, he wears a duffel coat, he has been suspected, perhaps with foundation, perhaps not, of molesting a child. His wife, though warned by Mrs. Mitchell that a man had been seen observing the children in the swings field, did not inform the police. On the afternoon of February 25th he could have been in Mill Lane. His wife and his eldest son certainly were. All the family were in the habit of going into their cottage just when it pleased them— and Mrs. Rushworth's Christian name is Eileen."

The doctor stared blankly. "I don't follow any of this. So what if her name is Eileen?"

"Last Sunday," Wexford went on, "I went down to Colchester to see Mr. and Mr. Scott, the parents of Bridget Scott. At that time I had no suspicion at all of Rushworth. I simply had a forlorn hope that one or both of the Scotts might be able to give me a little more insight into the character of Ivor Swan. But Scott, as you know, is—was, I should say—a very sick man."

"*I* should know?"

"Of course you should know," said Wexford severely. "Really, you're very slow." Having for once the whip hand over his friend was cheering Wexford up. It was a pleasant change to see Crocker at a disadvantage. "I was afraid to question Scott. I was uncertain what might be the effect of alarming him. Besides, for my purposes, it seemed adequate to work on his wife. She told me nothing which increased my knowledge of Swan, but unwittingly, she gave me four pieces of information that helped me solve this case." He cleared his throat. "Firstly, she told me that she and her husband had been in the habit of staying for holidays with a relative who lived near Kingsmarkham and that they had stayed there for the last time last winter; secondly, that the relative lived in an eighteenth-century house; thirdly, that in March, *a fortnight after he had been taken ill,* her husband was a very sick man indeed; fourthly, that the relative's name was Eileen. Now, sometime in March might well be a fortnight after February 25th." He paused significantly for all this to sink in.

The doctor put his head on one side. At last he said, "I'm beginning to get this clear. My God, you'd hardly believe it, but people are a funny lot. It was with the Rushworths that the Scotts were staying, Eileen Rushworth was the relative. Scott somehow induced Rushworth to make away with Stella in revenge for what Swan had done to his own child. Offered him money, maybe. What a ghastly thing!"

Wexford sighed. It was at times like this that he most missed Burden, or Burden as he used to be. "I think we'll have another drink," he said. "My round."

"You don't have to act as if I was a complete fool," said the doctor huffily. "I'm not trained to make this sort of diagnosis." As Wexford got up, he snapped vindictively, "Orange juice for you, that's an order."

With a glass of lager, not orange juice, before him, Wexford said, "You're worse than Dr. Watson, you are. And while we're on the subject, though I've the utmost respect for Sir Arthur, life isn't much like Sherlock Holmes stories and I don't believe it ever was. People don't nurse revenge for years and years nor do they find it possible to bribe more or less respectable estate agents, fathers of families, into doing murder for them."

"But you said," Crocker retorted, "that the Scotts were staying with the Rushworths in their cottage."

"No, I didn't. Use your head. How could they have been staying in a house that was let to another tenant? All that made me consider that house was that it dated from about 1750. I had forgotten all about the Scotts' relative being called Eileen—it was only mentioned in passing—but when I heard Rushworth call his wife Eileen, then I knew. After that I only had to do some simple checking."

"I am so entirely in the dark," said Crocker, "that I don't know what to say."

For a moment Wexford savoured the experience of seeing the doctor at a loss. Then he said, "Eileen is a fairly common name. Why should Mrs. Rushworth be its only possessor in the district? At that point I remembered that someone else had told me she had two Christian names, was called by the first by half the people she knew and by the second by the rest. I didn't care to enquire of her personally. I checked with Somerset House. And there I found that Mrs. Margaret *Eileen* Fenn was the daughter of one James Collins and his wife Eileen Collins, *née* Scott.

"Beyond a doubt, it was with Mrs. Fenn that the Scotts had been staying in February, at Saltram Lodge which is also an eighteenth-century house. They stayed with her, and on February 25th, after saying good-bye to Mrs. Fenn before she left for work at Equita, they too left by taxi to catch the three-forty-five train from Stowerton to Victoria."

Crocker held up his hand to halt Wexford. "I remember now. Of course I do. It was poor old Scott who had that stroke on the platform. I happened to be in the station, booking a seat, and they sent for me. But it wasn't at a quarter to four, Reg. More like six o'clock."

"Exactly. Mr. and Mrs. Scott didn't catch the three-forty-five. When they got to the station Scott realised they had left one of their suitcases behind at Mrs. Fenn's. You ought to know that. It was you who told me."

"So I did."

"Scott was a strong, hale man at that time. Or so he thought. There wasn't a taxi about—mind you I'm guessing this bit—and he decided to walk back to Mill Lane. It took him about three quarters of an hour. But that wouldn't have worried him. There wasn't another train that stopped at Stowerton till six-twenty-six. He had no difficulty in getting into the house, for Mrs. Fenn always leaves her back door unlocked. Perhaps he made himself a cup of tea, perhaps he merely rested. We shall never know. We must now go back to Stella Rivers."

"She called at Saltram Lodge?"

"Of course. It was the obvious place. She too knew about the unlocked back door and that Mrs. Fenn, her friend and teacher, had a phone. It was raining, it was growing dark. She went into the kitchen and immediately encountered Scott."

"And Scott recognised her?"

"As Stella Rivers. Not knowing what her correct name was, Mrs. Fenn spoke of her sometimes as Rivers, sometimes as Swan. And she would have spoken of her to Scott, her uncle, and pointed her out, for she was proud of Stella.

"As soon as she had got over her surprise at finding someone in the house, Stella must have asked to use the phone. What words did she use? Something like this, I fancy: 'I'd like to phone my father'—she referred to Swan as her father—'Mr. Swan of Hill Farm. When he comes, we'll drive you back to Stowerton.' Now Scott hated the very name of Swan. He had never forgotten and he had always dreaded

a chance meeting with him. He must then have
checked with Stella that it was Ivor Swan to whom
she referred and then he realised that here he was,
face to face with the daughter—or so he thought—of
the man who had left his own child to die when she
was at the same age as this child."

22

When they came back to Eastover from their drive the sun had set, leaving long fiery streaks to split the purple clouds and stain the sea with coppery gold. Burden pulled the car into an empty parking place on the cliff-top and they sat in silence, looking at the sea and the sky and at a solitary trawler, a little moving smudge on the horizon.

Gemma had withdrawn more and more into herself as the days had passed by and sometimes Burden felt that it was a shadow who walked with him, went out with him in the car and lay beside him at night. She hardly spoke. It was as if she had become bereavement incarnate or, worse than that, a dying woman. He knew she wanted to die, although she had not directly told him so. The night before he had found her lying in the bath in water that had grown cold, her eyes closed and her head slipping down into the water, and, although she denied it, he knew she had taken sleeping tablets half an hour before. And today, while they were on the downs, he had only just succeeded in preventing her from crossing the road in the path of an oncoming car.

Tomorrow they must go home. Within a month they would be married and before that he would have to apply for a transfer to one of the Metropolitan divisions. That meant finding new schools for the children, a new house. What kind of a house would he find in London for the price he would get for his Sussex bungalow? But it must be done. The mean, indefensible thought that at any rate he would only have two children to support and not three, that in her state his wife would not vex him with riotous parties or fill the place with her friends, brought a blush of shame to his face.

He glanced tentatively at Gemma, but she was staring out to sea. Then he too followed her gaze and saw that the beach was no longer deserted. Quickly he started the car, reversed across the turf and turned towards the road that led inland. He didn't look at her again, but he knew that she was weeping, the tears falling unchecked down those thin pale cheeks.

"Scott's first thought," said Wexford after a pause, "was probably just to leave her to it, flee back the way he had come away from these Swans. They say murder victims—but this wasn't really murder—are self-selected. Did Stella point out that it was pouring with rain, that he could have a lift? Did she say, 'I'll just phone. He'll be here in a quarter of an hour?' Scott remembered it all then. He had never forgotten it. He must stop her using that phone and he got hold of her. No doubt she cried out. How he must have hated her, thinking he knew what she meant to the man he hated. I think it was this which gave him strength and made him hold her too tight, press his strong old hands too hard about her neck ..."

The doctor said nothing, only staring the more intently at Wexford.

"It takes half an hour to walk from Rushworth's cottage to Saltram House and back again," the chief inspector resumed. "Less than that from Saltram Lodge. And Scott would have known about the fountains and the cisterns. He would have been interested in them. He was a plumbing engineer. He carried the dead child up to the Italian garden and put her in the cistern. Then he went back to the lodge and fetched his case. A passing motorist gave him a lift back to Stowerton. We may imagine what sort of a state he was in."

"We know," said Crocker quietly, "he had a stroke."

"Mrs. Fenn knew nothing of it, nor did his wife. Last Wednesday he had another stroke and that killed him. I think—I'm afraid—that it was seeing me and guessing what I was that really killed him. His wife didn't understand the words he spoke to her before he died. She thought he was wandering in his mind. She told me what they were. 'I held her too tight. I thought of my Bridget.' "

"But what the hell are you going to do? You can't charge a dead man."

"That's in Griswold's hands," said Wexford. "Some noncommittal paragraph for the press, I suppose. The Swans have been told and Swan's uncle, Group Captain what's-his-name. Not that he'll need to pay up. We shan't be arresting anyone."

The doctor looked thoughtful. "You haven't said a word about John Lawrence."

"Because I haven't a word to say," said Wexford.

Their hotel had no rear entrance, so it was necessary to come at last out of the hinterland on to Eastover's little esplanade. Burden had been hoping with all his heart that by now, in the dusk, the beach would be empty of children, but the pair who had brought tears to Gemma's eyes were still there, the child that ran up and down at the water's edge and the woman who walked with him, trailing from one hand a long ribbon of seaweed. But for the slight limp, Burden wouldn't have recognised her, in her trousers and hooded coat, as the woman he had seen before, or indeed as a woman at all. Inanely, he tried to direct Gemma's gaze inland towards a cottage she had seen a dozen times before.

She obeyed him—she was always acquiescent, anxious to please—but no sooner had she looked than she turned again to face the sea. Her arm was touching his and he felt her shiver.

"Stop the car," she said.

"But there's nothing to see . . ."

"Stop the car!"

She never commanded. He had never heard her speak like that before. "What, here?" he said. "Let's get back. You'll only get cold."

"Please stop the car, Mike."

He couldn't blind her, shelter her, for ever. He parked the car behind a red Jaguar that was the only other vehicle on the sea front. Before he had switched off the ignition she had got the door open, slammed it behind her and was off down the steps.

It was absurd to remember what she had said about the sea, about a quick death, but he remembered it. He jumped from the car and followed her, striding at first, then running. Her bright hair, sunset red, streamed behind her. Their footsteps made a hard slapping sound on the sand and the woman turned to face them, standing stock still, the streamer of seaweed in her hand whirling suddenly in the wind like a dancer's scarf.

"Gemma! Gemma!" Burden called, but the wind took his words or else she was determined not to hear them. She seemed bent only on reaching the sea which curled and creamed at the child's feet. And now the child, who had been splashing in shallow foam to the top of his boots, also turned to stare, as children will when adults behave alarmingly.

She was going to throw herself into the sea. Ignoring the woman, Burden pounded after her and then he stopped suddenly, as if, unseeing, he had flung himself against a solid wall. He was no more than ten feet from her. Wide-eyed, the child approached her. Without seeming to slacken her speed at all, without hesitation, she ran into the water and, in the water, fell on to her knees.

The little waves flowed over her feet, her legs, her dress. He saw it seep up, drenching her to the waist. He heard her cry out—miles away, he thought, that cry could have been heard—but he could not tell whether it brought him happiness or grief.

"John, John, my John!"

She threw out her arms and the child went into them. Still kneeling in the water, she held him in a close embrace, her mouth pressed hard against his bright golden hair.

Burden and the woman looked at each other without speaking. He knew at once who she was. That face had looked at him before from his daughter's scrapbook. But it was very ravaged now and very aged, the black hair under the hood chopped off raggedly as if, with the ruin of her career, she had submitted to and accelerated the ruin of her looks.

Her hands were tiny. It seemed that she collected specimens, botanical and marine, but now she dropped the ribbon of weed. Close to, Burden thought, no one could mistake her for a man—but at a distance? It occurred to him that from far away even a middle-aged woman might look like a youth if she were slight and had the litheness of a dancer.

What more natural than that she should want John, the child of her old lover who had never been able to give her a child? And she had been ill, mentally ill, he remembered. John would have gone with her, quite willingly, no doubt, recalling her as his father's friend, persuaded perhaps that his mother had temporarily committed him to her care. And to the seaside. What child doesn't want to go to the seaside?

But something would happen now. As soon as she got over her first joy, Gemma would tear this woman to pieces. It wasn't as if this was the first outrage Leonie West had committed against her. Hadn't she, when Gemma was only a few months married, virtually stolen her husband from her? And now, a more monstrous iniquity, she had stolen her child.

He watched her rise slowly out of the water and, still keeping hold of John's hand, begin to cross the strip of sand that separated her from Leonie West. The dancer stood her ground, but she lifted her head with a kind of pathetic boldness and clenched the little hands Mrs. Mitchell had seen picking leaves. Burden took a step forward and found his lost voice.

"Now listen, Gemma. The best thing is . . ."

What had he meant to say? That the best thing

was for them all to keep calm, to discuss it rationally? He stared. Never would he have believed—had he ever really known her?—that she would do this, the best thing of all, the thing that, in his estimation, almost made a saint of her.

Her dress was soaked. Oddly, Burden thought of a picture he had once seen, an artist's impression of the sea giving up its dead. With a soft, tender glance at the boy, she dropped his hand and lifted Leonie West's instead. Speechless, the other woman looked at her, and then Gemma, hesitating only for a moment, took her into her arms.

23

"It would never have worked, Mike. You know that as well as I do. I'm not conventional enough for you, not respectable, not good enough if you like."

"I think you are too good for me," said Burden.

"I did say once that John—if John was ever found I wouldn't marry you. I don't think you quite understood. It will be better for both of us if I do what we're planning and go and live with Leonie. She's so lonely, Mike, and I'm so dreadfully sorry for her. That way I can have London and my friends and she can have a share in John."

They were sitting in the lounge of the hotel where they had stayed together. Burden thought she had never been so beautiful, her white skin glowing from her inner joy, her hair mantling her shoulders. And never so alien in the golden dress Leonie West had lent her because her own was ruined by salt water. Her face was sweeter and gentler than ever.

"But I love you," he said.

"Dear Mike, are you sure you don't just love going to bed with me? Does that shock you?"

It did, but not so much, not nearly so much, as once it would have. She had taught him a multitude of things. She had given him his sentimental education.

"We can still be loving friends," she said. "You can come to me at Leonie's. You can meet all my friends. We can sometimes go away together and I'll be so different now I am happy. You'll see."

He did see. He almost shuddered. Go to her with her child there? Explain somehow to his own children that he had a—a mistress?

"It would never work," he said clearly and firmly. "I can see it wouldn't."

She looked at him very tenderly. " 'You'll court more women,' " she said, half-singing, " 'and I'll couch with more men . . .' "

He knew his Shakespeare no better than he knew his Proust. They went out on to the sea front where Leonie West was waiting with John in her red car.

"Come and say hallo to him," said Gemma.

But Burden shook his head. No doubt it was better this way, no doubt he would one day be grateful to the child who had robbed him of his happiness and his love. But not now, not yet. One does not say hallo to an enemy and a thief.

She lingered under the esplanade lights, turning towards him and then back again to where John was. Torn two ways, they called it, he thought, but there was little doubt who had won this tug of war. That light in her eyes had never been there when they looked at him, was not there now, died as soon as she ceased to face the car. She was parting from him not with regret, not with pain, but with *politeness*.

Always considerate, always ready to respect another person's conventions—for they were in a public place and people were passing—she held out her hand to him. He took it, and then, no longer caring for those passers-by, forgetting his cherished respectability, he pulled her to him there in the open street and kissed her for the last time.

When the red car had gone he leant on the rail and looked at the sea and knew that it was better this way, knew too, because he had been through something like it before, that he would not go on wanting to die.

Wexford was genial and sly and almost godlike. "What a fortunate coincidence that you happened to be in Eastbourne with Miss Woodville and happened to go to Eastover and happened—Good God, what a lot of happenings!—to meet Mrs. Lawrence."

He added more gravely, "On the whole, you have done well, Mike."

Burden said nothing. He didn't think it necessary to point out that it was Gemma who had found the lost boy and not he.

Quietly, Wexford closed the door of his office and for a few moments regarded Burden in silence. Then he said, "But I don't much care for coincidences or for melodrama, come to that. I don't think they're in your line, do you?"

"Perhaps not, sir."

"Are you going to go on doing well, Mike? I have to ask, I have to know. I have to know where to find you when you're needed and, when I find you, that you'll be your old self. Are you going to come back and work with me and—well, to put it bluntly—pull yourself together?"

Burden said slowly, remembering what he had once said to Gemma, "Work is the best thing, isn't it?"

"I think it is."

"But it has to be real work, heart and soul in it, not just coming in every day more or less automatically and hoping everyone will admire you for being such a martyr to duty. I've thought about it a lot, sir, I've decided to count my blessings and . . ."

"That's fine," Wexford cut off his words. "Don't be too sanctimonious about it, though, will you? That's hard to live with. I can see you've changed and I'm not going to enquire too closely into who or what has brought that change about. One good thing, I'm pretty sure I'm going to find that the quality of your mercy is a lot less strained than it used to be. And now let's go home."

Half-way down the lift, he went on, "You say Mrs. Lawrence doesn't want this woman charged? That's all very well, but what about all our work, all the expenditure? Griswold will do his nut. He may insist on charging her. But if she's really a bit cuckoo . . . My God, one culprit dead and the other crazy!"

The lift opened, and there, inevitably, was Harry Wild.

"I have nothing for you," Wexford said coldly.

"Nothing for me!" Wild said wrathfully to Camb. "I know for a fact that . . ."

"There was quite a to-do in Pump Lane," said Camb, opening his book. "One police van and two fire engines arrived at five p.m. yesterday—Sunday, that was—to remove a cat from an elm tree . . ." Wild's infuriated glance cut him short. He cleared his throat and said soothingly, "Let's see if there's any tea going."

On the station forecourt Wexford said, "I nearly forgot to tell you. Swan's uncle's going to pay out the reward."

Burden stared. "But it was offered for information leading to an arrest."

"No, it wasn't. That's what I thought till I checked. It was offered for information leading to a *discovery*. The Group Captain's a just man, and not the sort of just man I mean when I talk about his nephew. That's two thousand smackers for Charly Catch, or would be if he wasn't a very sick old man." Absently, Wexford felt in his pocket for his blood-pressure tablets. "When Crocker arrived in Charteris Road last night there was a solicitor at his bedside and Monkey keeping well in the background because a beneficiary can't also be a witness. I must work out sometime," said the chief inspector, "just how many king-size fags you could buy with all that boodle."

"Are you all right, Mike?" said Grace. "I mean, are you feeling all right? You've been home every night this week on the dot of six."

Burden smiled. "Let's say I've come to my senses. I find it a bit hard to put my feelings into words, but I suppose I've just realised how lucky I am to have my kids and what hell it would be to lose them."

She didn't answer but went to the window and drew the curtains to shut out the night. With her back to him she said abruptly, "I'm not going in for that nursing-home thing."

"Now, look here . . ." He got up, went over to her and took her almost roughly by the arm. "You're not to sacrifice yourself on my account. I won't have it."

"My dear Mike!" Suddenly he saw that she was not troubled or conscience-stricken but happy. "I'm not sacrificing myself. I . . ." She hesitated, remembering perhaps how in the past he would never talk to her, never speak of anything but the most mundane household arrangements.

"Tell me," he said with a new fierce intensity.

She looked astonished. "Well . . . Well, I met a man while we were in Eastbourne, a man I used to know years ago. I—I was in love with him. We quarrelled . . . Oh, it was so silly! And now—now he wants to begin again and come here and take me out and—and I think, Mike, I think . . ." She stopped and then said with the cold defiance he had taught her, "You wouldn't be interested."

"Oh, Grace," he said, "if only you knew!"

She was staring at him now as if he were a stranger, but a stranger she had begun to like and would want to know better. "Knew what?" she said.

For a moment he didn't answer. He was thinking that if only he had the sense to realise it now, he had found his listener, his one friend who would understand, because of her experience of many sides of life, the simple daily joy his marriage had been to him and understand too the blaze of glory, the little summer, he had found with Gemma.

"I want to talk too," he said. "I've got to tell someone. If I listen to you, will you listen to me?"

She nodded wonderingly. He thought how pretty she was, how like Jean, and that, because she was like Jean, she would make a wonderful wife for this man who loved her. And because there could now be no misunderstanding between them he hugged her briefly and rested his cheek against hers.

He felt her happiness in the warmth with which

she returned the hug and it infected him, almost
making him happy too. Would it last? Was he finally
finding a sense of proportion? He couldn't tell, not
yet. But his own boy and girl were safe, sleeping behind those closed doors, he could work again, and he
had a friend who was waiting now, still tightly clasping his hands, to hear what he had to tell.

Grace led him back to the fire, sat down beside
him and said, as if already she half understood, "It'll
be all right, Mike." She leaned towards him, her face
serious and intent. "Let's talk," she said.

ABOUT THE AUTHOR

RUTH RENDELL is the author of fourteen previous mystery novels, including *The Face of Trespass, Some Lie and Some Die, Murder Being Once Done, Shake Hands Forever, No More Dying Then* and *One Across, Two Down.* Her latest novel, *A Demon in My View,* was awarded the 1976 Golden Dagger Award by the British Crime Writers Association. In July 1986, Bantam will publish *A Dark-Adapted Eye,* written by Ruth Rendell under the pseudonym of Barbara Vine. A former journalist, she lives with her husband and son outside of London.

Dear Reader,

There is nothing unusual in having two Christian names, but perhaps it is less common to be called by each of them equally. This is what happened to me. Ruth was my father's choice of name for me, Barbara my mother's. Because Ruth was difficult for my mother's Scandinavian parents to pronounce, her side of the family called me Barbara, and since this sort of duality was impossible in one household, my father finally started calling me Barbara too.

I tend to divide friends and relatives into the "Ruth people" and the "Barbara people." Both names are equally familiar to me, equally "my" names. If either were called out in the street I would turn around. And I don't mind which I am called so long as people don't try to change in, so to speak, midstream. There is for me something grotesque in a Barbara person trying to become a Ruth person, or vice-versa. Only my husband knows as well as I do into which category each friend falls. He can write the Christmas cards and always get them right. But he never calls me by either of my Christian names.

It has always interested me—I don't think my parents realized this—that both my names mean or imply "a stranger in a strange land," Ruth who was exiled into an alien country, Barbara that signifies "a foreigner."

Growing up with two names doesn't make you into two people. It does give you two aspects of personality, and Ruth and Barbara are two aspects of me. Ruth is tougher, colder, more analytical, possibly more aggressive. Ruth has written all the novels, created Chief Inspector Wexford. Ruth is the professional writer. Barbara is more feminine. It is Barbara who sews. If Barbara writes it is letters that she writes.

For a long time I have wanted Barbara to have a voice as well as Ruth. It would be a softer voice speaking at a slower pace, more sensitive perhaps, and more intuitive. In *A DARK-ADAPTED EYE* she has found that voice, taking a surname from the other side of the family, the paternal side, for Vine was my great-grandmother's maiden name. There would be nothing surprising to a psychologist in Barbara's choosing, as she asserts herself, to address readers in the first person.

The novel itself is the story of Faith Severn, and her exploration of circumstances that led to a terrible murder in her family more than thirty years before. I hope you will enjoy reading this book, as much as Barbara Vine enjoyed writing it.

Sincerely,

Ruth Rendell

Ruth Rendell

1

On the morning Vera died I woke up very early. The birds had started, more of them and singing more loudly in our leafy suburb than in the country. They never sang like that outside Vera's windows in the Vale of Dedham. I lay there listening to something repeating itself monotonously. A thrush, it must have been, doing what Browning said it did and singing each song twice over. It was a Thursday in August, a hundred years ago. Not much more than a third of that, of course. It only feels so long.

In these circumstances alone one knows when someone is going to die. All other deaths can be predicted, conjectured, even anticipated with some certainty, but not to the hour, the minute, with no room for hope. Vera would die at eight o'clock and that was that. I began to feel sick. I lay there exaggeratedly still, listening for some sound from the next room. If I was awake my father would be. About my mother

I was less sure. She had never made a secret of her dislike of both his sisters. It was one of the things which had made a rift between them, though there they were together in the next room, in the same bed still. People did not break a marriage, leave each other, so lightly in those days.

I thought of getting up but first I wanted to make sure where my father was. There was something terrible in the idea of encountering him in the passage, both of us dressing-gowned, thick-eyed with sleeplessness, each seeking the bathroom and each politely giving way to the other. Before I saw him I needed to be washed and brushed and dressed, my loins girded. I could hear nothing but that thrush uttering its idiot phrase five or six times over, not twice.

To work he would go as usual, I was sure of that. And Vera's name would not be mentioned. None of it had been spoken about at all in our house since the last time my father went to see Vera. There was one crumb of comfort for him. No one knew. A man may be very close to his sister, his twin, without anyone knowing of the relationship, and none of our neighbours knew he was Vera Hillyard's brother. None of the bank's clients knew. If today the head cashier remarked upon Vera's death, as he very likely might, as people would by reason of her sex among other things, I knew my father would present to him a bland, mildly interested face and utter some suitable platitude. He had, after all, to survive.

A floorboard creaked in the passage. I heard the bedroom door close and then the door of the bathroom, so I got up and looked at the day. A clean white still morning, with no sun and no blue in the sky, a morning that seemed to me to be waiting because I was. Six-thirty. There was an angle you could stand at looking out of this window where you could see no other house, so plentiful were the trees and shrubs, so thick their foliage. It was like looking into a clearing in a rather elaborate wood. Vera used to sneer at where my parents lived, saying it was neither town nor country.

My mother was up now. We were all stupidly early, as if we were going away on holiday. When I used to go to Sindon I was sometimes up as early as this, excited and looking forward to it. How could I have looked forward to the society of Vera, an unreasonable carping scold when on her own with me. and, when Eden was there, the two of them closing ranks to exclude anyone who might try to penetrate their alliance? I hoped, I suppose. Each time I was older and because of this she might change. She never did—until almost the end. And by then she was too desperate for an ally to be choosy.

I went to the bathroom. It was always possible to tell if my father had finished in the bathroom. He used an old-fashioned cut-throat razor and wiped the blade after each stroke on a small square of newspaper. The newspaper and the jug of hot water he fetched himself but the remains were always left for my mother to clear away, the square of paper with its load of shaving soap full of stubble, the empty jug. I washed in cold water. In summer, we only lit the boiler once a week for baths. Vera and Eden bathed every day, and that was one of the things I *had* liked about Sindon, my daily bath, though Vera's attitude always was that I would have escaped it if I could.

The paper had come. It was tomorrow the announcement would be, of course, a few bald lines. Today there was nothing about Vera. She was stale, forgotten, until this morning when, in a brief flare-up, the whole country would talk of her, those who deplored and those who said it served her right. My father sat at the dining-table, reading the paper. It was the *Daily Telegraph*, than which no other daily paper was ever read in our family. The crossword puzzle he would save for the evening, just as Vera had done, once only in all the years phoning my father for the solution to a clue that was driving her crazy. When Eden had a home of her own and was rich, she often rang him up and got him to finish the puzzle for her over the phone. She had never been as good at it as they.

He looked up and nodded to me. He didn't

smile. The table had yesterday's cloth on it, yellow check not to show the egg stains. Food was still rationed, meat being very scarce, and we ate eggs all the time, laid by my mother's chickens. Hence the crowing cockerels in our garden suburb, the fowl runs concealed behind hedges of lonicera and laurel. We had no eggs that morning, though. No cornflakes either. My mother would have considered cornflakes frivolous, in their white and orange packet. She had disliked Vera, had no patience with my father's intense family love, but she had a strong sense of occasion, of what was fitting. Without a word, she brought us toast that, while hot, had been thinly spread with margarine, a jar of marrow and ginger jam, a pot of tea.

I knew I shouldn't be able to eat. He ate. Business was to be as usual with him, I could tell that. It was over, wiped away, a monstrous effort made, if not to forget, at least to behave as if all was forgotten. The silence was broken by his voice, harsh and stagy, reading aloud. It was something about the war in Korea. He read on and on, columns of it, and it became embarrassing to listen because no one reads like that without introduction, explanation, excuse. It must have gone on for ten minutes. He read to the foot of the page, to where presumably you were told the story was continued inside. He didn't turn over. He broke off in mid-sentence. 'In the Far,' he said, never getting to 'East' but laying the paper down, aligning the pages, folding it twice, and once more, so that it was back in the shape it had been when the boy pushed it through the letterbox.

'In the far' hung in the air, taking on a curious significance, quite different from what the writer had intended. He took another piece of toast but got no further towards eating it. My mother watched him. I think she had been tender with him once but he had had no time for it or room for it and so her tenderness had withered for want of encouragement. I did not expect her to go to him and take his hand or put her arms round him. Would I have done so myself if she had not been there? Perhaps. That family's mutual love had not usually found its expression in outward show. In other words, there had not been embraces. The twins, for instance, did not kiss each other, though the women pecked the air around each other's faces.

It was a quarter to eight now. I kept repeating over and over to myself (like the thrush, now silent), 'In the far, in the far'. When first it happened, when he was told, he went into paroxysms of rage, of disbelief, of impotent protest.

'Murdered, murdered!' he kept shouting, like someone in an Elizabethan tragedy, like someone who bursts into a castle hall with dreadful news. And then, 'My sister!' and 'My poor sister!' and 'My little sister!'

But silence and concealment fell like a shutter. It was lifted briefly, after Vera was dead, when, sitting in a closed room after dark, like conspirators, he and I heard from Josie what happened that April day. He never spoke of it again. His twin was erased from his mind and he even made himself—incredibly—into an only child. Once I heard him tell someone that he had never regretted having no brothers or sisters.

It was only when he was ill and not far from death himself that he resurrected memories of his sisters. And the stroke he had had, as if by some physiological action stripping away layers of reserve and inhibition, making him laugh sometimes and just as often cry, released an unrestrained gabbling about how he had felt that summer. His former love for Vera the repressive years had turned to repulsion and fear, his illusions broken as much by the tug-of-war and Eden's immorality—his word, not mine—as by the murder itself. My mother might have said, though she did not, that at last he was seeing his sisters as they really were.

He left the table, his tea half-drunk, his second piece of toast lying squarely in the middle of his plate, the *Telegraph* folded and lying with its edges compulsively lined up to the table corner. No word was spoken to my mother and me. He went upstairs, he came down, the front door closed behind him. He would walk the leafy roads, I thought, making detours, turning the half mile to the station into two miles, hiding from the time in places where there were no clocks. It was then that I noticed he had left his watch on the table. I picked up the paper and there was the watch underneath.

'We should have gone away somewhere,' I said.

My mother said fiercely, 'Why should we? She hardly ever came here. Why should we let her drive us away?'

'Well, we haven't,' I said.

I wondered which was right, the clock on the wall that said five to eight or my father's watch that said three minutes to. My own watch was upstairs. Time passes so slowly over such points in it. There still seemed an aeon to wait. My mother loaded the tray and took it into the kitchen, making a noise about it, banging cups, a way of showing that it was no fault of hers. Innocent herself, she had been dragged into this family by marriage, all unknowing. It was another matter for me who was of their blood.

I went upstairs. My watch was in the bed-side table. It was new, a present bestowed by my parents for getting my degree. That, because of what had happened, it was a less good degree than everyone had expected, no one had commented upon. The watch face was small, not much larger than the cluster of little diamonds in my engagement ring that lay beside it, and you had to get close up to it to read the hands. I thought, in a moment the heavens will fall, there will be a great bolt of thunder, nature could not simply ignore. There was nothing. Only the birds had become silent, which they would do anyway at this time, their territorial claims being made, their trees settled on, the business of their day begun. What would the business of my day be? One thing I thought I would do. I would phone Helen, I would talk to Helen. Symbolic of my attitude to my engagement, my future marriage, this was, that it was to Helen I meant to fly for comfort, not the man who had given me the ring with a diamond cluster as big as a watch face.

I walked over to the bedside table, stagily, self-consciously, like a bad actress in an amateur production. The director would have halted me and told me to do it again, to walk away and do it again. I nearly did walk away so as not to see the time. But I picked up the watch and looked and had a long, rolling, falling feeling through my body as I saw that I had missed the moment. It was all over now and she was dead. The hands of the watch stood at five past eight.

The only kind of death that can be accurately predicted to the minute had taken place, the death that takes its victim,

> ... feet foremost through the floor,
> Into an empty space.

Murder, that most foul of crimes, appears to be the most British of crimes in the hands of these two Bantam authors:

From Patricia Wentworth:

Maud Silver, Private Enquiry Agent, is everybody's favorite spinster-detective. From her Edwardian hairstyle to her beaded shoes, she is the very model of a governess, her occupation before she decided to take on the more challenging occupation of a private enquiry agent. Armed with stubborn British common sense and an iron will to succeed, she is one of the best at tracking murder . . . and so will you be as you follow close behind her on the trail of clues in each of these Patricia Wentworth mysteries from Bantam:

From Catherine Aird:

The charm and wit that have made Aird's Detective Inspector C. D. Sloan a classic among British Sleuths will draw you into the tangled webs of clues, misdeeds and intrigues that Sloan must unravel in each of these fine titles from Bantam:

Look for them at your bookstore or use this handy coupon: